RESISTANCE!
a speculative near-future novel

Gretchen Cassel Eick

RESISTANCE!
Copyright © 2025 by Gretchen Cassel Eick

This is a work of fiction. Names, characters, businesses, places, events, locales, and incidents are either the products of the author's imagination or used in a fictitious manner. Any resemblance to actual persons, living or dead, is purely coincidental.

All rights reserved. No part of this book may be reproduced in any form or by any electronic or mechanical means, including information storage and retrieval systems, without permission in writing from the publisher except for brief quotations quoted in critical articles and reviews. Inquiries should be addressed to:

Blue Cedar Press PO Box 48715
Wichita, KS 67201
Visit the Blue Cedar Press website: www.bluecedarpress.com
10 9 8 7 6 5 4 3 2 1

ISBN: 978-1-958728-33-8 (paper)
ISBN: 978-1-958728-34-5 (ebook)

Cover and interior design by Gina Laiso, Integrita Productions

Library of Congress Control Number: 2024952859
Printed in the United States of America at IngramSpark.

Table of Contents

PART 1
Chapter 1   Launch 1
Chapter 2   Porte Saint-Denis.. 11
Chapter 3   Summer... 17
Chapter 4   The Sorbonne and the National Youth Movement..21
Chapter 5   War? 33
Chapter 6   Assignment.. 39
Chapter 7   Complications 45
Chapter 8   Elise Brevard... 49
Chapter 9   Aidan, Orly Airport, Dec 18, 2027 57
Chapter 10   Return 65
Chapter 11   Reassignment.. 75
Chapter 12   End of the Holidays... 81
Chapter 13   Daniel's Assignment.. 83
Chapter 14   London.. 87
Chapter 15   Who is safe? 91
Chapter 16   The Growing Refugee Crisis 95
Chapter 17   What happened to Anthony Jones? 99
Chapter 18   Conversation in the University of London
             Lunchroom 101
Chapter 19   Paris—The National Front flexes its muscle. 105
Chapter 20   London—Homesick.. 111

PART 2
Chapter 21   A Surprising Alternative................................... 117
Chapter 22   Cora Meets Professor Benet 123
Chapter 23   Hanafi's husband 127
Chapter 24   Clarity?... 129
Chapter 25   Working for the NYM 139
Chapter 26   The Girl from Niger 147
Chapter 27   Hanafi's Message... 151
Chapter 28   The Day After.. 157
Chapter 29   Regional Trainings 159
Chapter 30   The Plane Trip 163

Chapter 31 The Training Camp	167
Chapter 32 Alone	171
Chapter 33 Brown-Eyed Iris	177
Chapter 34 The Deportation Camp	183

PART 3

Chapter 35 Escalation	187
Chapter 36 Jacques Thibault's List	195
Chapter 37 Occupation	199
Chapter 38 Prison	209
Chapter 39 Daniel's Parents	211
Chapter 40 Herding Cats	219
Chapter 41 Daniel in Porte Saint-Denis	223
Chapter 42 Amir Makes Contact	229
Chapter 43 Respite	233

PART 4

Chapter 44 Amir at the American Embassy	241
Chapter 45 Arrest	241
Chapter 46 The National Assembly Convenes	251
Chapter 47 Wichita, Kansas	255
Chapter 48 Stones or Flowers?	259
Chapter 49 What We Can Do	263
Chapter 50 Prison	267
Chapter 51 The U.S. Embassy	271
Chapter 52 The National Assembly	275
Chapter 53 The Weekend	281
Chapter 54 May Day	287
Chapter 55 Family Reunion	291
Chapter 56 May 8, Victory Day	297
Chapter 57 Daniel's Future?	307
Chapter 58 Family	311
Chapter 59 Crisis and Opportunity	319

Acknowledgements	325
About the Author	327

*For
Ronda Miller,
Laura Tillem, and
jazz artist Joan Minor*

PART 1

# A LAUNCH

She wanted to say, I've always loved you, Mama—your wildly curling hair, your quirky obsession with history, your beautiful, passionate intensity. But—to see your suffering, Mama—it wears me out and tears me up.

But she couldn't say that. Nor could she say that leaving would remove her from everything that reminded her of Dad's death, Mama's devastation, and Caleb's rebellion. She could not say that she needed a break from feeling responsible for them. *What could she say?*

Mama looked up from where she stood at the kitchen counter of the house Cora had lived in all her life. Mama was chopping vegetables for stir-fry, her cheeks wet from the onions. As Cora approached, Mama nudged an unruly strand of her thick black hair behind her ear and smiled affectionately.

"Dinner in half an hour. Your favorite, steak stir-fry. Want anything to snack on now?"

Mama was smiling but Cora knew what Mama was about to say.

Mama set three places for dinner. "It's our last summer together as a family." She turned to face Cora. "It's only ten weeks till you'll be off to university. I so wish you'd stay home with Caleb and me through the summer."

Cora looked at Mama, tears gathering in her eyes. The words that came to her protected Mama like Cora had protected her for the past three years. "I just need to leave home now so I can experience living on my own before I take on the stress of the University."

She pinched the skin between one thumb and forefinger while she waited for Mama's reply. How could Mama understand that Cora had stumbled through her adolescence trying to escape that April morning, trying to take care of her grieving mother and rebellious younger brother? Cora knew that had to change. At eighteen she had outgrown that Self.

Mama seated herself on a barstool and ran her fingers through her unruly curls. Typically, she asked for more information. Her face wore not a hint of self-pity, only her familiar Mother-Love expression. "Help me understand, Cora…"

Cora turned away to fill her water bottle, avoiding Mama's eyes and trying to find words that would be clear but not hurtful. "I feel like I've been an emotional zombie, and I can't live my life like that anymore. I have to figure out how to change, and I have to do that on my own, by myself. Does that make sense?"

To Cora's surprise Mama said calmly, "Yes. All right, then." That was all. But it was enough.

Within a week Cora had accepted the job as a live-in summer nanny for researchers at the University of Chicago and moved from their home in Evanston, north of Chicago, to the south side of the city where she began caring for Becca 8, Amy, 6, and Seth, 4. No drama. No tears.

Being a nanny was a strange job for one so introverted, but the children were loving and funny. When she was with them her curious, playful, and adventurous self returned, which felt good. And safe.

But in her second week once again just before dawn the memory resurfaced.

Unfamiliar voices downstairs, male voices wafting up the stairway. She opened her bedroom door and saw a group of uniformed men leaving the house and Mama, standing in the doorway with a woman officer. Mama turned away from the door. Something was wrong with her face. Then a sound like the earth was opening up to swallow them and the woman catching Mama as she slumped to the floor. She heard herself wailing, "Mama!" as she rushed down the stairs and saw Mama looking through her for a long moment, before reaching out to grab hold of her.

Cora always tried to wake herself up before Mama said those terrible words but she never could. "Dad was killed last night on the subway coming home from his gig."

Now, in her employers' upscale brownstone, she stood up, shaking, and moved to the bathroom where she splashed cold water on her face. The mirror showed an attractive young woman with intelligent-looking eyes her hair in a cultivated Afro, but the dream reminded her she was damaged.

~ ~ ~

When she wasn't at work Mandy Zablocki, the children's mother, was zany and full of energy. Once she proposed they all dress like monsters for dinner and served them green mashed potatoes and purple milk, with cutout paper teeth surrounding their plates to make it look like their forks were entering a monster's mouth. Another time, she sent them out for a walk in the park to find the food for her make-believe Malasaureses, small, friendly-to-children dinosaurs. Most of the time, however, like her husband Matt, Mandy was away at work.

When Mandy was out of town, Matt worked in his study after he returned from his office, emerging to interact with his children over dinner and for an hour or so before disappearing back behind the closed door of his study. He was tall and lean. Handsome for an older man and kind, Cora thought. Like her father. Cora observed Matt closely, wondering just how much like her father he really was.

One night when Mandy was at a meeting "at the U.N.," Cora put the children to bed and worked on her laptop until ten. Feeling a need to nosh, she went downstairs to the kitchen, surprised to find that she wasn't the only one needing "a little something." Matt sat at the table nursing a glass of wine and munching on mixed nuts, studying his phone.

"You hungry too?" He motioned to the fridge. "Help yourself."

She opened the fridge, took out the milk, and poured herself a glass. She took an apple from the broad wooden bowl on the counter and washed it.

"You can join me," he said smiling.

She sat.

"The kids like you. Mandy does, too."

She felt slightly uncomfortable. "I like them also."

Silence.

"You're from Evanston?"

"Yes."

"What will you do when summer ends?"

"Go to the University of Chicago. Study math."

"Good for you. That was my major, Mandy's, too. Now Mandy and I both work in Artificial Intelligence at the University of Chicago. In these times the world is desperate for bright young people like you to go into that career."

"What does it involve?" She took a bite of apple, beginning to relax a little.

"Understanding algorithms, analyzing data to find discrepancies, training machine learning models to recognize patterns associated with corrupted data. That's what I work on."

"Why did you choose that line of work?"

He laughed. "I wanted to save the world, be part of the relay race."

"Relay race? I don't understand."

"We work on our little bit and pass the baton to the next person. Ever run track?"

"Briefly in eighth grade."

Their conversation expanded as he told her why discovering corrupted data was so important. "Nuclear and biological weapons could be easily triggered by corrupt data traveling through multiple channels—satellite, Wi-Fi, cell towers, underwater cables." She felt excited listening to him talk about his work. She asked a lot of questions, intrigued by what she was learning.

At one in the morning, Matt yawned and stretched. "I'm beat," he said. "Unlike you, young lady, I need my beauty sleep."

They put their dishes in the dishwasher and went upstairs, but Cora lay awake a long while reviewing their conversation. *I want to do what he and Mandy do! I can use my love of higher math to make the world less dangerous.* The thought brought shivers. She wanted to hug Matt and tell him he'd changed her life. Of course, she wouldn't do that. He might not understand. Her last thought as she fell asleep was that her fantasies about him had changed with their conversation. Instead of wanting to climb onto his lap like he was Dad, she wanted to climb into his mind.

~ ~ ~

Five years later—after she finished her bachelor's and master's degrees—Cora arrived in Paris to study Artificial Intelligence at one of the world's premier universities for A.I. As she stepped into the coach that carried passengers from the jet to the terminal at Orly she recalled that conversation with Matt about his work. *I must text Matt and Mandy and let them know how important working for them that summer was for me*, she thought.

Resistance! 5

A month later she exited the Metro at the Eiffel Tower and stepped into the dazzling light show of April in Paris. In front of her sprawled the River Seine, and on the other bank, a breathtaking canvas of intense greens fractured by light and shadow, the grand garden of Trocadero. She walked along the Seine to the bridge, absorbing the energy of people sitting on the riverbank or strolling alone or in twos, celebrating this first glorious spring day. She had stayed at first with Aunt Joan, who was a local celebrity singing jazz in the major jazz club in the city, and then settled into her own flat just around a few corners from Aunt Joan and Uncle Andre. Small, yes, even tiny, but her own space.

She was back in the city that had captured her heart when she had spent one Christmas holiday there visiting Aunt Joan and Uncle Andre. Now she was enrolled in the Sorbonne's Artificial Intelligence Ph.D. program. But worry over whether her University of Chicago degrees had adequately prepared her for this work caused her heart to accelerate and distracted her from the spectacular spring day. She barely noticed the massed faces of daffodils bobbing in the playful breeze, brought back to life after the unprecedentedly cold winter.

Set those anxieties aside, Cora! You know they'll return, but you have the power to dismiss them. Focus on now. You can do this! She heard Mama's voice in her heart.

And her grandma's: *You have the gift of a job at Apple France, a break from academia until classes start in October, and time to work at perfecting your French in your favorite place on earth.*

And the great-grandmother for whom she was named: *Gratitude, Cora. It will always get you through.*

She refocused.

She turned left at the Pont D'Iena and walked briskly across the Seine and into the Jardin de Trocadero, following a footpath through the gardens. She made herself *notice* the scent of lilacs, the sounds of bicycle tires against pavement, children's voices as they played hide-and-seek amongst the hedges, laughter of little ones as the grass tickled their feet. Everything coming back to life!

She strode along Av. D'Iena toward Apple France Corporate Headquarters. She didn't want to be late.

She felt more than heard someone behind her. He was tall and fit, wearing running shorts and a T shirt and pricey running shoes. He was running fast. When she tried to get out of his way, they both moved right and instead of passing her he plowed into her, his momentum knocking her down.

"*Mon Dieu*, what have I done?! I am so sorry Mademoiselle." The voice spoke French but with a familiar accent. He held out a hand to help her up. Reluctantly she accepted his help. Drops of sweat flew from his face and flickered momentarily in the sunshine.

She apologized for obstructing his run, though she felt more cross than apologetic. After all, *he* ran into *her*. She checked her pants for grass stains and, seeing none, turned away, picking up her pace to get back to work on time.

Enough excitement for one lunch hour, she thought as she entered the glass doors and made her way to her office cubicle.

The next day as she walked in the opposite direction along the Seine, she saw him running toward her. This time they faced off and, recognizing her, he made an exaggerated diversion to his right waving to her as he passed.

Now that she had lived here a month, she rarely paid attention to the people she passed on her lunch hour walks. She was an internal person, quite happy living inside her head when in familiar surroundings. But this man, who ran past her nearly every day, began to attract her attention. Gradually she began to watch for him. Was it her imagination or was he watching for her also? Their nods progressed to one-word greetings, "Salut."

On a Thursday, three weeks after their collision, she strolled through the Jardin taking delight in the tulips, azaleas, and rhododendron. His voice with its oddly accented French interrupted her reverie.

"I think it's time we met. I'm Daniel. Who are you?" He had come up behind her, but he did not set off her alarms because he no longer seemed a stranger. Proximity in their brief daily intersections had softened her boundaries. Smiling, she replied, "Cora."

"Do you want to go for coffee sometime? Like tomorrow?" His question came with a smile that felt open and welcoming. He had shifted to English. *How does he know I am American? Is it so obvious? Or is he more comfortable speaking English?*

"I would like that," she replied, feeling strangely demure and somewhat awkward, a bit shaken by the beauty of his smile.

They agreed to meet at noon on the corner across from Apple France and he resumed his run, smiling over his shoulder as he called, "Tomorrow, then!" It occurred to her that she might not recognize him in street clothes.

Their coffee-time was comfortable. He was also American. Like her, from the Midwest, although from a smaller city in the middle of Kansas. They shared why they were in France and what they did at their respective jobs. An intern with the National Front Party, he worked on International Outreach. The National Front Party had almost won the Presidency in 2022, came close in the "snap election" of 2024, and was favored to win the elections this month. He talked at some length about the charismatic 30-something woman who led the Party. Cora suspected their political views would be very different, but he was interesting and attractive. They exchanged business cards before heading back to work.

Cora found herself thinking about Daniel on and off for the next week, but he didn't text her and, to her surprise, they didn't cross paths during her lunch hour walks.

Two weeks later when she stopped to observe a May Day demonstration in the St. Deny neighborhood where she lived, there he was. The National Front Party had won the elections and hospital workers had taken to the streets to protest the cuts in benefits the National Front government had announced the previous day. They gathered, hundreds strong, outside the hospital, waving their homemade signs and chanting their opposition.

"I'm surprised to see an Apple France employee here." She recognized his voice and its playful, slightly mocking inflection.

"Your presence here is even more remarkable," she replied. "Isn't this protest *against* the policies of the National Front?"

But he had turned back to a tall blond woman standing beside him and was conversing animatedly with her. Cora felt dismissed. She left the protest, collected some groceries from the small Moroccan market down the block, and walked back to her flat feeling grumpy and annoyed.

She didn't hear from or see Daniel and told herself she didn't care if she ever saw him again.

PORTE SAINT-DENIS

Porte Saint-Denis, in the 10th Arrondissement, was Paris' most diverse neighborhood. The multiple languages she heard while walking its streets reminded her of New York City. Shops selling falafel and babaganoush sat next to shops selling Pho and bun noodles. Others offered croissants and French pastries. She had wondered as she walked from the Metro to Aunt Joan's why most of the restaurants didn't open until 7 p.m. Aunt Joan said it was Ramadan and during Ramadan Muslims fasted, not eating or drinking until the sun set. The staff and clientele of these restaurants and shops were mostly Muslim.

Those first weeks she had paid attention to the people out on the street in Porte Saint-Denis. Women in hijabs and men wearing fez and keffiyehs greeted each other with a warmth that

Resistance! 11

surprised her in so large a city. She wrote Mama how much she loved living among and learning about this array of people from around the world who lived in Porte Saint-Denis.

Aunt Joan introduced her to a childcare center near her apartment that cared for kids from immigrant families, and Cora began spending Saturday afternoons there. The children's families had come to France from Syria, Iraq, Iran, Sudan, Yemen, Niger, Chad, Algeria, Morocco, and Palestine. When she talked with Mama each Sunday, Mama, always the historian, said the program sounded like the settlement houses that existed in the U.S. at the end of the Nineteenth Century when so many immigrants were flooding into the country. Mama was always adding historical notes to their conversation.

One of the mothers at the center, through her son, invited Cora to their apartment for tea at the end of Ramadan. They sat on the floor leaning against giant colorful pillows drinking tea and eating pastries. Sami, the seven-year-old, translated.

"My mother is embarrassed to speak in French now," he explained. "When my baby sister was sick, we took her to the hospital. But the staff complained they couldn't understand Ommi. Where we come from, Morocco, everyone speaks French. Ommi has always talked in French and Arabic!" Sami asserted, glancing at his mother for a nod of agreement.

"But since that experience, she has felt ashamed and afraid to speak to French people?" Cora tried to understand. Sami's mother lowered her eyes.

"Sami, please tell her that her French is fine. I'm not from France either. I'm American. So I doubt they would approve how I speak French," Cora replied. She was rewarded with a hesitant smile from the woman Sami called Ommi.

The afternoon went well, slowed by their need to concentrate to understand each other. Sami looked quite proud of himself as he shifted from French to Arabic and back. His mother brought out her wedding jewelry to show Cora, heavy gold necklaces and opulent head decorations that must have been worth a fortune.

When the tea ended, Cora returned to her apartment feeling happy.

She entered the code, climbed the tall stairs, and entered her snug apartment. She would not dwell on that year. "That was then. This is now." Another of her great-grandmother Gran Cora's aphorisms.

As she closed and locked her door a wave of nostalgia swept over her. She lowered herself into the overstuffed chair she'd bought at the outdoor market and hauled up the steps to her place. Gran Cora, the woman for whom she was named, had died five years ago at the age of 98. She had profoundly influenced Cora's life.

When Cora was born back in 2004, her dad had started calling Mama's step-grandmother, "Gran Cora." They were so fond of her they'd named their daughter after her. Cora recalled a balmy afternoon when the whole family had gathered in Nashville at Gran Cora's for a meal. Dad had referred to Gran as "Cora the First."

"I need to correct you, Richard. I'm actually *Cora the Fourth* in my family, and in our family the name was hallowed. For generations my family gifted girl babies with that ancestral name to inspire the newest someday-woman to be like the original."

Of course, Mama wanted to hear the story of the original Cora, so Gran Cora told it while they sat in the back yard drinking lemonade.

"The original Cora was an enslaved woman who, according to family lore, had run away twice and been twice apprehended, publicly flogged, and branded. Nothing would deter her, so drawn she was to the taste of freedom. After her second futile attempt to escape, she escalated her resistance and turned to sabotage.

"Like most of the women around her, the first Cora, even at fourteen, knew how to recognize poisonous plants: deadly nightshade, castor beans, white snakeroot, pokeweed, tobacco, mushrooms, jimson. She concocted a wine of sweet nightshade and pokeberries that brought paralysis that could stop the heart."

Sitting in her Porte Saint-Denis apartment, Cora remembered interrupting the old woman with a question. "She was enslaved?"

"Yes, child. All of her family were."

"And she learned to make a poison?"

"Yes."

Cora recalled how this information had sharpened her attention as Gran continued.

"Well, she decided she wouldn't give it to the owner of the farm because, if he died, they would be sold to cover his debts. But the man who delivered life threatening punishments for the least infraction, their overseer? She would serve it to *him* next time he ordered her to come to his cabin after dark." Gran's face showed how much she relished retelling this story.

"They discovered him the next morning sprawled on his back inside his cabin, his face contorted and a froth of reddish pink bubbles on his lips. It was clear he would never wield a whip—or anything else—again. No one knew the cause of his death. Or why the man who succeeded him perished one hot August day some weeks later."

Cora remembered Dad nearly choked on his lemonade at this revelation.

"In the quarters people whispered that the second man passed after consuming greens he'd ordered Cora to prepare and bring to him after dark. Some suspected she'd substituted the root of hemlock for its lookalike, wild carrot. Regardless, Cora developed a reputation among Blacks and Whites. She was clever, careful, and she was a survivor, attributes essential for young Black women, attributes that made her a woman to be wary of, no matter the color of your skin."

Gran said all the succeeding Coras were strong women not to be messed with, women determined to make their own path in this world, although the later generations of Coras shifted to nonlethal means to achieve their goals. (Unless the situation was dire.) Cora Number Three and Cora Number Four were born into freedom, but they had seen the swinging bodies of Black women hanging beside the mutilated bodies of the Black men who tried to protect them.

Even though she must have been only eight at the time, Cora remembered vividly Gran's words. "These women were determined they would not become that strange purple terror fruit. And that required skill in a region of the country saturated with violence."

Later Cora had asked Mama to explain "purple terror fruit" and Mama had told her that some bad people in long ago times would hang Black people for very little reason. "That was a very long time ago. You don't need to be worried," Mama had reassured her. From what she saw in Mama's eyes, Cora wasn't convinced.

Cora remembered being glad when Gran finally got to her own story.

"At thirteen I left my family's farm to move to Nashville to attend high school. No high schools in rural east Tennessee admitted Black students in those days. I did well in school and took to music. Which was how I met Booker. That man was as ambitious and serious about religion as I was. We married and I gave birth to Edward. Then Booker went to fight in Korea leaving me and two-year-old Edward behind."

Gran had stopped telling her the story and dabbed her eyes with a handkerchief, the linen kind with embroidered borders that no one younger than Gran used. She seemed to rush through the next part of the story.

"When a Korean landmine blew apart my beloved husband, I was nineteen… Somehow, I got a college education while raising my little boy and then, with the help of Arthur, Booker's best buddy in Korea, finished graduate school. I taught at a Black college. That was when Arthur's half-Korean daughter joined our little family. Later Arthur moved in. And, in 1967, when it finally became legal for Blacks and Whites to wed, I married my best friend. We had nearly four decades together, that dear man and I.

Resistance! 15

"That I've coped and excelled I credit to God, my church, and the Civil Rights Movement. They kept me focused. And, of course, to the heritage of my name." Gran had winked and smiled at young Cora.

When Arthur, her second husband, was reunited with his long-lost son, Gran welcomed the son, his wife, and his daughter—Keisha, Cora's Mama—into their family. *No wonder they named me for you. Oh, Gran, I never told you that your weekly calls to me after Dad died kept me going! Mama was barely functioning from grief and without your support I don't think I would have made it.*

In the tiny Porte Saint-Denis apartment so far from home, Cora Johnson-Allen huddled in her worn, overstuffed armchair and wept for her great-grandmother.

Later she phoned Mama. "Remember the photo of Gran you keep beside your bed?"

"The one of her in her nineties leading her church ladies to meet with state legislators in Tennessee to demand they protect voting rights?"

"Yes, that one. Could you have a digital copy made for me and send it? I'd like to have it here."

"Of course. Do you want me to send her cane too?" Cora could hear Mama's smile.

"I don't think that's necessary. If I need one, I can get one here."

"Hang in there, Cora the Fifth!"

"I will, Mama."

**SUMMER**

When the National Front won the election, some people speculated life in France would change dramatically. More people talked about the weather.

The summer was, well, *hot*. And the heat wave began in May. In Paris thermometers reached unprecedented highs. There was a noticeable decline in tourists and those who braved the extended heat wave took taxis for even short, walkable distances, rushing from cabs to air-conditioned public spaces and constantly wiping their shiny faces and fanning themselves. The L'Orangerie and the Louvre museums recorded the lowest numbers of visitors in two decades and the press reported the National Assembly was considering a large subsidy to enable them to remain open.

The media featured daily stories about the Riviera where the Mediterranean was encroaching on the coastline of France's major resort areas. The sea had crossed the beach and risen to the boulevard that separated it from the pricey high-rise hotels of Nice and Cannes. Everyone was talking about it.

Everyone was also talking about the fires that simultaneously devoured so many areas across Europe. Ignited by the slightest spark—a car whose ignition was faulty, or a cigarette not smudged completely out—climatologists warned this was a region-wide natural disaster. The unprecedented high temperatures and drought created much more extensive damage than in 2024 and 2025, when the European Union had called on member states to come to the aid of Italy and France by loaning their bombers to drop chemicals to extinguish the fires.

Even July 14, Bastille Day, was subdued. According to Aunt Joan, families preferred to remain in their apartments and watch the parade on television. The fireworks were canceled. Too dangerous.

Carbon emissions from the fires left a haze over Paris and the countryside, and a quarter-of-a-million people were evacuated from the south of France. Through most of July and August you could see people pulling roller bags and gripping children as they exited the Metro. They resembled refugees from Ukraine and the Baltic States, but they spoke French.

People resumed wearing medical face masks against the air's dense load of carbon dust. Clouds of emissions sapped the color from parks and gardens, leaving Paris gray and grimy. This was not the Paris Cora had fallen in love with years ago. She was glad when the prolonged heat wave began to subside in mid-October, just as university classes began.

Classes starting meant reducing her hours at Apple France to parttime, afternoons only. No more lunch hour walks along the Seine. She was a student at the Sorbonne, France's most prestigious university that was almost one thousand years old! That, along with relief at the coming of cooler weather, elevated her spirits and she poured herself into this new chapter of the rest of her life.

Daniel was off her radar.

# THE SORBONNE AND THE NATIONAL YOUTH MOVEMENT

In late October, Cora sat at a street café with two other students savoring coffee and croissants enjoying the chance to converse with other international students. She loved this part of university life, loved conversing with students from around the world. It felt good to be making friends after all the years she had lived solitary.

Muhammed was talking about a youth movement he was studying that recruited young French people who felt endangered by the large number of immigrants coming into France from North Africa and the Middle East.

Muhammad was tall, lean, and self-confident. He spoke English with a near perfect British accent, which he attributed

Resistance! 21

to growing up in Qatar with a British tutor. He spoke with intensity about what he was learning. "It is truly brilliant how they're organizing—weekend cookouts in the countryside hosted by one of France's richest businessmen, fun activities interspersed with speakers who message the importance of returning to the values 'of our forefathers and mothers,' values of the heroes of the French Resistance. What young person would not be attracted by playing rich and thinking of themselves as a fighter in the Resistance? Whoever the National Youth Movement's leaders are, they're smart. They know how to attract young people—T-shirts with slogans, free tattoos, free membership in the Movement, food at every event, opportunities to play the games of today's nobility—shooting guns, fencing, feasting. Plus, they feature popular performers at these events chosen because of the messaging in their lyrics. I tell you, it is a phenomenon."

Muhammed stopped talking to sip his tea.

Was this the organization Daniel Cook worked for? Cora's interest sharpened. Beside her, Hanafi, her new friend and classmate, appeared to be pondering Muhammed's words as she stirred sugar into her tea and lifted her veil to sip without uncovering her face.

Hanafi was a Saudi student who'd acquired her BA and MA in chemical engineering at Northwestern University, the university where Cora's mother taught. Like Cora, Hanafi had come to Paris to pursue a doctorate. Unlike Cora, she came accompanied by her husband and two young children.

Discovering their shared connection to Evanston and Northwestern had bonded Hanafi and Cora when they first met. Hanafi wore a black burka and a veil that covered the lower half of her face when she was in mixed company, mixed meaning men as well as women. When they met up at Cora's apartment, she shed the burka. Cora at first was surprised to see that she wore blue jeans and sweaters under the burka and make-up. Cora thought Hanafi quite beautiful.

Now Hanafi set her teacup on its saucer and spoke, her voice skeptical. "Is there no one in the Youth Movement who is other than White?"

"Actually, there *are* people of color in the Movement. I think they want them to participate. After all, many people in their twenties living in France came here as refugees from the wars in Syria, Iraq, and Gaza when they were babies, or they were born here to refugee parents. They too can be attracted to 'the way things used to be.' Isn't that true in the U.S., also?" Muhammed looked to Cora for a response and behind her veil, Hanafi's eyes fixed on Cora.

"Yes, I think you're right. Immigrants to the U.S. from places like Vietnam, Cuba, Iran tend to come because their side in a conflict lost to anti-American or anti-capitalist groups, which may make them receptive to 'the way things were' appeals…. But I thought the National Youth Movement was modeled on Hitler's youth organization and white supremacist groups?" Cora looked puzzled.

"Not exactly. It's building an international movement, fascist, yes, but according to what I've read, it intends to send those of its recruits who are not European French back to their countries of origin. Almost like missionaries. They train them to operate in Europe but also in their home countries, around the globe. They're to recruit others. They have a large and lofty agenda."

"That's really interesting. It sounds similar to the Christian youth movements in the U.S. back in the Sixties my mom told me about—Youth for Christ, Young Life, The Jesus People." Cora had gone through a phase in high school when she had researched Christianity, searching for a spiritual community where she could experience her great-grandmother's deep belief and the strength Gran drew from it. She had learned a lot, but never found a niche where she felt she belonged. She was still looking.

Hanafi jumped in. "I suppose most effective movements organizing youth know young people are attracted to free food, the luxuries of the rich and famous, and an opportunity to rebel against their parents' generation. In Saudi Arabia the government operates a similar program. Its intent is to keep its young people pacified."

Cora thought Hanafi was grinning behind her black face covering.

Muhammad smiled conspiratorially. "You both know Adam, right? The guy who went with us to the Second Chance concert? Well, he is part of the NYM. He invited me to go with him to one of their country weekends. I said I'd think about it. It does intrigue me, as a subject of academic research. Hey. Why don't we all go? It's this weekend. I think Adam would be happy to bring us three 'prospective new recruits.'"

Sitting at the outdoor cafe crowded with people enjoying the rare October sunshine, it sounded like an interesting excursion.

When she got back to her apartment that evening, Cora felt both excited and apprehensive about having agreed to go to the NYM gathering on Saturday. But when Muhammad texted that Adam had replied immediately to his suggestion, saying that it would be fine for the women to come, she decided it could be a fun outing. Adam would meet them at 9 a.m. at the Gare du Nord to take the train together to two stops past Chantilly. They should bring water bottles and jackets. Everything else would be provided.

When she Skyped with her mom the next day, Cora didn't mention the upcoming excursion or the National Youth Movement. Mama wouldn't understand. And she would worry.

～～～

On Saturday, Hanafi, Muhammed, and Cora met Adam at the train station. They had agreed to let their curiosity guide their conversation with Adam and others at the NYM event and resist challenging what they heard. Cora squeezed Hanafi's hand. She was glad they were going together. On the train they chatted about classes and professors, and Hanafi entertained them with funny stories about her children. But once the doors opened and they stepped down to the platform and hailed a taxi to the estate, no one spoke. Cora wondered if the others were as anxious as she was.

The estate was rumored to belong to Jacques Thibault, the conservative billionaire who owned France's largest media group and modeled his media empire on FOX News, promoting commentators who were right-wing. Adam told them one of the network's celebrities was scheduled to speak at today's event.

The estate was hidden behind ancient boxwood hedges too tall to see over.

"I think we've fallen through a rabbit hole," Cora whispered to Hanafi.

They pushed the digital entry box after Adam entered a code and the broad, wrought iron gates slowly opened to reveal a curving entry road that wound up hill to where a large manor house sprawled, commanding a view of the extensive grounds. The house was imposing and magnificent.

A golf cart raced toward them. The driver called out a welcome as he stopped beside them.

"Climb aboard. I'll give you a ride and include a guided tour of the estate. It's massive. Where are you from?"

The question offended Cora. Plenty of French citizens were dark skinned. And plenty of covered Muslim women were French. Nevertheless, Muhammed, Hanafi, and Cora answered dutifully as they stepped into the golf cart, "Qatar," "Saudi Arabia," "The United States." Adam said nothing and the driver didn't ask him. Cora wondered if he even noticed the assumption behind the question.

On all sides lay beautifully maintained, undulating lawn. Here and there mini-gardens with benches for conversation broke the sea of green. On the left was a boxwood maze and behind it a grove of trees. The driver was talking. "There is an apple orchard beyond the maze and," he gestured to the right, "tennis courts and an Olympic-sized pool behind the manor house."

This was clearly Rich and Famous territory.

"The pool is open as are the tennis courts. There are suits, towels, and rackets in the changing rooms you that should feel free to use. Also fencing equipment, although I doubt you fence. There are paths into the forest if you prefer hiking or jogging, and archery and target shooting on the right beyond the house. Drinks and refreshments over there. Just do whatever appeals to you until 11:30 when the plenary session begins—speakers, music, lunch." He eased the golf cart to a stop in front of a large tent filled with people milling about tables loaded with food. "Enjoy your day!"

Cora had never been to such a lavish place. Hanafi and Muhammad were speaking in Arabic to each other. When the golf cart and driver were out of sight, Hanafi explained that they had been comparing this place to similar "playgrounds" back home, only there the play spaces were air-conditioned.

By consensus they walked the grounds to view their options, stopping to play a game of doubles tennis. Adam was by far the best player, although Hanafi's burka definitely disadvantaged the women's side.

When it was nearly 11:30, they moved to the amphitheater for the plenary. The crowd of young adults was breathtakingly large and mostly White. "Should we leave now?" Hanafi joked in a whisper.

First came the musicians, including some well-known groups. They performed their hit songs and the crowd went wild. People moved to the music, whistled, and called out. When the music ended, the news analyst from station BFMTV, moved to the microphone and introduced the speaker, who was greeted with more cheers and whistles. Hanafi said she had expected Eric Zemmour to speak, but this was a young, blonde woman who appeared to be in her early 30s. She was obviously a celebrity.

Her message was clear. France was being overtaken by immigrants, including Muslims and Hindus who were changing the demographics of the country and threatening French culture.

"We are being replaced," she asserted. "I want to be clear. I am not anti-immigrant or anti-Muslim. I just believe we have taken in more people than our national resources can adequately serve. Which means they are consigned to living in squalor despite their educations and the professions they trained for in their homelands. We need to make their homelands safe for them and their children. All of us understand that the occupation of your homeland by a foreign group that does not speak your language or adapt to your customs and behaviors destroys the very nature of your country, whether it is France or Syria or Algeria or Mali. That is the message of today's anti-colonialism—let people govern their own countries and live there without outsiders dominating them. And that is what the National Front Party will do. You, as its youth cadre, will lead the way. Right?"

The crowd roared its agreement.

"The National Youth Movement exists to help people across the globe make their homelands free of outsiders who wish to dominate them. We must revive Patriotism across the globe, in Africa, Asia, Latin America, the Middle East, and in Europe."

Cora's mind was buzzing. Who wouldn't agree that outside occupiers should leave sovereign nations? Especially now with Russian troops on the eastern border of the Baltic states and knowing what happened to Ukraine? But the speech seemed too simplistic to her. She wanted to question the woman, perhaps make some points of her own.

She wanted to say that immigrants are an *international* phenomenon. Wars and drought and starvation force them to leave their homelands across the world. Yes, they often faced poverty and were unable to continue to work in their professions in the countries that received them. But like a centrifugal force the conditions that produce them keep going, throwing off millions of new refugees every year. If France reached its limit and closed its doors, and the rest of Europe did the same, what would happen to them? And with climate crises drying up huge areas of the globe and coastal cities threatened by rising sea levels, especially in the global south, how could they return to their home countries? Besides, many of their countries of origin were run by military governments with terrible human rights records. Her head was full of points she wanted to make.

The woman's speech was short and to the point. There was no opportunity to ask questions.

As they filed out of the tent, Cora and Hanafi agreed the speech was inspiring but left too many questions unanswered.

The plenary was immediately followed by a banquet served at long tables set up in the shady back yard of the manor house. Beer and wine flowed. The crowd moved to the tent, where the banquet was laid out, collecting food and drink, and then breaking into small conversation groups.

Cora noticed two of her work colleagues from Apple France. They were engaged in conversation and didn't acknowledge her.

"What do you make of her message?" Adam asked when they were seated in the sunshine on the lawn nibbling *fromage* on croissants, fruit, quiche, and raspberry custard tarts.

Muhammad responded first. "She's charismatic and convincing. She drew the group in with statements they would find it hard to disagree with."

Hanafi jumped in. "But the conflicts that create immigrants are not reduced by everyone remaining in their country of birth. Take me. I'm Saudi, but I'm also a Shi'a Muslim, and the government of my country is Sunni. The Sunni government persecutes my people while buying the cooperation of our best and brightest with scholarships, professional jobs, and houses with swimming pools. Remember the war against Yemen? That was against Shi'a. Religious identification divides people as much as ethnic background and language. So developing patriotism in countries like mine and organizing the youth to govern and maintain order is complicated, maybe impossible." Hanafi spoke softly, her gaze swiveling between them, then resting on Muhammad. Muhammed was Sunni, like the majority of Muslims.

"Isn't it similar in other parts of the globe? It's not just the

Muslim world that faces this." Muhammad sounded defensive. He turned to Cora for affirmation.

Cora took time to sort her thoughts. "In the U.S. of course there are many cultures and colors of people. And I agree that applying her vision to my country raises all sorts of questions. Which culture grounds patriotism? On my mother's side half of my ancestors are from Africa. On my father's side they were from Europe. And while we have mixed our cultural traditions, they remain somewhat distinct. Especially for indigenous Americans, those who have lived in North America the longest. We don't go to war against each other, but in our *feelings* about each other we sometimes come close."

Muhammed's shoulders relaxed and he lowered his defenses. "Anti-colonialism attracts me, but Hanafi is right that when you take it deeper and look within a nation at the diversity on the inside, it gets complicated…Take my country. In Qatar we are proud that we don't have poor people. But we designate the lower-level jobs for immigrants and recruit them to come to Qatar. So Qataris are not poor, but our immigrants are another story."

Adam interrupted. "So why do they come to Qatar?"

Hanafi and Muhammad answered simultaneously. "Because they make more money there than in their home countries."

"You're saying they're poor or almost-poor at home, so migrating helps them feed their families? Sounds like immigrants to the U.S. coming from Central America and the Caribbean!" Cora loved making connections. Was she channeling Mama the historian?

"Do I hear someone speaking of my country?" A shadow fell over Cora from behind. She turned, thinking she recognized the man's voice. The shadow darkened the grass between them and the sun's glare prevented her from seeing his face.

"*Cora?* What are you doing here?"

Now she recognized the voice. She felt acutely uncomfortable, wishing he would go away. "We were invited," she said without warmth to Daniel and turned away. He stood for several minutes,

Resistance! 29

presumably hoping to join them. When no one invited him to sit, he walked away heading for the food tent.

"Who was that?" Muhammad sensed her discomfort. She could tell he wanted to protect her.

"Just someone I used to see when I walked on my lunch breaks last spring."

Hanafi looked a question at Cora and Cora nodded. "Another American," Hanafi said to the men before turning to ask Adam a question. Hanafi was very good at signaling when a conversation was over.

Cora decided she needed to take a walk to sort out the conflicting emotions she was feeling. She told her friends she'd return in an hour. After thirty minutes she was no less confused. Seeing a pergola, she strolled toward it and, as no one else was there, settled on the bench. Within minutes an older gentleman wearing a cashmere sports coat asked if he could join her. What could she say?

He sat across from her studying her face. She felt uncomfortable. "*Excusez-moi, s'il vous plaît. Je suis Jacques Thibault.*" He switched easily to English. "This is my estate. I had to get away from all these people for a short while. You also, perhaps?"

She gazed at the ground without replying. She wanted time alone. He did not take the hint.

"And you are?"

"Cora Johnson-Allen."

"American?"

"Yes."

"I am honored to welcome you to my place, Mademoiselle Johnson-Allen. I hope you are finding what you are learning about the National Youth Movement to your liking."

Cora tried to be noncommittal. She was not interested in talking with this man. She faked noticing the time and excused herself with the explanation that friends were waiting for her. *Manners, Cora.* (Mama's voice.) She turned toward him as she walked away. "Thank you for hosting a lovely party."

Later that afternoon, as Adam, Hanafi, Muhammed, and Cora walked through the boxwood maze, they overheard a heated argument from the other side of the hedge.

"There is no room for them in our movement. We will not let them replace us."

"But if we train them to work in their home countries, they won't replace us."

"And those who remain here? Will we simply let them stay? They are reproducing while our people suffer an epidemic of infertility. We will soon be outnumbered!"

"Those who stay will assimilate. We can make that happen."

"And that means the mongrelization of our people. NO! That is not acceptable. They must be forced out!"

The four graduate students stood quite still, listening. Cora wondered what Adam was thinking. Gradually the voices receded as the two men moved on.

"Apparently not all NYM members agree with the speaker," Adam mumbled. "Actually, I'm not convinced that our speaker agrees with herself. I've heard her on CNEWS arguing replacement rather fiercely for someone who says they are not anti-Muslim or anti-immigrant."

At this anti-Muslim sentiment acknowledged so casually by his French friend Muhammad picked up his pace. Of course, he knew it existed, but most of the time he stayed focused on his research, confidant that as an upper-class Qatari and a graduate student at the Sorbonne, he would be protected from this disdain and even hatred. His discomfort was evident in the way he strode ahead of the others, his body coiled as though ready to sprint to safety. Hanafi watched him. Her eyes looked troubled as she called to his retreating back. "Shi'as and Sunnis may have more in common than we think." She spoke loud enough for Muhammad to hear her. Then she walked rapidly ahead of him and the others, her long skirts whooshing as they swept the grass. They could almost see steam rising around her.

A WAR?

That November the news was full of the Russian and Belarusian invasion of Latvia. NATO convened an urgent meeting to consider the situation and what it should do. In its long life—since 1946—only once had NATO considered an attack on one member nation an attack on them all. That was after September 11, 2001, when Saudi terrorists attacked three U.S. targets—the Pentagon in Washington, DC, the Twin Towers in New York City, and planned to attack the White House, only passengers took over the plane and forced it to crash in a Pennsylvania field.

France had not been a member of NATO at that time, having withdrawn its membership in 1966 under President De Gaulle. But NATO had launched Eagle Assist, its first ever anti-terror operation, a month after 9/11, in mid-October 2001. NATO

AWACS radar aircraft helped patrol the skies over the United States. For seven months 830 crew members from 13 NATO countries flew more than 360 sorties. It was the first and only time that NATO had deployed military assets in support of Article 5, the provision of its charter that pledged all member states would come to the aid of a member who was militarily attacked.

France had rejoined NATO in 2009. Now, in late 2027, the Russian invasion of Latvia and the decision NATO faced regarding how it would respond were of great interest to the French. Latvia's capital might be one thousand miles from Paris, but most French people had heard from their childhoods about the devastation brought to their soil by Germany's invasion of France in both world wars. No one remained alive who had lived through the last great war that ended in 1945, but the stories remained. They flavored succeeding generations' response to this 2027 threat. For those who followed politics, the first three decades of the Twenty-First Century felt like one long, protracted attempt to hold back World War III.

A major blizzard followed the Russian blitz attack on Riga, the Latvian capital. Commentators surmised Russia had moved its troops into Latvia to show Europe what it was prepared to do in the rest of northern Europe come spring 2028.

Fourteen years earlier, NATO had implemented the biggest increase in collective defense since the Cold War following Russia's annexation of the Crimea in 2014. NATO also increased its air policing over the Baltic and Black Sea areas and tripled the size of its Response Force (NRF), a technologically advanced multinational force. A NATO strike force 5,000-strong had been readied and multinational battlegroups deployed off the coasts of Estonia, Latvia, Lithuania, and Poland.

But NATO's increasing surveillance of the area, the multinational forces, and Sweden and Finland joining NATO in early 2023 had not deterred Russia from attacking Latvia. Latvia's neighbors, the other Baltic states of Lithuania and Estonia, prepared to be attacked. Anxiety spread like a forest fire across Europe.

Many pundits of the Twentieth Century had speculated that Russia's loss of 27 million people in World War II, made Russia war averse. But that assumption *mis*read Vladimir Putin. When he invaded Crimea in 2014 and Ukraine in 2022 and began killing off those who opposed him and imprisoning those who demonstrated against his wars of aggression, all bets were off about how Russia would behave in the world. Putin appeared to be modeling himself on Joseph Stalin, who had eliminated all of his opponents after Lenin's death and imposed absolute rule on what was then the Soviet Union. For the Baltic nations it was a nightmare, evoking 1941 when the Soviet Union seized their territory.

Amidst the fears of a global war, Cora, Hanafi, and Muhammed, along with the rest of the international students in Europe's universities, discussed whether to remain in Europe or return to their home countries. Cora thought her mother and grandparents would be less alarmed if she pointed out that Latvia's capital city was a bit farther than the distance between New York City and Chicago, but when they group-phoned to ask when she was coming home, Mama was not mollified. Buttressed by her parents and utilizing the historical knowledge Mama could be counted on to trot out in defense of her arguments, Mama was insistent. "Cora," she said, "in the U.S. Civil War the Union Army traveled that distance to take New Orleans within one year, *and that was 166 years ago, when armies had no tanks, aircraft, drones, or tactical nuclear weapons.* Surely you remember how quickly Russia conquered areas of Ukraine?"

Mama's caution hit home. Cora had been a high school senior when Russia invaded Ukraine. She had devoured news of the war. Images of exploded hospitals, schools, and apartment buildings, and of young and old women and children sheltering in place despite the bombing, or attempting to find refuge in neighboring countries, were seared into her memory alongside images of Israel's 2023-25 war against Palestinians in the Gaza Strip.

Resistance! 35

While the prospect of war alarmed Cora, she decided to remain in Paris. She hoped that her research might help end the conflict. She wasn't sure how, but that was her intention.

~ ~ ~

On the fourth Thursday in November, Cora received a text from Daniel. "Happy Thanksgiving! Want to try to find a turkey sandwich to celebrate?"

How dare he contact her now after six months of no contact—other than interrupting her conversation with her friends at the NYM event a month ago. She didn't reply. Instead, she fumed as she sat in the library of the Artificial Intelligence Department of the Sorbonne. She found it hard to concentrate on what she was reading. That annoyed her even more.

It was already dark outside, when she began putting away her laptop and notepad. At home the family would be gathered at their house in Evanston: her grandparents, Gran Cora's son Uncle Edward, Mama, and Caleb, Cora's brother. Maybe also Femi and Jacob, her cousin Aidan's parents. Feeling wistful, she pulled on her parka and eased the backpack over one shoulder. As she turned to leave, she noticed a man seated at the opposite end of the study table. He looked up as she passed and said just loudly enough for her to hear, "If the mountain won't come to Mohammad, Mohammed will have to go to the mountain."

It was Daniel.

"How did you know I would be here?" She felt completely blindsided and out of control. "You do know that that statement is nowhere in the Qur'an. It's totally apocryphal, some Englishman expropriating Islam and getting it wrong!"

"I do believe the lady is distressed." He threw her a sardonic smile. He was playing with her now, pretending to have a conversation with an invisible person. "She has good cause, I suspect. I did disappear last spring. Then I accosted her from behind at the NYM gathering, and now I appear to be stalking her."

Ignoring him, she walked past him, down the stairs, and out into the night. She heard him call from behind her, "It still is Thanksgiving, and if she'd let me take her to a place I found that serves an American turkey dinner, I can explain, though perhaps not to her satisfaction."

Her cheeks burned. She felt a hot mess of conflicting feelings. Nevertheless, she stopped walking, though she didn't turn around. When he caught up to her, his face looked woebegone and apologetic. Was he mocking her?

"I asked Adam where I might find you. Adam, the guy you were with at the NYM last month…The restaurant is around the corner near the Metro stop. You've probably eaten there? The American Café? I was hoping that the prospect of turkey and dressing and apple pie would override your irritation at me, at least for the time it takes to enjoy the meal!"

She looked at her feet, uncertain how to respond, which was enough for Daniel. He took her elbow and led her around the corner and down the steps to the café. She had to admit he was funny. And good looking. And speaking English felt good.

Over turkey, dressing, mashed potatoes, green beans, cranberry sauce, yams, and apple pie they talked.

"I was out of France for four months running a training program for Canadian and U.S. youth, and when I returned to Paris, the NYM promoted me. I'm no longer an intern but the assistant director of outreach for the National Youth Movement." He watched for her reaction. Seeing none, he continued. "I looked for you where we used to meet up when you went walking during your lunch hour and where I went running. But you didn't show up. No Cora. I went to Apple France and asked for your contact information, but they refused to supply any information about their employees, present or past."

Cora set down her fork. His explanation surprised her. Perhaps she was too hard on him. He at least deserved a response.

"I resigned my job at Apple France at the end of October. It was too much, working while attending the University. The

Artificial Intelligence program at the Sorbonne is too demanding for even a part-time job."

He smiled happily at her explanation, and she felt weak and disoriented, like the ground was opening and she was falling in. She concentrated on the surrounding diners, attempting to subdue the relief and excitement roiling in her.

The café was festive, decorated with fall colors and fake fallen leaves. A candle lit each table, softening her irritation. He *was* a perfect gentleman. They talked comfortably. He asked about her work at the Sorbonne, and she asked about the training he had led and how he liked his new job. Both feeling a bit homesick, each talked about their families and what they would be doing this Thanksgiving Day.

Their conversation shifted to Russia's invasion of Latvia and the pressure both felt from their families to leave France and return to the States. Like Cora, Daniel wanted to remain in France.

After nearly two hours, she said she should get back to her apartment.

"Let me ride with you back to Porte Saint-Denis. Some people say that neighborhood isn't safe for a young woman living alone." Daniel's voice was half-mocking.

Cora laughed but accepted his company. She did not invite him in. He was still on probation despite the dinner and his persistence. But she did like him, probably more than was wise.

Back in her apartment Cora reflected on the evening. She wanted to tell Mama about Daniel. This evening reminded her of her parents' story about how they had met. One party angry and offended, the other apologetic and determined to make things right. But maybe the similarity would be too painful for Mama. Might she and Daniel someday be telling their children about tonight? *Where did that question come from? It was just a pleasant evening,* she told herself. *Anyway, the turkey dinner did taste a little like home.* When Mama called, she didn't mention her dinner with Daniel.

Assignment

The last week in November, Professor Benet, Cora's advisor, called her in to discuss her dissertation research. Cora sat on one side of her professor's large desk, waiting for Professor Benet to initiate the conversation. Without looking at Cora the woman said that she was proposing that Cora take on a special project that would "help prevent war."

Cora's eyes widened. *What?*

"NATO has partnered with universities in the European Union to develop defense against cyber-attacks. NATO maintains a Cooperative Cyber Defence Centre of Excellence in Tallinn, Estonia that does accredited research and development and training. It also conducts educational programs for member states and collects intelligence. The Centre is NATO's premier expert on cyber defense. It organizes cyber exercises for NATO Allies and their partners."

Now she looked at Cora. "We have noticed how well you've done in your coursework here. We believe you will be an asset to this field. AI is the cutting edge of cyber warfare and cyber defense." She paused to assess Cora's reaction to what she was saying, but Cora's face was impassive.

"Your professors have suggested that you become our liaison to the Tallinn Center."

"*Me?* What would that involve?"

"You would be assigned to the Center in Tallinn for four weeks to be trained in their state-of-the-art research. Then you would return here to work with Professor DeLun, testing their results with aerospace companies that have contracts to supply NATO members with secure aircraft. That work would form the center of your PhD work. Of course, your dissertation will have to be classified."

Cora's advisor could see from Cora's expression that the young woman was astounded.

"Why wouldn't you want to send a French student rather than an American? And is it safe to be in Tallinn now?"

"I've already told you why you were selected—your impressive work in our program—and our program is the best in Europe, in my opinion, perhaps the best in the world." Her face wore a proud, smile. "Also, we believe our new government will be less likely to monitor an American. Frankly, we are concerned that the National Front Party government may pull France out of NATO, which could jeopardize our program here at the Sorbonne. We need to get one of our top students trained by Tallinn as soon as possible, and if it is you, we believe it is less likely for there to be reprisals."

Cora's confusion was obvious, so Professor Benet expanded her answer.

"And as a young woman of indiscernible ancestry, you will be less likely to be suspected of being engaged in such a high security operation by those watching." Professor Benet looked uncomfortable. She seemed to be implying that Cora's ethnicity had been a factor in her selection, that a young woman of color would not be involved in a "high security operation." Cora puzzled over how she felt about that.

Professor Benet stood and walked to the window, her back to Cora before she continued. "NATO has already done a security check. You have no behaviors that would compromise our security."

This information stunned Cora. *How do they know my "behaviors"? What does it mean that NATO has done a security check on me?* Cora forced her mind back to Professor Beret's proposal while her fingers beat a silent tattoo in her lap where her professor could not see them.

"You want me to go to Tallinn for a month to study at NATO's AI Center there?"

Professor Benet nodded.

"When?"

Professor Benet turned toward her. "In three days…One of the reasons we are accelerating this program and sending our liaison now rather than waiting until mid-2028, as we had planned, is that NATO expects Russia to move against Estonia in early spring. And to move rapidly, now that they have a foothold in Latvia and have alarmed the European Union. Our intelligence says the E.U. will appease the Russian Bear, at least for the next month or two, and the Russians know that. Neither NATO nor Russia would want military action before spring because of the complicated logistics of winter warfare. And of course, the E.U. and NATO need time to negotiate with Putin. That means we need our liaison trained *now*, before the thaws of early February when the Russians move on Tallinn and the AI Center there will have to be destroyed to keep it from the Russians."

Cora leaned her head against the back of the chair, her eyes scanning the ceiling while her brain processed what she had been told. How should she respond? She struggled to take in the urgency of the situation: The world on the verge of war with a short window to secure NATO's cyber intelligence before the Russian army could take it over. The request that she accept this assignment terrified her, even as she felt proud to be selected.

Professor Benet moved back to her desk and picked up a covered glass dish that she opened and offered to Cora. "Jacques Genin chocolates, made right here in Paris and, in my opinion, the best chocolates anywhere."

Is she trying to normalize the situation? Does she know that I rely on chocolate to get through disturbing moments? I mustn't be distracted. This is too important. She declined the chocolate.

"If the worst-case scenario materializes and they launch an all-out invasion of Estonia and Lithuania in the spring—remember, with the warming of the planet spring begins in February—we will have time to destroy the Tallinn Cyber Center and secure its R&D in other NATO research facilities ahead of Russia's invasion. Do you understand the urgency?" Benet moved around her desk to stand directly in front of Cora. Leaning back against her desk she looked directly and imperatively at her. Waiting.

Cora gave her an almost imperceptible nod.

"What do you say?"

"Can I talk with my family before I decide? My cousin is coming to Paris to spend the Christmas holidays with me. I haven't seen him in a very long time."

Professor Benet returned to her desk chair, her face stern. "My dear girl, I don't think you understand. This operation is **top secret**. *No one* can know where you are or what you are doing. We will provide you with a convincing cover story to keep your family from worrying and you will be back in your apartment by New Year's Eve. Hopefully your cousin can see you then?"

"Can you please repeat the time frame? When would I leave?"

"In three days… Short enough for you not to reconsider," she said with a slight smile.

"Can I tell you tomorrow?"

Professor Benet smiled. "Nine in the morning?"

"All right." With that Cora stood and put on her coat. She helped herself to two chocolates and stuffed them in her pocket. Then she fled the office.

COMPLICATIONS

She could not fall asleep. The assignment terrified and excited her. She would be doing something important that could save lives, even prevent war, Professor Benet had said. But four weeks… Four weeks could be a lifetime. She thought back to her fifteenth year, the year her dad left. She preferred to think of it as "left." "Was murdered" she did not say. Ever. That year weeks had gone on forever.

Yet when she went away to college, even months sped by. *Probably they would pass quickly in Tallinn, too?* She'd be super busy learning so much and concentrating on doing it right.

Her phone alerted her to a text.

"Outside. Can I come up? Miss u."

Cora looked out the window. Daniel stood on the sidewalk shuffling his feet and shaking the rain from his face as he scanned the windows of the third floor. She tried to open the window to call down to him, but it wouldn't budge. She knocked on the glass and he looked up and saw her. She signaled she was coming, pulled on jeans and a sweater, and hurried out of her apartment and down the stairs to let him in, silencing the voices in her head arguing caution.

She pushed open the heavy door and he stepped into the entryway, water puddling on the tile floor around him. He looked happy to see her.

"I'm so glad..." he pulled her gently into a very wet embrace. She surprised herself by not protesting. *I am an adult and can make decisions on my own how I will behave,* her heart told her. They mounted the stairs clinging to each other and she laughed at how wet he was, how wet she was becoming. She didn't let herself question what she was doing.

The next few hours were like nothing that had come before. He was careful to check if she wanted what he wanted. Careful as he joined her on her narrow bed, careful as he touched her. When she answered, "No. Can we just hold each other?" he stopped moving against her.

"You're right. It's too soon," he whispered. They lay close together on her bed, gently and carefully caressing each other. She suspended her disbelief that this was happening, banished lingering reservations, and savored the feel of his arms around her, his scent, and his respect of her wishes. Her lips parted to invite his tongue. His mouth moved from her lips to her neck, her shoulders, her breasts, and back to her mouth.

They talked idly while they held each other, and she felt safe, like they'd been together this way before. It felt natural, comfortable. Eventually they fell asleep lying like two spoons in her narrow bed.

~ ~ ~

They didn't awaken until sunlight spilled over them, and with it, awareness of where they were and what had happened.

"*I'm late! I must have forgotten to set my alarm. I have a meeting with my professor!*" Cora untangled herself from his arms, bolted from the bed, and threw on yesterday's clothes. Daniel pulled her close and kissed her once more before doing the same, and together they rushed out of the apartment and back to their separate worlds.

The morning was damp and cool but unusually sunny as they entered the Metro station. Neither spoke. She tossed him a quick smile as each headed for the trains that would take them in different directions.

During her ride to the Sorbonne, she turned her attention to the decision she had to make. Many questions remained, but by the time she arrived, the most important one she had decided.

ELISE BREVARD

Smiling broadly, Professor Benet said she had believed Cora would accept the assignment. From her desk drawer she drew out an iPhone and handed it to Cora. She also gave her a receipt for round-trip e-tickets to Tallinn, a wad of Euros, a credit card issued in the name Elise Brevard, and a Canadian passport bearing that name and a fictitious Canadian home address.

"You were that sure I'd agree to do this?" Cora studied the passport. It all felt so final and frightening. There was no changing her mind now.

Professor Benet nodded and held out her hand. "I need your cell phone and laptop. Do you have any other digital devices? We don't want anyone to be able to track you. This iPhone is only for emergencies. You will make no calls on it, only to Yanis, your contact there. Hopefully you won't use this phone at all in the next month. I'll store your phone and laptop safely and we'll respond to texts with a general message 'from you' that you have a chance to go on a ski holiday in Turkey with a friend and will have spotty Wi-Fi and cell service. You and your friend will travel the Turkish national parks after skiing and will be out of contact until sometime in mid-December. We'll monitor your texts and generate replies in your 'voice.' I am certain that your family and friends will accept what 'you' tell them. Artificial intelligence is a marvelous thing!"

Cora shivered involuntarily. Not because of the temperature in Professor Benet's office. Realization of what she had agreed to landed in her gut with a thud.

"And what about my cousin Aidan who will arrive before I return?

"Yes, you mentioned your cousin is coming. Do you want him to stay in your flat while you are gone?"

"Yes. I can give my code and door key to my Aunt Joan and ask her to meet him and take him to my place. I'm worried he'll be upset that I'm not in Paris when he arrives. My choosing to be gone could hurt his feelings."

"We—'you'—will message him that you have the chance of a lifetime to travel to Turkey with a friend for the next two weeks. Then we—'you'—will message him that while there your friend had an accident. You are fine but your friend needs to be in the hospital until late December and has no family near. You feel obligated to stay with her. You'll return to Paris on the 31st. You so regret this change of plans but look forward to seeing him on New Year's Eve and for the following week. Will that work?"

Cora thought it sounded plausible. Professor Benet seemed to have thought of everything.

"We have issued a rail ticket to Turkey in your name and an air ticket for your return from Ankara so anyone who tries to check will see that is where you are. I think we can address any contingencies and your contact in Tallinn will alert you to what we have told people before you arrive back here."

"I guess that would satisfy the family and my friends, although Mama will likely try to phone me at the hospital. What happens then? It's not like me to be out of communication with my family."

"AI will generate your voice response from the hospital. It will sound very authentic. I doubt she will worry too much. And on your return, we will tell you what 'you' told them."

Professor Benet poured two glasses of Dubonnet, even though it was still morning. She handed Cora one. Suddenly Cora remembered Mama telling her that the Japanese military toasted their young kamikaze fighters just before they boarded their plywood planes for their suicide bombing missions. She forced herself to remain outwardly calm.

"Remember that you are to have no contact with *anyone*, other than the one number in your new iPhone, the number for Yanis, your emergency contact. It's super-secure. Only use it to call if anything goes wrong. But make sure you pick up any calls you receive from that number. The number is your protection. It is how our liaison will keep you safe. When you arrive in Tallinn, take the airport transit bus #15 into the city and get off at The Sitting Woman Sculpture just outside the Old Town wall. Yanis will meet you at the sculpture and get you settled into your accommodations. He will be able to answer your questions. Please remember: Yanis is the only person you are to contact."

She stood and lifted her glass, toasting Cora. *"Bon voyage, ma chere. Tu es redoutable!"*

There was little time for anxiety once she got back to her flat. She had too much to do. She packed her roller bag, straightened her apartment, changed the sheets for Aidan, cleaned out the fridge, discarding produce and milk that would spoil in the weeks before Aidan arrived, and walked to Aunt Joan's to leave a key for Aidan. No one was at home, thankfully, so she texted, explaining that she'd be incommunicado on a ski trip in Turkey with another student. Would Aunt Joan please introduce Aidan to Paris if her return was delayed. She slid the key with a tag bearing the codes to her building and apartment into Joan and Andre's mailbox.

She felt naked with no screens. There was no way to check if Daniel had texted her and she couldn't text him. Back in her flat she wrote a note to Aidan welcoming him to Paris, using a cheery tone she hoped would sound normal. She said she was eager to show him the city she had come to cherish and hopefully would be home before he arrived. She left the note on the table under a small French flag, a souvenir she'd picked up at the National Youth Movement event.

As she left the apartment her knees were wobbly. *What am I doing? Will I see this place again?* At Orly Airport she boarded the plane and sank into her seat feeling a rush of homesickness for Mama. *Too late for second thoughts, girl. Get a grip. It's only a month.*

~ ~ ~ ~

The flight to Tallinn from Orly was bumpy due to an ice storm, which increased the anxiety that flooded her now that she was actually enroute. When the jet landed, she took the airport transit bus into town and made her way to The Sitting Woman Sculpture, following Professor Benet's instructions. She sat on a park bench shivering in the cold and reviewed her profile. She was a French Canadian, from a village south of Montreal. One younger brother, only one parent living, her father, a teacher in a secondary school. She liked that, it was easy to remember. It gave her a chance to imagine what her father would be like if he had lived. She conjured a fifty-something man, tall and kind, interested in people, a composer and conductor, creative, imaginative, and affectionate. Her eyes burned and she blinked away the pain of missing her father. *Our whole family lost Dad,* she reminded herself.

She was shaking in the brisk December air. It was much colder in the Baltics than in Paris, perhaps from the salty dampness of the nearby Baltic Sea. Traces of yesterday's snow-turned-mush chilled her feet despite her sherpa-lined boots. She heard the soft hum of tires rolling through the wet streets and the staccato spattering of the ice crystals they kicked up against the sidewalk.

The iPhone rang. She answered in French to stay in character. It was becoming her default language anyway. A low, rich baritone suggested she look to her left where she would see him seated on a bench just meters away. "Meet me at the fountain."

A lean man in a dark wool coat that a sailor might wear with a blue-plaid woolen muffler encircling his neck, got up from the bench and walked to the fountain. He did not look in her direction.

As she approached, the man turned toward her, his eyes brown, warm, and friendly. "Let me get you to your flat, Elise Brevard." He guided her by one elbow through the slush to the opposite side of the park, to a dark blue late model Honda CRV, and opened the passenger door for her.

The man identified himself only as "Yanis." He delivered her to an apartment building and walked with her up three flights to the furnished efficiency that would be her home for the next four weeks. It was immaculate. The spare furnishings included a single bed and armoire, kitchen table, chairs, and a futon, all in Baltic contemporary—blond pine wood, minimalist, but brightened by colorful woven throw cushions in geometric designs. The apartment was equipped with basic foodstuffs. He suggested she shop the covered market on the next block for perishables.

"Please remember at all times, you are Elise Brevard, Canadian, including when you are at the Center. Avoid conversation beyond small talk. You can't be too careful. We suspect spies are monitoring activity at the Center." He handed her a walking map with her path to the Center and to the Market marked. "They will expect you at 8 a.m. tomorrow. There is no time to waste. You have a lot to learn. Call me if there are problems but call no one else."

"I understand."

She expected to have a hard time sleeping, her mind crowded with colliding questions, but sleep came on suddenly and her alarm awakened her just in time for a croissant and instant coffee before she hurried along the route Yanis had marked to the Center. She went through security and met the staff with whom she would spend the next month. The first instruction she received at the Center was how to get to the underground bunkers if the siren sounded.

The days were long. She crammed so much new knowledge into her head that exhaustion overcame her by the time she reached her flat at the end of each workday. She was learning the other side of Artificial Intelligence, how it could be and was being manipulated by countries and corporations. How the various safeguards might fail and provide an opening for incorrect data, deliberately fed into the computers, to potentially be used to launch a nuclear attack, perhaps in response to fabricated aggression from a particular international player. Or, with a clever hack, AI could be used to launch worldwide economic catastrophe by disrupting international equity markets. Cora immersed herself in the latest research in how to identify corrupted algorithms and how to use CRCs to verify the authenticity of data transmitted or stored. The more she learned, the more it boggled her mind the precariousness of the world. How limited her knowledge of this had been!

Fortunately, the weeks passed rapidly. When she entered the Center before eight in the morning, it was dark, and it was dark when she returned to her apartment at the end of the day, which made her feel she was in one of those surrealistic *film noirs* her parents had enjoyed watching. Days of intense concentration and no personal conversation. Nights lying in bed reviewing what she'd learned and shuddering at the seriousness of it all. She took to eating chocolate every night, often more than one piece at a time. She was rewarding herself for her spartan existence. It helped to pass the time, although by the end of month zipping up her pants was a challenge. But the time did pass. The siren didn't sound. The Russians and their Belarusian allies stayed in place in Riga. She received no calls from Yanis, her liaison, and felt no need to contact him.

On December 30, with a minute storage device and its yottabytes of data embedded in her upper left arm, she left Tallinn. There had been no time to wander the medieval Old Town or to visit the city's renowned jazz clubs where Aunt Joan had sung. But she had learned so much in such a short time. She only hoped she had learned enough and in time.

AIDAN, ORLY AIRPORT, DEC 18, 2027

There was no blue sky as Aidan's plane landed in Paris. Only thick gray smog. People deboarding glanced furtively at each other as they hustled through the airport. It was not the normal anxiety international travelers show when they must navigate their way to baggage carousels and then Customs. They funneled into their designated lanes—EU passports? British passports? Other?—like cattle moving into trucks at feedlots. Avoiding eye contact as their bodies crowded the lanes.

Aidan collected his bag, displayed his passport, and completed the Customs check. He followed the signs to the exit and the Paris Metro, grateful for the French his tired tenth grade teacher had taught him. As he moved out of the sliding glass doors, the odor of woodsmoke and its acrid taste on his tongue disconcerted him. This was to be a joyous return to the city of light and beauty, a city he had loved to hear about from Aunt Joan, to read about, and to see in movies. Leslie Caron and Gene Kelly dancing deliciously along the embankment of the River Seine. What lay before him was not that Paris, and his disappointment was palpable. He'd read that Europe continued to experience annual fires that raged across the region devastating wide swaths of the land. But this was well past fire season. And he'd never thought about how those fires would change the feel of Paris.

He texted Cora before boarding the Metro and, when he didn't hear back, texted Aunt Joan that he had landed and was on his way to Cora's flat.

The Metro was crowded, especially as it roared into the city limits. There he changed to the line that would carry him to the St. Denis neighborhood. People pushed into the cars even when the doors were half-closed. As every seat was taken, most clung to the chrome bars that spanned the middle of the car or shared the hand-straps that dangled from the bars like nooses. The car's inhabitants rocked and swayed with the movement of the train, colliding with each other. They were mostly young, abundantly pierced, and tattooed. Eyes downcast, glued to their digital wrist devices, or closed while their earbuds carried music to their brains.

Aidan gripped the handle of his bag. This was a perfect environment for pickpockets, and he was a perfect target with a white Chicago O'Hare Airport tag on his suitcase that marked him as a stranger carrying cash for his overseas trip. The pressure of bodies on all sides felt oppressive.

A young man bent over suddenly and then re-emerged in the sea of heads holding Aidan's phone. In fluent English he said, "I think you dropped this, sir." His face was intelligent, eyes smiling. The utter confidence his eyes held made Aidan uncomfortable, wary. He wore a black hoodie, and as the train slowed approaching a station, he pulled the hood over his curly dark blond hair and turned away from Aidan toward the door.

"Thank you," Aidan said to his back as the doors opened and he left the train. Then Aidan felt for his fanny-pack that held his passport and the money he'd changed into Euros at the airport. His passport and the Euros were not there! His eyes scoured the door to the platform. It was nearly closed. He could make out two figures in black hoodies and jeans—one of them the blond man who retrieved his phone—talking animatedly as they hurried to the exit.

Another man wearing a suit and carrying a leather shoulder bag made eye contact. "They scammed you," he said in French but using the word everyone knew regardless their language—"scammed."

He motioned to the two hooded men and mimed the one retrieving Aidan's phone while the other unzipped his fanny-pack while Aidan focused on his phone. "*C'est ce qui se passe tous les jours à Paris, l'emploi principal pour quelques!*" [It happens every day in Paris, major employment for some.]

Aidan felt overwhelming frustration at this devastating development. But there was something about this man's face that made him feel hopeful. He appeared so calm. And friendly. The outer edge of his eyes deeply crinkled and his mouth wore a half-smile, as though good humor was his default.

Aidan clutched his phone, his one link to survival. When he left the train at Porte Saint-Denis station, the suited man followed him. "*Direction?*" he asked, his half-smile intact.

"Rue de Bartolome, merci."

The man pointed right and counted on his fingers to show how many blocks to the street: "*un, du, trois.*"

Aidan thanked him and began walking into the neighborhood where his cousin and his aunt both lived.

Porte Saint-Denis was like a bear, equal parts friendly and scruffy. Its streets splayed out from the Metro station in five directions, as though the animal was stretching every which way. Its sound was deep bass, punctuated with the treble high notes of car horns and the startling screeches of brakes halting the profusion of vehicles at the central stop light. He heard the hum of animated voices speaking in probably a dozen languages. Porte Saint-Denis was no *caged* bear. It was boundaryless and bountiful.

As Aidan walked toward Rue de Bartolome, he smelled curry—turmeric, coriander, cumin, cinnamon—and roasting lamb. Restaurants framed the boulevard advertising in hand-scrawled signs the day's special, often in Arabic, French, and English. Sometimes in Urdu and Hindi as well. He imagined the bear that was Porte Saint-Denis living in a garden of culinary delights, savoring the smells and flavors—a medley of cultures and voices and colorful, distinctive apparel. Ahead of him strode a woman of indeterminate age in a dark coat. Underneath, a red and orange print lappa. She carried a small child secured to her back by another lappa and tied securely over her winter coat. She was brown-skinned like Aidan and smiled at him. Another woman passed her, acknowledging her with a slight nod. That woman wore black from head to foot. Even her face was covered, except for her eyes. Was she from Saudi Arabia?

At #57 Rue de Bartolome Aidan pushed the buzzer for Apartment D. There was no answer. He buzzed again. He checked his texts. To his surprise, he had not heard from either Cora or Aunt Joan. He texted them both again, including that he'd been robbed and could not get into Cora's apartment building. Then he sat on the concrete step in front of the apartment and waited.

Several people stepped around him to enter the building: a mother with two young children who looked Middle Eastern, a young Asian man in a leather jacket and studded leather pants wearing headphones, and an elderly man with a white beard who carried cloth bags of groceries from which pita and a bottle of olive oil protruded.

The smog that filled the Paris sky combined with the smoke and the exhaust of rush hour streets, and he felt slightly nauseated. Cold rose from the sidewalk and he shivered. Farther down the street he watched workers in scrubs pulling puffy down jackets around them as they scurried out of a hospital. Must be a shift change.

This had been a day of mounting disappointments. He had expected Paris to glitter and glow, not to sputter and be nearly extinguished by the heavy air and lowering sky. He had expected to arrive at Cora's flat and be greeted by this cousin who had won his heart when they first met years ago. She was fifteen then and they'd stayed close for nearly nine years, but this was the first time since her university graduation they were to have a block of time together. *Where was she?* He had certainly not expected to be sitting on a cement stoop a few days before Christmas in an immigrant neighborhood where the only people he knew in the entire city were nowhere around. And with no passport, no credit card, no cash, other than the five Euro note in his pocket, his change from buying his Metro ticket. He pulled his roller bag closer. From another pocket he extracted a woolen muffler and coiled it around his neck. He was cold and tired from flying all night. Why had he watched two movies instead of napping?

He listened for the voice in his head, his mother Femi's voice. He didn't always appreciate her, but in these circumstances, he reached for her reassuring aphorisms. She had one for every occasion. He concentrated on remembering them.

"When God closes a door, God opens a window."

"When life gives you lemons, make lemonade."

"We don't have problems, we have situations."

That one would do. At least for a few more hours. Damn! What an introduction to two weeks of Christmas vacation in the city of his dreams that he had planned to spend with his special cousin.

~ ~ ~

Generally easy-going and accommodating, Aunt Joan was unaccustomed to irritation. But when she arrived home from the corner grocer, and the lift to the 4th floor wasn't working, she felt irritation in spades. That was before she belatedly read Aidan's texts and learned that Cora had not notified him she would not get back to Paris until the 31st. Irritation was too mild a word for what she felt.

Aidan was Joan's favorite nephew and the black sheep of her sister Femi's family. He did everything the hard way. He had overcome a great deal—foremost, five years in prison for a crime he did not commit—that occupied nearly all of his teenage years! When he was released at 21, he had to live dependent on his parents, with no job. Gang members threatened his life when he broke with them. But the man was tenacious. When a lucky break came—a federal program allowing him to transfer to Dallas to work for a relative who would supervise his probation—he'd taken it, although it meant working as a nanny for a year. A nanny! How many Jamaican American men would do that? But as he said at the time, compared with incarceration, caring for his small nieces and nephews was a dream job.

After his supervised parole ended, he attended a community college, where his intelligence and diligence were recognized. A professor there suggested he look into the foreign service, and he'd applied through the U.S. State Department. When last Joan talked to Femi, Aidan was waiting to hear if he'd been accepted.

Such courage he'd shown. Such tenacity. She was very proud of him. But what if the foreign service didn't accept him? Would his felony conviction preclude his acceptance? *How could Cora not have notified this poor, dear man of her absence, knowing the uncertainty and anxiety he would be feeling as he waited to hear from Washington about his future?*

Joan's irritation grew. She felt like a woman betrayed by the person she thought best understood her. She paced her apartment giving vent to her feelings. *How could Cora decide that staying with a hospitalized friend from university was more important than being here to welcome Aidan?*

Suddenly, Joan's irritation morphed into worry. Her love for Aidan took over. Aidan was alone, his funds and passport stolen. He was probably huddling in the cold darkness on his absent cousin's doorstep. What am I thinking pacing this apartment when Aidan needs me!

She was Mother Love again. Her hard-luck nephew Aidan was a son of her heart, and her Mother Love was mama bear protective. Her adrenaline surged until she was ready to battle anyone who might harm him. Powered by the urgent need to find him and bring him Home, she pulled on her boots and jacket and raced down the stairs and across the street, hurrying the five blocks to Cora's place. There she found him, huddled, head in his hands.

"Aidan! I'm so sorry!" She pulled him to his feet and smothered him in a too-tight embrace.

A RETURN

On December 31st, Cora left the NATO Center on Artificial Intelligence dragging her roller-bag behind her and headed through the gray smog that hunkered over Tallinn to the train depot. She had finished her weeks of training and carried in her head—and in the device embedded in her arm—the data that the Center's top scientists could not risk committing to other channels of communication. *Ironic,* she thought. *Tomorrow is 2028, the AI revolution is booming, and AI's top experts are relying on individual humans to carry critical intelligence instead of utilizing the digital, satellite, and solar channels that made AI the state of the art.*

She understood better after these four weeks why the AI experts were reduced to this "backward" step. Sabotage of AI was real and that changed everything. AI controlled so much of what the world knew, how the world received information, and how nations, media, educators, militaries, and scientists made choices. Once it was corrupted, its information could no longer be trusted. Worse than that, manipulation of artificial intelligence by a nation or even an expert scientist could start international panics, world wars, economic collapse.

As she hurried toward the train station, Cora cowered under the weight of what she now knew. The lowered sky magnified the weight of dread she carried. Like gravity on steroids, it held her down and she felt that she walked like a much older woman, bent over as though carrying a heavy load.

On the high-speed train she tried to distract herself with anticipation. She had the New Year's holiday weekend "off" before reporting to Professor Benet. She would soon see Aidan, who would be waiting for her at her flat in Porte Saint-Denis. Of course, she could not tell him what she knew. But in the past, whenever she was with him, she felt calmer.

When she first met Aidan, technically her mother's cousin, she was fifteen and he was twenty-one. His clarity that they must remain friends, when her adolescent self yearned for more, kept her from making an impetuous mistake that might have altered the trajectory of her life forever. He did not embarrass her as he let her know that theirs would not be a romantic relationship. He told her that deep friendship was more important, more valuable, rare. And he had been right. Being Aidan's close friend *was* more important.

Another time, he had assured a young and depressed Cora that bad things happening did not mean you caused them to happen. "The universe has its own rules of cause and effect; consequences come from factors influencing people that can be minute and unrecognized," he had said. "The gang members who beat your father and left him to bleed out on that subway car might have taken one too many drinks, or been screamed at by a frustrated parent the previous hour, or triggered by a verbal challenge from a brother that engaged their latent anger and insecurity. The sudden storm that night may have scrambled the ions in the air—even that may have altered their behavior. That doesn't excuse them, but it complicates who and what to blame for terrible things."

But what could Aidan say now that might calm the thudding of her heart and ease her fear of the consequences unknown actors could put in motion to threaten life on this planet? Maybe threaten her life? She folded her arms and hunched her shoulders, trying to make herself unnoticeable while she considered what she now knew and carried under the skin of her arm.

When the train arrived at her stop, she forced herself to assume a confident veneer and strode purposefully through the station and along the slushy streets to her apartment.

She shivered from the bitter cold of the damp near-darkness covering the city. Why hadn't she noticed, really noticed, the changes she was living through? She recalled Gran Ann—Mama's mother—recounting the story of how to kill a frog: put it in a pot of water and *gradually* turn up the heat; "before he knows it his body stops functioning." Was that what had happened to her and most of the world? Slow changes that were not noticed in the busyness of living one's life?

At #57 Rue de Bartolome, Cora entered the code and pushed open the door, dragging her bag behind her up the stairs to her flat. She leaned against her door, marshalling her resources before entering and reuniting with Aidan, the man whose wise soul could read her truth before she herself knew it.

On the other side of the door Aidan heard someone clanking up the stairs and saw his cousin through the peephole. He sighed seeing the worry lining her face as she sagged against the door before opening it. This was not the Cora he remembered. Something was very wrong.

Settled inside the apartment, the cousins tentatively reconnected. It had been so long since they had seen each other. Maybe good news would help bridge those years apart? He would try it.

Resistance!

"A few days ago I heard from the State Department. Drum roll, please. They've accepted me into the foreign service! My training starts the 5th!" Aidan's eyes were shining. Cora felt a surge of joy for him. He spread his Aidan-magic just by being here.

He jumped off her sofa to fetch a bottle of champagne and two glasses. "I thought we could celebrate." Aunt Joan had ordered dinner for them delivered by a local Moroccan restaurant. They ate, drank, and talked, taking a break to watch the New Years Eve fireworks at the Eiffel Tower from her front window. So much catching up to do.

Was it the champagne or his good news that made them giddy?

She asked him why he wanted to be a foreign service officer.

"I got through those years in prison by imagining my life in exotic places. When I got out and couldn't find a job, I read all I could find about history and politics outside the United States. It was my solitary passion. I think you know I am a solitary person." He smiled at her conspiratorially. "You, too, right?"

She nodded. "But with a felony conviction, can you be a foreign service officer?"

"In certain circumstances. If you score high enough on the exam, demonstrate skills the State Department needs, and have a legislator supporting your application, they'll admit you. It helped that my record was expunged three years ago thanks to my lawyer brother, who watched closely for the brief window Illinois allows for expungement after you serve your time and demonstrate you have reformed. I've been lucky."

Cora thought about Aidan's years of *bad* luck. He was such a special person, so caring and bright, yet he had been through so much pain. She blinked rapidly to keep back the tears she could feel welling. She chided herself. *This is his time to celebrate. Don't spoil it with your own sadness for what he has experienced. Just be happy with him tonight.*

Over the next hours while they sipped champagne and sparkling water, she listened to him unspool the past four years and the rocky path he had followed to pursue what had seemed a totally unrealistic dream for a man who had spent five years in adult prison for a gang crime he'd been present for at sixteen.

When the bottle was empty, Aidan laughed.

"I can't believe I've gone on and on about my saga when you've just returned from a holiday that turned into a nightmare, keeping watch over your friend in a hospital in a remote town in Turkey. But if you'd rather not talk about that, tell me about your experience here in Paris. How is the Sorbonne treating you?"

She kept her reply brief. "The Sorbonne's AI program is the best. I'm learning a lot and loving it." She deterred his follow-up questions by talking about the friends she was making from around the world, which led to a lively account of her holiday skiing in Turkey. Totally fabricated, of course. She wished she could talk with him about what she had really done this past month, her time in Tallinn.

They broke into a second bottle of champagne and the conversation shifted to their personal lives.

"Is there anyone special in your life, Cora?"

"I don't know how to answer that…I've met an American here who I'm attracted to, but he works for the youth movement of the National Front. Yes, I know. Scary group. He's funny and intelligent and I don't know what to make of him. Mama doesn't know anything about him. And Aunt Joan warned me to stay away from him. But…"

"You don't want to."

"Yes."

"Have you talked with him about what he believes, how he sees the world?"

"Not yet. There hasn't been time. It's early days."

"Sounds like that conversation may be needed before you get in deeper."

"I know. It's hard to do. It probably would be a deal breaker for me."

"Take the National Front seriously, Cora. They're fascists. It may be that he's uncomfortable with what he's learning about them. Or maybe not."

Cora was quiet. Her head spun from the past four weeks, the questions Aidan raised, and all that champagne. "I can't talk more about this tonight. My knees are going wonky from the alcohol, and I do believe that dawn is lighting up the window. Let's talk more after we've slept. I made up the bed for you."

"Of course. I am looking forward to seeing Paris with you tomorrow—no, *today!* Happy New Year, Cuz." He gave her a brotherly hug and moved his bag beside the bed. "Mind if I use the toilet first? All that champagne is working on my bladder. I'll be quick so you can shower."

Cora collapsed onto the futon, too tired to unpack. Shower? The thought brought anxiety and she gingerly touched the device in her upper arm. *Can I shower properly while it is in place? Should I wrap my arm in plastic first?* It was all too complicated. She lay back, pulling the duvet over her, still fully clothed. The last thing she remembered was hearing the water running as Aidan brushed his teeth.

On New Year's Day they walked the city, stopping at a cafe when they needed a rest. The weather was chilly and overcast and her numb fingers soaked in the warmth emanating from her large cup of take-out cappuccino.

"Aidan, is there anyone special in *your* life now? It's a fair question!"

"You sound like my mother! She'd like nothing better than to see me settling down and producing more grandchildren... There *was* someone. I'd have liked to spend the rest of my life with him, actually. But my foreign service work is classified."

"Are you in intelligence?"

"You know I cannot answer that. Lots of jobs in foreign service are classified. Even your spouse can't know much about what you do. He said he couldn't accept living with such a chasm of secrets. Felt it would erode the intimacy of our relationship. Maybe he's right... We agreed to take a break from our relationship while I discern if this is really the path I want to be on."

"Sounds painful."

"It is."

"The pull between what you want, even need, to do with your life and what your partner wants/needs from you—that must be difficult thing to negotiate."

"We tried negotiating, but he is clear what he needs, and I am clear that I need to try this calling. Yeah, it really feels like a calling, not only a job. There you have it. An impasse. Something had to give, and that something was our relationship."

"I'm so sorry, Aidan. You just recently broke up?"

"Just as I boarded the plane to fly here. But I think it's permanent."

Cora paid for their coffee. They shrugged on their winter jackets, pulling up the hoods against the drizzle that had begun. "Let's see if we can walk off some of your pain, or rather give you blisters that will move the pain from your heart to your heels, at least for a while. Lady Paris has some wonders to distract you, Cuz."

They walked quickly, heading for the Arc de Triomphe. The crowded streets had emptied as the drizzle turned into sleet. Rounding the corner of Avenue de Friedland, they saw ahead of them six young men wearing armbands with the NF logo that was noticeably similar to the swastika. Cora picked up her pace to get past them and Aidan followed her lead.

Voices assaulted them. "Hey! Who do you think you are? Don't you know your place?" "Where are you from, jungle bunnies? Paris is for the French, not for baboons from Darkest Africa." "Get off the sidewalk, shitface." The largest man blocked their path while the other young men began to chant, "Frenchmen only. Go back to where you came from."

The leader shoved Aidan into the street and knocked him down. Tires screeched as cars traversing the traffic circle in the sleet applied their brakes and swerved to avoid hitting Aidan. The men were laughing, loud, mocking laughs.

Cora helped Aidan up and hurriedly whispered what to do. Without looking back, they dashed through the crazy traffic circling the monument and ran to the Arc. Twelve avenues splayed out from the Arc like spokes on a bicycle wheel. Huddled under the Arc they could still hear the raucous laughter of their assailants.

The sign on the Arc de Triomphe said CLOSED. "Damn! I thought we could go inside to escape them, but it's New Year's Day."

Aidan stood beneath the arch looking out to his right. He was studying the frieze carved into one wall of the monument. A winged woman warrior dramatically urging men to fight the invader. Cora heard him chuckling. He pointed to the sculpture. "Perhaps our French patriots were inspired by this."

Cora was grateful he could see the irony in La Libertie leading men to battle the invader 240 years ago in the French Revolution. She felt herself channeling her mother, the historian, as she told him, "That valiant effort cost France a million civilian casualties." She shuddered imagining the carnage and looked across the street just in case. The men who accosted them were gone. "I don't think they're coming after us. Let's move on from this mighty icon of French patriotism and walk that way," she pointed left. "We can catch a bus to my favorite restaurant."

Over a meal of coq au vin and ratatouille, crusty bread, and red wine they talked about their encounter with the hoods of the National Front. Cora felt appalled and confused.

"This is the first time I've personally experienced racism in Paris, but then my skin is lighter than yours and I live in Porte Saint-Denis, Paris's most diverse neighborhood."

"I'm not totally surprised they went after us." Aidan had turned very serious. "That is what I meant when I said the NF is fascist. Its program, its tactics, even the armbands and tan shirts they wear."

"It seems to be getting more aggressive…I'm so sorry, Aidan. I wanted this trip to be a really good experience for you… A month ago I got tickets to take you to see the Catacombs tomorrow. It's the enormous underground maze of rooms and halls built just before the French Revolution from the bones of Frenchmen buried in the city's biggest cemetery. The city needed more space for expansion and was experiencing a public health crisis that the leaders thought was related to unhealthy conditions in the cemetery. So, they dug up all the bones and used them to build a huge underground maze nearly a mile long, lots of winding corridors all built with human bones and skulls. It's spooky and phenomenal, the stuff of nightmares… But maybe today provided enough nightmare for this trip?"

"No, that sounds like fun. After all, they're only bones. It's the living that I worry about. I'm game."

That evening Cora spoke with Mama who was spending the New Year in Cleveland with her parents. To Cora's surprise, Mama did not complain about having no conversation with Cora for four weeks. She simply asked about the ski trip in Turkey and her time with Aidan. Mama had her own exciting news—she talked extensively about a conference at the University of Winnipeg in February at which she would be giving a lecture on the Dakota refugees living in Canada in the 1860s. Cora attempted to show enthusiasm and support without giving Mama an opening to launch into yet another history lesson.

"How's your mom?" Aidan asked when the call ended.

"Actually, she sounds really well. She's busy with her own life. I can tell she's enjoying it, which is good. Do you ever feel glad when your mom doesn't ask you much about your life?"

"All the time," Aidan replied, grinning. "We all need to have our secrets from our parents, no?"

A REASSIGNMENT

Cora's few days with Aidan were full of walking, talking, and sightseeing—after they visited the U.S. embassy and secured his new passport. Thank God, there were no further encounters with the skinheads of the NF. On Tuesday, the 4th of January, she took the Metro and train with Aidan to see him off at Orly Airport, feeling tearful as he walked away through security and turned back to wave. *When will I see him again?* she wondered.

Next, she took the Metro to the Sorbonne to meet with Professor Benet and report on her time in Tallinn. The holidays were definitely over, and life in Paris had returned to its familiar brisk pace. It was her fourth day feeling the device embedded in her arm and she wanted it removed!

When she arrived at the professor's office, she was startled by the grim expression on Benet's face. No pleasantries or even, "Happy New Year." Professor Benet was pacing her office, her brow crinkled, and her voice rough-edged.

"The National Front pulled France out of NATO a few minutes ago. We have intelligence that they plan to expropriate our university's AI program, privatize it, and place it under their appointees—the businessmen who make billions from supplying militaries around the world with the means of war. The very people we've suspected of corrupting our intelligence to increase their profits will control our program!"

She stopped in front of Cora who had seated herself in front of the desk. "What you learned in Tallinn won't be safe here now, Cora. *You* are no longer safe here. We must get you and your information to London where we have been given temporary working space to continue our research and monitoring without the National Front and its agenda controlling us."

Cora tried to process this.

Professor Benet fidgeted, rubbing the forefinger of her right hand back and forth on the edge of her left thumbnail. Cora had never noticed this nervous habit before. Benet's urgency stunned her. Apparently, Benet noticed her surprise.

"I'm sorry to be so abrupt. I fear I cannot hear your report. The walls may have ears, and we don't have much time. The Front is deputizing citizens to enforce their new decrees, which include forcibly expelling foreigners thought to be a threat back to the former colonies. That might include you. We must get you safely out of Paris *tomorrow*."

"You can't be serious. How could they get away with that?" Then Cora remembered their assailants from two nights ago. Could they have been deputized citizens?

"It's been part of their playbook all along. People who study them have read their position papers on foreigners, their hatred of international alliances. They say alliances only cost money and draw France into wars and entanglements that don't benefit the people. They are strongly isolationist, as long as they can continue making money from selling armaments to all sides." She paused, inhaled, and changed direction. "But let's talk about you. Can you resume your identity as Elise Brevard and pack up your flat to leave by tomorrow night?"

Cora didn't speak. What about Aunt Joan? Would she be safe? What about Hanafi and her family, Muhammed, the others? What about Daniel? Did he know about this? Did he approve of these drastic policies?

"What about the other international students? My friends, and my family members?"

"The Sorbonne's lawyers are trying to bring a challenge through the courts while the university develops contingency plans for evacuating any student affected by these horrendous policies. This is unfamiliar territory. We've not faced anything like this since the days of the Vichy government and that was a very long time ago—1941-44. The people alive during those times have all. I assume you know what I am referring to, the Vichy government?"

"Yes. The government of southern France that chose to collaborate with Hitler after he invaded France. My mother is a professor of history."

Professor Benet smiled briefly, then reset her face to dead serious. "So, can you leave by tomorrow night?"

"Yes." The word slipped out almost on its own. Internally, Cora felt appalled that she had so readily agreed to uproot her life again. She yearned to have breathing space, to savor her time with Aidan, get back in touch with Daniel, talk with Mama and reconnect with Aunt Joan, sort through what she'd learned in Tallinn. But Professor Benet faced a far greater crisis than Cora's personal life, so she remained silent, although two questions circled her brain on a continuous loop: *What am I thinking? Do I really want to do this?*

Professor Benet passed her another cash card, a hefty wad of British pound notes, a paper with an address in London where she was to live, and the name of her contact there. "You still have the iPhone and passport?"

"Yes."

"I'm returning your phone and laptop. They may not be safe with me. But please be very careful using them. What you are doing in London must be shared with no one." She walked around her desk and opened her arms to Cora, kissing her on both cheeks.

"*Ma chère*, you have been most accommodating and helpful in this precarious time. I hope I will be able to continue to advise you on your research once the current crisis passes. And it must pass. For now. . ." She stood and extended her hand, taking Cora's in both of hers. "May we all survive." She said it like a benediction and the emotions flooding her face frightened Cora, who could find no words other than *"Merci,"* which she muttered as she left the office to return to her apartment and begin packing.

So now I will go to London. Alone for who knows how long. More weeks away from my friends and Aunt Joan. Still unable to talk with Mama. Why did I agree to go? Some overblown sense of responsibility? Oldest child syndrome?

The questions swirled as she packed. She would be more alone than she had been in Tallinn. With the Sorbonne requisitioned by the Party, how would she stay in touch with Professor Benet? Would they invent a new charade to reassure her family, or would the whole support apparatus that was her lifeline in Tallinn disappear? She made a brief call to Mama and another to Aunt Joan, telling them about her last few days with Aidan and saying she would be on another research trip for a while, unclear for how long. When they wanted more information, she begged off, saying she had to catch an early train and wasn't finished packing.

She saw that Daniel had texted but resisted the desire to call him. *What can I say? That the party he works for regards me as a public enemy? That I have to flee France for my safety? That the whole world could self-destruct?* She scratched her arm where it itched and felt the small device just under the surface. *And I'm still wearing this damn device!* At that moment she did not care if she was Cora the Whatever. Not in the least.

In the morning, she lugged her suitcases from her apartment and caught sight of herself in the downstairs hall mirror. *I will not give up chocolates!* She spoke the words aloud not caring if anyone heard them.

END OF THE HOLIDAYS

January 6th, 2028, Orly Airport swelled with travelers returning from holiday. Hanafi and her husband Raza firmly held the hands of their children, Khadija and Hassam, as they followed the crowd to the baggage claim. So many people were irritated that their vacation was over and impatient to get home! Hanafi wished the French weren't so surly.

They collected their luggage and moved to the exit to hail a cab, shivering as they stepped into the night air. Sleet fell like ice needles and stung their faces. Such a contrast to the persistent heat of Riyad. The children were shivering. Raza gave her a why-are-we-doing-this look, and she heard a torrent of angry words in French directed at them from the pavement in front of the taxi area.

"Get back in line!"

"We were here first!"

"Go back where you came from, you carpet kissers!"

The taxi driver released the doors of his cab without getting out. He, too, was an Arab, and they scrambled in, grateful for his unspoken understanding and shaken by the French people's ugly words. Back home in Saudi Arabia with their families, they had spoken of Paris in superlatives, forgetting this side of their experience in the city of enlightenment.

When Hanafi asked the driver to stop at a corner grocery so she could buy some basic groceries, he cautioned, "Be careful, Madame. There have been some nasty incidents in some of the shops over the holidays."

The driver unlocked the cab only as he stopped in front of the store to let Raza out. Raza instead of Hanafi dashed into a shop, returning with eggs, milk, vegetables, and fruit. The driver relocked the cab once Raza was safely back inside the cab with his purchases.

"Welcome 'home,'" Raza said to her.

DANIEL'S ASSIGNMENT

Daniel received instructions to appear at the office of the National Youth Movement Chief Executive's Office at 11 a.m. That was unusual. He had never had a meeting with her one-on-one. He wasn't sure whether to be excited or nervous as he knocked on her door. When he heard her "Entrez!" he entered the room. His hands felt clammy.

She was a striking woman in her thirties, carefully groomed and expensively dressed. Her appearance announced she was in control. She stood behind her desk and seemed to float when she moved around the desk toward him, her arm extended, a look of authority chiseled on her face.

"It's an honor to meet with you," he said, sitting where she indicated. She asked several questions about how his work was coming along before leaning forward in her chair and fixing her gaze on him. She switched effortlessly to English.

"Daniel, I understand you have a woman friend who is studying at the Sorbonne in the Artificial Intelligence program. Correct?"

"Yes."

"How well do you know her?"

"Not very well. We've only gone out a few times."

"She could be very useful to the National Front. We would like to see you focus on recruiting her. I understand that she is a… shall we say a 'person of color'? We want you to find out what she knows. Artificial Intelligence is very important to our movement. It is not exaggerating to say it is the future, so we must be familiar with it and identify persons we can place in positions of authority within AI."

"Actually, we've not talked much about her work."

"It is time to remedy that, Daniel. You can report directly to me what you learn. We have reason to believe she is engaged in high level research that has taken her to the AI research center in Tallinn. That's Estonia, in case you didn't know. I've been told that your French is improving to the point one forgets you are American and therefore geographically challenged."

Daniel swallowed his irritation at the insult. "I planned to contact her tonight."

"Good. Please let me know what you learn." She stood, indicating their meeting was over. "Good afternoon, Daniel. We'll meet again soon."

He recognized he was dismissed. No questions permitted.

That evening he texted Cora, who texted back that she would be spending the next semester in London. A sudden opportunity had opened up. Not Estonia. London. What was happening? Was she brushing him off?

He texted to ask if they could meet before she left, but she said she was catching the early train. He thought she sounded sorry, but what can you tell from a text?

How could he carry out his new assignment if she was in London? How would his job be affected if he couldn't? A whole semester until could see her again! She could be married to some Brit by then. Why did that thought pop into his head?

A LONDON

The morning of January 7th the clouds broke open to reveal a dazzling blue sky as Cora made her way to the Gare du Nord Rail Station. After days of gray sleet and rain, Cora chose to take this splendid display as a sign that things would be all right. She longed for such signs.

The train would carry her through the world's longest undersea tunnel, twenty-three miles, to London. The train was full of people, all heavily bundled against the winter cold, all peeling off layers of clothing and unwrapping mufflers in the warmth of the car. At this early hour no one talked. Commuters, probably, for whom this half-hour, high-speed trip under the English Channel was routine. Not for Cora. She had never done this before. She found she was holding her breath as the train descended into the earth and sped beneath the sea, gliding smoothly from Paris to London. She smiled to herself when she realized what she was doing. It was the child's game Dad had them play when they approached tunnels. "See if you can hold your breath till the end of the tunnel." She sent a silent prayer to Dad to stay near her and then blushed, thinking how silly it was to pray to Dad and expect he'd respond.

In no time a cheery voice announced in French and English that they were arriving in England. Cora, like everyone else, busied herself rebuttoning, rezipping, rewrapping, readying herself for the cold.

She pulled two roller bags this time, since she was bringing everything with her. It was possible she would not be allowed to return to Paris. She pulled the bags through the station to the taxi queue. In no time a taxi deposited her at a block of nineteenth century stone walk-ups on Woburn Place. She pulled her bags to the third floor and entered the high-ceilinged efficiency apartment Professor Benet had booked for her. By the time she unpacked and made herself a cup of tea, it had begun to snow.

She felt a sudden rush of homesickness. Christmas had slipped by while she worked nonstop in Tallinn. Her time with Aidan had been lovely but too brief. And in less than a week her life had again altered profoundly. She was far from her family, in an unfamiliar city where she knew no one, and the world was on the verge of a multinational war. The worst thing was being unable to talk with anyone about it. She lay on the narrow bed in the small flat and let her tears come. She felt so homesick that she hurt, everywhere. *What am I doing? All I want is to be with the people who love me.* She cried until she fell asleep.

Hours later she awakened feeling hungry. *Okay, Cora, get a grip. There's a map here showing where to get groceries. This is your life now. Move, girl!*

She consulted her phone. *Mon dieu!* A major blizzard was beginning. The news said it was another example of weather extremes caused by the warming of the planet. She pulled on outerwear, sped down the stairs and out the door, carefully making her way along the treacherous icy sidewalk. To the right of her building, several blocks ahead and across the street, she thought she saw a grocer. She moved toward it through the snow blanketing the city. She opened the door to the shop, gathered an assortment of food that would get her through several days, and paid. Thank God, they accepted her cash card. Back outside, she reviewed how to get "home"; cross the street and walk left to the building. But all landmarks were obscured. Was this Woburn Place? It must be. The entrances looked identical. She tried one and, when it rejected her code, the next. At the seventh walk-up her code worked. Grateful, she hurried up the three flights, her bags of groceries bumping into her calves as she climbed. She was thinking, *I'm home!* Funny word. But it would do for now. She felt relieved at her resourcefulness, finding the store and making her way back to the apartment. Was it resourcefulness or just luck?

The following three days "the storm of the century" settled over London, obliterating everything. The world beyond her window was whited-out, as though erased and replaced with giant piles of chalk dust. She peered out her window at the snow that rose higher and higher until some drifts reached the second story of her building. She scurried down the stairs to the basement laundry room and back up again for exercise (and to keep her sanity). She tried texting her contact, but cell towers were down. Wi-Fi also. Occasionally her tablet screen produced wavering images of BBC reporters cautioning people not to leave their homes because this blizzard was life-threatening. The reporters appeared faded, themselves white-washed and unreal. At night her window gave off an eerie glow from moonlight on the vast expanse of white.

Day four the sky was so low that clouds floated outside her window. The heat in the building gave out and she put on layers of sweaters and jackets and huddled on the bed with the duvet pulled around her wondering if she would ever see her mama and grandparents, Aidan, brother Caleb, Hanafi, or Daniel again.

She tried to read, but without power, she could not charge her devices to bring up anything to read. She probably could not have concentrated anyway. The storm seemed to have taken over every aspect of her life in this tiny, unfamiliar space that confined her.

Day five she awakened to hear a low voice. Someone was knocking insistently on her door.

"Miss, are you all right? We're checking on everyone in the building to be sure they've made it through this crisis. Are you in there?"

Her voice sounded scratchy from not being used for days and it took a moment for her to recognize it belonged to her. "I'm fine. Is there any news?"

"Cell and Wi-Fi should be back by noon, they say. The forecast is for an unusually warm day, if you can believe it. Since you are all right, I'll be on to the next flat. Cheers." She heard footsteps receding and then a knocking, more faint this time, and the voice repeating its message as it moved down the corridor.

Outside the sun shone, melting the white dunes with surprising alacrity. The street had become a gray river on which floated the detritus of city life: paper, umbrellas, plastic bins grocers used for their outdoor displays, bicycles. Even small electric cars rode the current. The green awning over the entrance to the building beside hers had collapsed and lay half-buried under the weight of snow, bits of green canvas showing through its white cargo like the possibility of grass. There would be no venturing outside today. She wondered how long it would take for the river of melting snow to be absorbed by the sewers and the thawing ground.

She turned on the electric kettle, grateful that it worked, grateful for a cup of instant coffee, disoriented by the changed world beyond her window.

WHO IS SAFE?

Cora shifted into a routine similar to what she had in Tallinn. The AI center she reported to was attached to the Imperial College London Innovation Hub. Once the streets returned to normal, she could easily walk the short distance to work. The offices were in the bowels of the building, four floors down. Her colleagues were businesslike, courteous, and impersonal. They asked nothing about her. She wondered if they were always like that. Were they as worried as she was?

They thoroughly debriefed her after removing the device from her arm and scanning it. She was included in a meeting with the top brass who were assessing next steps now that France had requisitioned the Sorbonne's AI program and assigned it to private AI experts working under the National Front Party.

They assigned her to the team monitoring France. Her days were sometimes monotonous. Other times she felt totally absorbed in her work of developing algorithms to reconstruct corrupted data based on redundant information, error correction codes, or statistical interpolation techniques. She also analyzed data looking for sudden shifts, unusual distributions, or unexpected patterns that might indicate corruption or tampering.

Most of her co-workers in London, like those in Tallinn, kept to themselves. Whenever she witnessed a warm or joking exchange between two or three of them, a pang of longing for connection assailed her. But she was not to have conversations with them other than about the work; Professor Benet had made that clear. So she stifled her loneliness, trying to drown it in long hours of work.

When she finally had an afternoon to herself, she visited the Imperial War Museum to tour the World War II exhibit. There she purchased a replica poster that read, "Loose talk can cost lives," featuring a man with someone's hand over his mouth. She stuck it up on the wall across from her bed as a reminder. She must manifest Elise Brevard at all times and speak only when spoken to. But she was lonely. Very lonely.

Five weeks after she arrived in London, on February 15th, 2028, Russian troops, tanks, and artillery fanned out from Riga across the Latvian countryside. The lunchroom buzzed with speculation. With France out of NATO, how would NATO respond? Would all the countries Russia had conquered and added to its Union of Soviet Socialist Republics in 1941 again fall, eighty-seven years later, to Russian troops?

Security intensified due to heightened concern that there might be moles for the Russians inside Britain's AI program. Five floors beneath her office was the top-secret bunker where a select group remained around the clock to watch for new activity that might indicate corruption of the messaging.

On March 1st, the Russians and Belarusians moved across the border into Lithuania. Within days, NATO's Artificial Intelligence Center in Tallinn was under Russian control. Cora's boss announced this. He said it was unclear whether the Tallinn staff had been able to destroy the facility in time. He didn't know whether the staff had escaped.

Images of the people she had worked with in Tallinn haunted her sleep. Imagining their fate left her numb with fear.

Yet, on the surface life went on with a surprising degree of normalcy. Everyone waited for the other shoe to drop. Would NATO respond militarily? No one wanted World War III. And no one wanted to see the Russians expand across Europe with impunity the way Germany had in those long-ago days of World War II. NATO continued delaying its decision as to how it would respond, unable to reach consensus.

As suddenly as the blizzard had descended on London the day Cora arrived, spring showed up. It stayed only two weeks before the temperatures rose to uncomfortable. April was especially warm. Cora began buying lunch at an outdoor café around the corner from her office where there were fans.

One lunchtime while she nibbled her salad with brie and crusty bread, an older man entered the café who she thought looked familiar. He headed her way, stopping at her table to ask if the seat across from her was taken. "No," she mumbled. To her chagrin, he pulled out the chair and joined her.

She hoped he couldn't tell how his next words terrified her. Looking directly at her and smiling, he said. "We met last fall, I believe. You came to a National Youth Movement event held on my estate, no?" The voice was carefully modulated with a distinctive Parisian accent.

"I'm afraid you have me confused with someone else, sir. I live here in London." She turned back to her tablet, afraid to pick up her latte for fear he would see her hands shaking. *I never have been able to lie. Damn it. I must stay in character. I am Elise Brevard. I am Elise Brevard. I am Elise Brevard.*

"Then you must have a double. I am certain I met someone who looks exactly like you in the pergola beyond my tennis courts. I believe you have a man friend named Daniel Cook?"

She forced herself to show no reaction, although hearing Daniel's name sent a shock through her. Was this the businessman who funded the NYM? How could he have located her here in London? Why would he remember her?

In her smoothest British English, she replied. "Like I said, sir, you have mistaken me for someone else. I must return to work. Have a good day." She left half her salad, carried her latte to the counter to request a to-go cup, and exited the café, deliberately taking a circuitous route back to the Imperial College London Innovation Hub in case he was following her.

"You did the right thing coming to me immediately," her pasty-faced supervisor said. "The man is Jacques Thibault, who now controls the Sorbonne's AI program."

Did I do the right thing telling him? Professor Benet said to tell nothing to anyone, other than the London contact in my iPhone. The weeks that followed Cora watched warily for Jacque Thibault but did not see him again. Her anxiety mounted as she worried that she may inadvertently have done something wrong.

THE GROWING REFUGEE CRISIS

They had been coming for decades as great swaths of Africa, Central Asia, and the Middle East baked in the heat, no potable water to be found. Their worried, drawn faces struck fear in the hearts of northern hemisphere Europeans and of Americans, who were convinced that their presence threatened life as they had known it. It was not a new problem, but it had grown dramatically decade by decade in the twenty-first century and the numbers were staggering. Fifty million people from more than one hundred nations had flooded into the northern hemisphere. People from as far south as Cameroon and Kenya, and from the Arabian Peninsula, Central Asia, India, China, and Central America. All came with only what they could carry. They fled starvation, desperate that their children be able to survive. They ran, too, from fights over resources that convulsed their nations as land once capable of supporting farming people dried up and the deserts expanded by miles each year.

International Agencies had done all they could to provide temporary help, but without an end to the use of fossil fuels, there was no holding back the march of the deserts that absorbed more masses of land. After years of the worst droughts in more than a hundred years, torrential rains had flooded vast areas of land in Asia, Africa, and the Middle East, wetting and rendering inedible families' meager food supplies, destroying their possessions, and forcing them to leave their temporary encampments on foot, their children in hand and tied to their backs.

The human suffering was too disturbing to see, so most in the global North chose not to look at the footage documenting this refugee crisis. Many popular politicians maintained the crisis was "fake," "manufactured by the media."

As the youth outreach director for the National Front, Daniel Cook met people from across the world. His job was to cultivate their trust in the Party's leadership. He excelled at one-on-one conversations with potential recruits, usually over coffee. That was a fact, and he was proud of it. Occasionally his recruits voiced their concern about the refugee crisis, sharing their personal experiences of it with him. Last week, while he had coffee with Abu Mohammed, one of his recruits, the man surprised him by suddenly gripping Daniel's arm, his voice lowered. He spoke with urgency.

"My brother was to come from Chad. He should be here by now. There is no water at home and our neighbors raid our villages stealing what livestock we have left from the drought. My brother thought the only chance our family had was for him to come here and send money back. He was to arrive two weeks ago, but I've heard nothing."

The coffee bar was loud with the festive voices of young people celebrating Mardi Gras. Daniel had to strain to hear Abu.

The man's face contorted with distress. "I've seen images from the deportation camps and from the rickety boats that try to make it across the Mediterranean undetected with too many people crammed on board. I keep thinking he is in one of those camps or dead somewhere under the sea. I don't know what I can do to help him." The usually stoic young man's eyes could not hold back his tears. Daniel had found the conversation disturbing.

Others shared similar worries with Daniel, once they came to trust him. Their confidences stirred in him a desire to know more about what was happening beyond the boundaries of the insular community of the National Front that was his world. These conversations disconcerted him and eroded his usual self-assured confidence that he knew what he was doing and had it together. He could think of nothing to say to calm their worries.

A WHAT HAPPENED TO ANTHONY JONES?

The Imperial College London Innovation Hub was abuzz over the disappearance of Anthony Jones, a man Cora had been assigned to work with. He had not come to work the previous week, supposedly ill with the latest round of Covid. But by day seven, his supervisor had called Jones's home where no one answered. The landlord reported he'd not seen the man for at least a week, and the police found Jones's apartment empty.

When Cora entered her flat that night, she found a small, folded piece of paper on the floor, as though someone had slid it under her door. "HIGHGATE KARL" it read in hand-printed letters. Perplexed, she googled the words. What popped up was "Highgate Cemetery, Karl Marx." Reading on, she learned that Karl Marx, the philosopher whose ideas evolved into the philosophy of Marxist communism, was buried in Highgate Cemetery in North London.

Why would someone slip her this note? What did it mean?

Cora cooked herself a simple supper, puzzling over the strange message. In the next few days work allowed her little time to speculate, but when Saturday dawned sunny and promising, she decided to have a look.

She took the Piccadilly Line to Kings Cross St. Pancreas and changed to the Northern line, exiting at Archway. It was an eleven-minute walk in unusually warm spring weather to the overgrown cemetery, the last resting place for a number of luminaries, according to her Google search. The tall wrought iron gate groaned as she pushed it open enough for her to slip inside.

Walking toward the back of the cemetery, an over-sized bust of the bearded Karl loomed before her. It diminished everything around it, compelling and stunning. She stopped to study him. His stone face was stern and intelligent, very like photos she'd seen of the original Marxist. She moved nearer. To the left of the stone bust the ground appeared recently disturbed. She knelt to examine it and found a sticky note that bore twenty-one seemingly random numbers. She studied the numbers and then pocketed the note. When she'd seen enough of stone Karl, she moved on to locate the graves of other famous people. After a while, her curiosity satisfied for now and her feet aching, she left Highgate Cemetery.

On Monday, she took the note to her strange supervisor, who again commended her for informing him of the note and of what she found at Highgate. "I will follow this up, Elise," he told her without making eye contact. He did not get back to her. No more was said of Anthony Jones' disappearance and no one in the office mentioned him again.

Spring rapidly turned into summer and wildfires again spread across Europe, Canada, South America, and the U.S. Cora, a.k.a. Elise, continued her AI research. She had begun to question what she was doing in London, where the research was taking her, and whether she wanted to go there.

A CONVERSATION IN THE UNIVERSITY OF LONDON LUNCHROOM

Two of Cora's co-workers sat at the next table deep in conversation. From their faces, their subject appeared important to them both. Curious, Cora edged her chair closer so she could listen.

"After Russia's illegal annexation of Crimea in 2014, with security challenges coming from the south, attacks by ISIL and other terrorist groups across several continents, NATO implemented the biggest increase in collective defense since the Cold War. It tripled the size of its high-tech multinational force, adding a 5,000-strong Spearhead Force. It deployed multinational battlegroups in Estonia, Latvia, Lithuania, Poland, and Romania." The younger man wearing tan cords and a wine red turtleneck spoke with passion.

"You think I don't know that? I remember NATO stepping up its air policing over the Baltic and Black Sea areas and increasing Joint Intelligence, Surveillance, and Reconnaissance. That's when our unit became central to NATO's strategic planning." The man with gray hair who dressed more conservatively was speaking, his voice low.

"So here we are twelve years after NATO recognized cyber defense as a new operational domain to better protect its networks, missions, and operations. Nine years after it declared space was a new operational domain and asked members to share satellite communications. And we do nothing while the Russians take over the Baltic states." The knife-edge intensity in the younger man's voice caused others in the lunchroom to turn and look at him.

"You certainly remember when Russia invaded Ukraine six years ago. NATO allies placed thousands of additional forces on high readiness and deployed additional in-place combat-ready forces on its eastern flank. It scaled up from battlegroups to brigade-size units, underpinned by rapidly available reinforcements. It prepositioned equipment and enhanced command and control. NATO declared Russia was 'the most significant and direct threat to the Allies' security and to peace and stability in the Euro-Atlantic area.' And then, while Russia laid siege to Ukraine, destroying the country and its civilian population, NATO did nothing. Why would you expect anything to happen now, given NATO's weakness? You know it relies on consensus?" Except for his flushed face the older man looked uniformly gray.

He pushed back from the table and went to refill his coffee, his movements quick and jerky like someone trying unsuccessfully to control their emotions. When he returned, he continued where he had left off. "Allied fighter jets patrol the airspace of Allies who do not have fighter jets of their own. They run on a 24/7 basis, every day of the year. So it's not like they do *nothing*. But they won't stand up to Russia, other than to remind Putin that they are there protecting weaker states."

"It's a damn catch-22. With the far-right taking power in the Netherlands, Hungary, and France, they've crippled NATO, either by withdrawing from their membership or refusing to reach consensus to take *any* joint military action! The world is impotent, and Russia gets a free pass to do whatever Putin pleases. It's a bloody nightmare! All summer the media has been predicting a mass exodus from NATO. More nations electing right-wing governments that want to avoid war at all cost!" The younger man held his fork above his plate, making no move to pick up another bite of his lunch. His face looked stark.

"Let's face it: NATO is terrified that any confrontation will lead to nuclear war. That's what we're afraid of, too, right?" The older man didn't wait for the younger man to respond. "We know U.S. nuclear weapons are housed in Belgium, Germany, Italy, the Netherlands, and Turkey. And France and the UK have their own nuclear arsenals. Not to mention Russia, India, China, South Africa, Israel. And, if there is a military confrontation, Russia has stated it will use them." The gray man took a sip of his coffee and did not raise his head. Steam from his cup rose like a small cloud around his face. Cora was reminded of Rodin's statuette, *Despair*, that she had seen the previous Saturday in the Victoria and Albert Museum. Such a look of desolation!

"I'm betting Russia will control all three Baltic countries by November," the younger man added. "Will NATO appease Russia then, or confront it? How long will NATO member nations remain paralyzed by indecision? It's like the immigration and climate crises—such a small minority of people are willing to honestly address the problem. I've thought about moving my family out of the U.K., but where could we go and be safe?" He placed his fork on his plate and gazed at the screensaver on his phone. From where Cora sat, she could see it was a photo of two small children.

"So we just plod on with our work and pray it makes a difference? Is there any alternative? I want to reassure you that it will be all right, but I can't tell you that. We have grandchildren, so I know how you feel. It is terrifying."

The two men paused before standing and picking up their trays to carry their half-eaten food to the conveyor belt that moved steadily into the kitchen. Silent, they left the lunchroom. Conversation in the lunchroom, which had ended during the last few minutes while they were speaking, slowly resumed with the sound of the door closing behind them.

A PARIS—THE NATIONAL FRONT FLEXES ITS MUSCLE.

Daniel sat in his running shorts sipping water while he read in the only remaining independent online newspaper in France that the National Front had seized the AI department of the Sorbonne, replaced its staff, and was arresting hundreds who protested this action. He wondered what this would mean for Cora's PhD. work. Perhaps it was good that she was at the Imperial College London this semester. In her text to him saying she was leaving Paris for a semester in London she'd written, "I hope things go well for you the next few months. I look forward to seeing you upon my return in June." Her tone implied they would not be in contact till then. But would she return at all now that her program was under NF control?

He was utterly confused about what to think of Cora. He had exited her life last year for opportunities abroad, and twice now she'd exited his life with a similar excuse. He liked to think their connection was strong, but would they ever have the time to pursue it? At least she wasn't living through the chaos of her program at the Sorbonne being taken over and rearranged by the government.

That same issue of the online newspaper reported that the National Front Party had declared a national emergency. It was the first declaration of national emergency in twenty-four years. The last time was when terrorists attacked Paris on November 13, 2015, attacking several locations, killing 130 people, and injuring 350. The story went into some detail about that earlier state of emergency and the attack on the stadium where it began… *Oh, my god! The stadium that terrorists attacked then is just north of Porte Saint-Denis, not far from where Cora lives!* Then he remembered that Cora was in the U.K. now and presumably safe. The intensity of the relief he felt surprised him.

Noticing the time, Daniel closed the newspaper website and walked rapidly to the kebab shop where he was to meet Amir. Amir was always on time. Daniel? Not so much.

Daniel thought it unusual that Amir called rather than texted him this morning asking to meet. Amir was one of Daniel's star recruits, already promoted to director of outreach for Cameroon. What was so urgent that he needed to meet on Saturday, Daniel's day off?

The tiny kebab shop was barely big enough to swing a cat. Most of its clientele came for take-away food, but in the back, beside the bold arrow pointing the way to the toilet, was a small table with two chairs. There Amir sat, his back against the wall. His eyes scanned the sidewalk through the shop window. The two embraced before sitting across from each other.

From the kitchen doorway with its curtain of colorful strings of jingling beads, a small, covered woman emerged carrying a copper tray with an open copper pot of coffee, a bowl of sugar cubes, another bowl of jellied cubes in primary colors, and two miniature porcelain cups. The strong aroma of Turkish coffee preceded her. She served them and backed away as they smiled their thanks.

Amir got straight to the point. He spoke rapidly and in English. "My uncle has contacted me. He is full of stories about the problems in our country. For several years Amazon, Meta, and Nvidia have offered jobs to our best and brightest young people, programming jobs. Our people expected they would receive promotions if they worked well in the world's largest AI companies. Instead, they are assigned stupid tasks like designing and managing those identity bots you must use to prove you are a human. They are paid very little and are never promoted. They can barely meet their personal expenses, much less assist their families. These are our university graduates! They speak multiple languages. They are our future. Uncle says today's *Le Monde* reported that these AI companies are earning enormous profits, as they have been for a decade. Meanwhile, those who are the key to Cameroon's future flounder."

Daniel did not understand what Amir's distress had to do with him, but he knew Amir well enough to wait and listen.

"On top of that, Uncle says the heat wave has made life at home unbearable. Yesterday the fishermen from Uncle's town returned with empty nets. The temperatures are averaging five degrees higher than three years ago. That makes the rivers too hot for the fish to survive. They harvest few fish, and sometimes, when there is a leak from the offshore drilling rigs, no fish at all because the fish float on top of the sea killed by an oil slick. Our town relies on fish for our people's diet and for export."

Usually Daniel took pride in his ability to read his recruits, but today he was completely lost. He slipped a green jellied sugar cube into his mouth and sipped the strong, dark coffee, letting the coffee soften the cube. He savored how the cube's melting sweetness offset the bitterness of the coffee while he tried to comprehend what Amir was telling him.

Detecting Daniel's confusion, Amir tried to explain. "Our government collaborates with the giant AI companies and gets a payoff—contingent on the government permitting these companies to operate unregulated. It's a new form of colonialism, and fossil fuel industries are today's colonizers."

"Whoa! What do fossil fuel companies have to do with any of this?" Daniel felt defensive. His grandfather and great-grandfather had started the largest privately owned oil company in the U.S., a company that he would likely run one day.

Amir ran his hand through his tight curls and, for a moment, looked lost. When he raised his eyes to meet Daniel's, he looked resolute. "I must find a way to make you understand." He took a deep breath before continuing.

"Please let me explain. Every year companies and governments, the fossil fuel suppliers—including the governments across the Persian Gulf: Saudi Arabia, Dubai, Qatar, the United Arab Emirates—pledge to reduce the warming of the planet, to keep it no more than 1.5 degrees higher than the average in the twentieth century. But they are allowed to buy carbon credits from other parts of the world to 'offset' their over-production of carbon dioxide. It is an elaborate trading scheme. Oil producers—countries and companies—buy and sell carbon emission credits (one credit for one ton of CO_2 removed from the atmosphere). They especially buy these credits from African governments that don't use as much fossil fuel and therefore don't produce much CO_2."

Amir leaned forward and his hand sliced the air between them landing on the tabletop with a bang. His voice was strident. "Purchasing carbon credits allows companies and foreign governments to go on producing petroleum and natural gas as usual without violating international climate agreements! Their over-production lets them continue to accelerate the warming of the planet, while the rest of the world believes they are actually reducing CO_2. They are not. It's a magic trick, mirrors and smoke, all fake. Do you understand me?" Amir took a sip of his coffee, his eyes locked on Daniel, who nodded.

"Also, the price they pay to African countries for these credits has dropped dramatically. They paid $18/ton in 2022. Today they pay less than $1/ton. They keep extracting fossil fuels virtually unregulated while Africa's temperatures continue to rise and its environment to degrade. African governments receive almost nothing in return. Our climate catastrophe is so much worse than Europe or America's. Yet the rest of the world doesn't give a damn. Our people suffer. And our best and brightest are employed in entry level jobs without hope of promotion. It's been going on throughout this century and it's getting so much worse. Of course, our government officials receive incentive 'bonuses' for selling our carbon credits. They grow wealthy and don't acknowledge the impact on our people of their kowtowing to foreign companies and governments."

Daniel said nothing. It was a lot to take in. He had heard allegations against oil companies, but the details in Amir's account implied abuses on a scale much larger than he had imagined.

At his silence, Amir stood up, his hands on his head. Daniel had never seen Amir look so distressed. The sound of his chair legs scraping the floor echoed loudly in the empty kebab shop.

"You're feeling you must do something about this?" Daniel asked.

"Of course!" Slowly Amir lowered himself to his chair. He did not make eye contact with Daniel.

"But what can you do?"

"I'm working that out." He looked directly at Daniel now. "What I can NOT do is continue working for the National Youth Movement, persuading our youth that they must believe their Big Lie."

Now Daniel felt lost and defensive. "What is the Big Lie, exactly?"

"That Europe, America, and the Middle East want what is best for Africa. Come on, Daniel! You must see it! They want us to serve them, to provide oil, natural gas, solar power, diamonds, iron ore, land for mining, and specialty foods for rich folks. To allow them to continue to pollute, raise temperatures in Africa, and hide behind the carbon credits scheme. To hire our best and brightest to do shit work for little pay and no ability to be promoted. To tell them if they follow the policies of the National Front, they will prosper… I can't be a part of that, no matter how glitzy the lifestyle you all offer me. I won't sell out my people. And I needed to tell you today, before my resolve is corrupted by all the perks of your new colonialism."

Amir stood again, pulled Euros from his pocket to pay for their coffee, forced a wan "I'm sorry" smile, and left.

The covered woman appeared in the doorway. No doubt she'd heard Amir's raised voice. The colorful beads hanging over the doorway chimed and tingled as she moved through them and toward their table. Her eyes questioned Daniel: Was everything all right? Was he leaving too? Should she clear away the coffee?

Daniel smiled and nodded, passing her Amir's Euros. Amir had paid for both coffees and he had left a substantial tip. Daniel thought Amir had been too generous in his tip. Did that make him complicit in what Amir was talking about? Uncomfortable with that thought, he swallowed the last of his coffee and tucked another jellied cube into his mouth before leaving the kebab shop.

He paid no attention to where his feet took him. His mind mulled Amir's words. Amir's experiences exposed him to a way of looking at the world that was so foreign to the perspective of his privileged family. But he trusted Amir. Hearing his account validated the questions Daniel had been asking himself. He felt like a sea change was going on inside him, altering how he understood the world. He needed to stay in contact with Amir, to learn from him. He tried to decide how to respond.

A young man on a skateboard collided with Daniel, which brought him out of his head. He looked around to see where he was. It was familiar in an odd pleasure/pain kind of way. Looking up, he recognized the third window to the right of the entrance. Cora's apartment. It looked identical to the other vacant windows looking down on Rue de Bartholome.

A LONDON—HOMESICK

Cora was sick of being Elise Brevard. No one talked with her at work. Her immediate boss was cold and business-like, never asking how she was or complimenting her work. She longed to be her real self with someone, anyone. Self-pity swamped her as she walked home to Woburn Place. Not even the "Cheerio!" from the Indian grocer on the corner raised her spirits. She had been in London six months, and nothing was improving. Certainly not the situation in France, which the news media reported was steadily worsening. Certainly not the prospects that their work at the Imperial College London Innovation Hub could deter an inevitable worldwide conflict. She'd listened closely to the senior researchers' conversations. If *they* were so discouraged, why should she remain here, isolated from family and friends, trapped in a false identity, and unable to talk with anyone?

Climbing the stairs to her flat, she felt grief rise from her throat to her eyes. She opened her door and fell onto the bed sobbing. She was twenty-five, single, and nowhere near the optimistic woman she had been when she'd arrived in Paris two years before. With the Sorbonne's program taken over by the French government and run by the National Front Party, Professor Bernard had disappeared from the Sorbonne's website and her dreams of a PhD in AI lay shattered. She wanted to talk to Mama. To Gran. To Aidan. To Hanafi. To Daniel.

She had no idea how long she cried. It felt like hours. When she went into the bathroom, she hardly recognized her ravaged face in the mirror. *I can't do this. I can't. I want to go home. Or back to Paris.*

She couldn't recall a single aphorism Gran had taught her for times like these. Which deepened her misery. She hadn't felt this low since she'd run away from home when she was fifteen.

That thought triggered a memory. The homeless woman who had befriended her and kept her safe that night. "You can get through just about anything, child," Lucy Jordan had told her. "It all depends on your attitude no matter the circumstances."

When the sky darkened, she realized it was close to midnight. It was June 23rd, the longest day of the year in Europe. In Tallinn, her colleagues had told her that Jaani, June 23rd, was a magical night. When a group of them had gone to lunch together shortly before the holiday, one mentioned that both of his children's birthdays were in late April. The others chortled and Cora's confusion must have shown because he continued: "Everyone goes to the countryside, drinks too much, sings, parties wildly… and nine months later our population increases." Everyone had laughed and nodded.

"Elise, you need to know about *Jaanilaupäev*, Jaani for short. It can change your life," a woman had added. "You never know what can happen June 23rd. Remember Shakespeare's *Midsummer Night's Dream*, people turning into donkeys and fairies?"

This day could change her life? Cora forced herself to sit up in bed. Supported by the Coras who came before her, she gave herself a talking to. *You can do this. You are Cora the Fifth. You can face the future whatever it brings and do your part to make it better.*

She could feel herself channeling Gran. That helped. Eventually she fell asleep. The last thing she remembered thinking was, *Bring on the life-changing magic. I'm ready.*

In the morning, she surprised herself by insisting that her unpleasant supervisor meet with her. "I am resigning," she told him. He did not ask why. He didn't even seem surprised, just told her to clean out her locker and return to him the university laptop she had been using for her work. That was all. Which was confusing. Shouldn't he urge her to stay? Tell her the future depended on her work? But that was it. Not even a muttered "Thank you." Just "Good day, Miss Brevard."

PART 2

A SURPRISING ALTERNATIVE

There were many gendarmes at the airport and rail stations when she returned to Paris. She texted Aunt Joan that she was home and went to Joan and Andre's apartment for a meal—Aunt Joan's delicious Afro-Mediterranean cuisine. She bought groceries and settled into her familiar flat. She had no work. Her advisor had disappeared, her department had new partisan leadership, and she wasn't certain she still had a place at the university. Still, she felt liberated. She called Mama and caught up on family news, ate, and slept late.

A few days after she returned to Paris, Cora found in her apartment mailbox a letter on embossed stationery inviting her to lunch with Jacques Thibault. *Wasn't he the wealthy businessman who hosted the frolic for the National Youth Movement that, Hanafi,*

Muhammed, and I attended with Adam more than a year ago? Was he the elegantly dressed man who had approached me in the café in London and claimed to remember me? She had read that he was the man now running the AI program at the Sorbonne. *Why would he invite me to lunch?* Curious, and figuring she had nothing to lose, she accepted. She told herself that Midsummer magic might show up in surprising ways.

On a Saturday morning, she entered the elegant restaurant where he'd asked her to meet him. He was waiting for her and rose as she approached, extending a carefully manicured hand. He looked the same as he had when he'd approached her Elise Brevard persona on her lunch break that day in London. He didn't mention that meeting, nor, of course, did she.

"Thank you for coming. I'm very glad you accepted my invitation, Ms. Johnson-Allen." He guided her to a table in the rear. No one was lunching nearby.

"Ms. Johnson-Allen, what will you have? The escargot are especially fresh here, the scallops also. Their truffle mousse and aubergine parmesan penne are the best I've had anywhere."

Cora went with his suggestions. She felt awkward, but they sipped wine and nibbled crusty bread and paté, while they awaited their entrées.

"Your mother is a professional historian, I believe, teaching at Northwestern University?"

"Yes." It was apparently futile to try to hide anything from this man.

"And your father was a composer, I believe, who died tragically, murdered, nine years ago?"

Cora felt her stomach lurch. Why would this French billionaire know these details of her life? She nodded, on guard and wary.

He maintained his suave demeanor but smiled as if to assure her that her secrets were safe with him.

The waiter served their entrée, which lived up to Jacques Thibault's description. They ate in silence for a while before he spoke, looking directly at her.

"I do believe you've recently returned from working at the Imperial College of London."

Cora nearly choked on her scallops. *No one was supposed to know where I was other than Professor Benet. He knows it was me in that London café.* He watched her with an amused half-smile. Was he enjoying her discomfort?

Cora remained silent, waiting to see what he would say next.

"You can trust me with your secret."

She never believed anyone who said, "trust me."

He leaned toward her, his voice lowered. He was no longer smiling. "Can I trust you with mine?"

"I don't know if I want to know your secret." The honesty of her reply surprised them both.

"Then I guess I'll have to take a chance. You know me as the CEO of one of the largest communication companies in the world. You may also know me as a major funder of the National Youth Movement of the National Front Party and as the current chair of the board of the Sorbonne program you are enrolled in. Those are not secrets." He wiped his mouth and took several sips of wine, then wiped his mouth again before saying more. The waiter was approaching but M. Thibault motioned him away.

"I am going to tell you some things in confidence, revelations about me that few people know. It is imperative that you tell no one, other than Professor Benet, who already knows. Revelation #1: I was not happy when the National Front requisitioned the Sorbonne AI program. I believe in the private sector, and I believe academia should not be controlled by any government— American ideas that I appreciate. Government, economic, academic, and religious institutions should be separate and not pollute each other."

She was unclear how he expected her to respond, so she remained silent, studying his face for clues.

The waiter collected their plates and returned with *salade*. When he was out of earshot, M. Thibault resumed speaking.

"Revelation #2: I secretly hired your professor, Madame

Benet, when she was 'released' from the Sorbonne program. She is an intelligent woman, and we have more in common than either of us had thought. Like her, I'm opposed to the National Front pulling France out of NATO. Of course, these are not views I share with my colleagues in the Party. I must be discreet to remain in their inner circle. And I do intend to remain there while I have even a shred of influence to exert. Influence relies on access, you know."

Cora's discomfort was acute. It irritated her to have such a spectacularly tasty meal ruined by anxiety. *Can I trust this man is telling me the truth?* She heard her mother's voice in her head. "There is no one truth, Cora, just a whole lot of competing and complicated truths from a whole lot of perspectives."

"I know you've been assisting NATO's AI program. I also know that one of your colleagues, Anthony Jones, went missing. You may not know this, but Anthony Jones is dead."

Her fork clanged loudly against her plate as it slipped from her fingers. Diners on the other side of the room craned their necks to see who was responsible for this *faux pas*.

"Yes, dead. You are fortunate you left London when you did. Remember your boss, that emotionless man you told about the note you received?"

How did he know any of this?

"He left London the day after you did. We suspect he's in Belarus, an agent the Russians managed to place in the Imperial College of London. Had you remained even a day longer, your safety may well have been compromised."

She remained silent, unwilling to affirm anything he'd said. *What have I gotten myself into? Does this mean Anthony Jones gave the information I brought from Tallinn embedded in my arm to the Russians?*

The waiter refilled their wine glasses, then silently, deferentially, disappeared.

"So, my dear American scientist, we come to Revelation #3. I want you to work for us, for the new French Resistance. To work with those of us like Professor Benet and me who are committed to preventing the corruption of AI and the onset of World War III." He paused to let her process his words before he continued. "What do you think of this proposal? Will you join us?"

"To do what?" Cora leaned back in her chair, twirling the stem of her wineglass, trying to collect her thoughts.

"To be our liaison to the National Youth Movement."

She could feel her stomach lurch as though the escargot wanted to escape. "I think I need to speak with my professor before I can answer that."

"Of course. We anticipated that. Just a moment. *Excusez-moi, s'il vous plait.*" He moved to the doorway leading to the toilets, fingering his iPhone, and spoke in French, his head turned away from her. Then he returned to their table. "She'll meet you in two hours at La Cantine de Bretonne, #22 Rue de l'Ourcq. She thought you might enjoy their exquisite *crepes au chocolat* after this meal." He was smiling, his confident veneer back in place. "She will meet you at the far left of the outdoor seating. The next two hours should give you time to gather your questions. I do hope you will decide to work with us, Mademoiselle. It would be an honor and a privilege to have you join us. You clearly have been doing important work for the future. Please remember that what I have told you is for your ears only."

With that he summoned the waiter, supplied his plastic card, and extended his hand to her. It felt soft, warm, and well cared for. Then he left the restaurant.

Cora remained seated, feeling stunned. After a while she sipped more wine and began scribbling questions on a small notepad. She didn't think she should commit her questions to a digital device that was likely being monitored.

Resistance! 121

CORA MEETS PROFESSOR BENET

She arrived at their meeting place to find Professor Brevard already seated, stirring a *café au chocolat*. She stood and took Cora's hand in both of hers, obviously delighted to see her.

"We have much to discuss, my brave Cora. Do you want to order? No? You enjoyed the scallops and escargot, I imagine."

Cora said the meal had been delicious, but she was too full for anything more.

"Then let's walk. The walls have ears." Professor Benet finished the last of her coffee, paid her tab, and led the way, walking briskly along the path that led into the park. Only when they were far removed from the restaurant did she speak again.

"You have questions, of course, and I believe I have answers."

"What happened to you while I was in London?"

"I was removed from my position at the Sorbonne, 'disappeared' into a black hole of sorts in that no one who tried to locate me could find me. Fortunately, I had known Jacques from childhood and, being well positioned in the Party, he knew what was happening to our program and to independent thinkers like me. He brought me into his company under another name with an office adjacent to his and immediate access to him so that I could brief him as I continued my research on the private, super-secure computer he provided."

"Why is this all so secret?"

"Pourquoi? Parce que tout va très mal. Pardonne moi.. I lapse into my mother tongue under stress. What those with great wealth and power and no empathy are involved in is evil. Their motivation is corrupt, and they will let nothing deter them. We are engaged in a great act of *l'histoire,* a struggle whose outcome will determine the fate of the world."

She stopped walking and turned toward Cora to see how she reacted to these words, but Cora was not reacting, just listening carefully, trying to understand.

"Fortunately, Jacques understands the seriousness of both the international and domestic situations and is well positioned inside the National Front to resist them."

Professor Benet flushed and smiled at Cora apologetically. "I'm sorry. I must sound like an extremist. What is happening in my country has me very distressed. Perhaps I sound overly dramatic." She turned back to the path and resumed walking.

They continued their conversation while Cora ticked off her questions. Benet confirmed what Jacques Thibault had said. A secret renegade group were collaborating to try to stop the National Front Party's full-on descent into fascism. It was all top secret, and they wanted Cora to work with them. Thibault had known of Cora's work in London through his friendship with Professor Benet, who trusted him implicitly. When he'd seen Cora there in the café, he was checking on her for Professor Benet, who had no way to be in touch with Cora once the Party took over the Sorbonne's AI Program. Then, believing Thibault to be a true Party man, the National Front had asked Thibault to run the Sorbonne program. This was a lucky break for those who secretly opposed the most extreme elements of the National Front.

A smokey blue haze was settling over the city. It penetrated the deep recesses of the woods that fringed the park, covering them in an eerie half-light. They stopped to sit on a bench. Cora probed why her mentor believed Jacques Thibault could be trusted. Professor Benet went on at length about him: his core humanity, the years she had known him and his family, his disillusionment with the National Party's leadership.

Then Professor Benet stood. "I think we must go now."

Before she could move away, Cora asked, "But exactly what do you want me to do? I need more information."

Professor Benet avoided the question and continued moving toward the entrance of the park. Cora accelerated her pace to keep up. The air felt heavy, laden with the opaque residue of ash from the fires again raging across Germany and Belgium.

"What should I do now?"

"You must decide that. Think about what I have told you. Ask more questions if you need to. In the end, trust your intuition. We will give you more information once we know your decision."

"I've been thinking about going home, running away from all this. It frightens me," Cora confessed.

"Of course. *Mon dieu*, if it wasn't terrifying, none of us would choose to be involved in resistance. My *grand-mere* was in the French Resistance in World War II, when Hitler occupied Paris and northern France. She paid a heavy price for her involvement. Several of her friends were executed, including the man she planned to marry. She spoke of it only once when I was eleven. She said she had no regrets. It had to be done and she could do it. I don't say this to force you to join us, just to share that, should you decide to join, there will be a price exacted. I hope you, like my *grand-mere*, will feel it is the right choice for you."

She turned to face Cora. "Here we must part. I'm a short walk from my apartment and I believe your Metro stop in Porte Saint-Denis is a dozen stops in the opposite direction. Shall we say in three days you will let me know?" She passed Cora a business card with a series of numbers. Then she walked away while Cora descended into the Metro.

That night, Cora could not sleep. She repositioned her legs dozens of times, moved onto her right side, her left, her back, her stomach, and finally surrendered to her sleeplessness, using the time to sort through what she had learned.

A HANAFI'S HUSBAND

In the morning, Cora texted Hanafi, whose return text was full of emojis showing her excitement that Cora was back in Paris. Hanafi suggested Cora come to her flat for a coffee. They had seen each other only once since Cora's assignment to Tallinn, more than nine months ago, but picked up their friendship without awkwardness.

Hanafi's husband had begun painting, and Hanafi was eager to show Cora his latest work.

"Times have not been easy since we returned from our holiday in Riyad. I think painting has helped him with his anxiety. He worries what the National Front will do next, a Muslim ban or even deporting immigrants like us even though we are here legally."

Hanafi showed Cora the huge canvas Raza had just completed. The painting reminded Cora of a Jackson Pollock, only the colors were dark purples and blues and shades of black with an occasional spot of green. Cora was not a fan of abstract art, but she found herself taking a lot of time examining this work. There was something compelling about the overwhelming dark of it, like a vortex leading the viewer into a deep, disturbing chasm. There was a heaviness about the work. She felt like a black blanket was lowered over her as she entered the painting.

Hanafi watched her. "It's like looking from inside a burka, no?"

"Yes! Exactly what I was thinking until I remembered I've never worn a burka."

"But watch this…" Hanafi lowered the shades and pulled the curtains closed, then switched off the light.

In the lower right quadrant of the painting something small and white was suddenly visible. Cora stepped closer. It was an evil eye, the kind sold in the street markets of Porte Saint-Denis, except those had blue irises and this iris was brown, a brown iris surrounded by shiny white, no larger than the nail of her thumb. When Hanafi turned the light on, it was gone.

"He's very proud of this painting. He's titled it 'Odyssey 2030.' What do you think?"

"It's powerful and eerie, intense. I like the title and the work."

The women chatted about the Sorbonne, Hanafi telling Cora how the changes were affecting the University and her program. When it was time for Cora to leave, they embraced. "I've missed you so much," Hanafi told her, and Cora's eyes filled with tears. She so longed to confide in Hanafi her loneliness in London and her confusion about this job offer from Jacques Thibault, how it would complicate any relationship she and Daniel might develop, but she knew that once again she must be silent about what was really happening in her life.

As she walked back to her apartment, the decision she must make occupied all the space in her mind.

A CLARITY?

With two days left before she must decide whether to join Professor Benet and Jacques Thibault, Cora went for a long walk along the Seine, stopping when her legs needed to rest. She settled on the grass under a linden tree and watched the water. She lay back and savored the lacy patterns made by the leaves above her.

Her mind wandered and into it walked her father. Not his corpse. That she had never seen. This was the tall, gangly, mystical musician-Dad, the man who she loved as she had never loved anyone, even Mama. He sat at his grand piano, shook out his hands, crouched protectively over the keyboard before his fingers descended to the keys. She startled as the music soared, throbbed, and cavorted. Suddenly it switched to discordant chords that set her teeth on edge. Tympani and electronic music in rapid cadences that stirred her. It was *that piece*! The piece he'd been so excited about, the one that was to be premiered at Northwestern's commencement. Only Dad was murdered on a subway car early one morning and never got to complete it.

Now she listened even more intently. The collision of sounds, the faint intrusion of sweet bells amidst the dark bass chords—this was new, not what she'd heard him trying out in his and Mama's bedroom where he often composed. Was this what he would have written had his life not been violently taken from him that April morning in what T. S. Eliot wisely called "the cruelest month"?

When the piece ended in an idyllic promise of something radiantly lovely, she began weeping.

After a while, she got up and made her way back to her flat.

When Mama answered on the third ring, Cora wasted no words. "I heard Dad playing his last piece, Mama, all of it. It was so powerful, so dark and deep, and the ending was like nothing I've ever heard in its beauty and fragility. I don't understand how I heard it, but I did, Mama. I did."

Across the Atlantic Ocean in their house in Evanston, Illinois, she heard Mama weeping. Eventually Mama got out some words: "I trust that you did hear it, Cora. Thank you for telling me."

On Decision Day, she discovered an old voice message she'd missed when she returned from London. She listened to it. It was Daniel wanting to meet.

Perhaps she should wait until she made her final decision and then call him? He worked for the National Youth Movement of the Party, so how was she to view him, if she accepted a job a working with those resisting the Party? As friend or enemy? Could she trust him? Those months of living under an assumed identity, keeping her life a secret from everyone, had worn down her capacity to be open with anyone.

She decided to wait. Instead, she phoned Professor Benet. "The answer is Yes," was all she said. Professor Benet asked her to come to Jacques' office at four that day so they could begin. That was all. In a call that lasted less than three minutes she had committed herself to a resistance that she did not understand, and her decision could lead her into serious danger.

She told herself, *I am Cora, the Fifth Cora, with a whole line of courageous Coras behind me who used unconventional means to fight for freedom. Now it's my turn.*

She felt that Dad and Mama understood in some unique, inexplicable way. Gran Cora often said, "Girl, don't discount the power of Signs." And Cora had received three of them: she saw Hanafi's husband's painting, she heard Dad's final composition, and Mama believed her.

~ ~ ~

Her meeting with Jacques and Professor Benet was very interesting. They assigned her to assess the National Youth Movement leadership to learn how committed to the Party's dogma they were. It would be her professional responsibility to pursue this with the NYM deputy director for outreach—Daniel—but, if she was honest, she had a personal interest, too. She needed to know if Daniel was comfortable with France's new fascism. For both personal and professional reasons the assignment felt important.

Daniel texted that evening.

"U in Paris? Meet @7 4 dinner? Our place?"

She liked the sound of "our place." She replied with a thumbs-up.

Dinner with Daniel after more than six months apart was surprisingly comfortable, although her heart raced seeing his broad smile and feeling his nearness when he greeted her with a kiss on both cheeks. They caught up on his new job and her dropping out of the Sorbonne and chatted about their families.

Just as the waiter approached with a tray of desserts, Daniel leaned across the table and lifted a strand of her hair that had come loose. "Have you any idea how good it feels to be with you again?" He smiled warmly.

The waiter discreetly backed away, saying he'd return later.

Suddenly Cora felt petrified. *How well do I know this man? He may fully agree with the National Front's philosophy, which would make him a disaster for me to get more involved with.*

"You do realize that your body language gives you away," he said laughing. "I can tell when you flee any kind of intimacy with me by the way your crossed leg starts swinging back and forth like it's on speed." He reached for her hand.

She reached for her wineglass, not looking at him. *Damn! Why am I so transparent? I hope I won't be a complete failure at undercover work! Calm down, girl. He's only a guy.*

"Cora, I'm happy to take it as slowly as you like. Maybe we could go together tomorrow to the opening of that new exhibit at the Louvre? No pressure, but I think it's something you'd enjoy."

Relief flooded her. After the past year of so little contact, she *was* glad that it would not be months before they saw each other again. And he was thoughtful and respectful. She stopped herself from adding a dozen other glowing qualities that popped into her mind. *Yes, we can take it slow, while I learn what I can about his views. It doesn't have to be black or white, all or nothing.*

"That sounds like fun," she answered with a smile.

They met beside the Seine where the flat boats loaded and unloaded tourists eager to float toward the Eiffel Tower and see Paris from its famed riverside. The sun was warm but there was a breeze off the water that balanced it. They climbed up the embankment toward the shiny glass pyramid that marked the City of Light's most famous museum, the Louvre, their steps against the pavement rhyming as they approached the entrance.

"The Louvre is open late Fridays, and I really wanted to see this with you. The exhibit just opened. It features works of contemporary artists from across the globe. It's called 'Justice Burning.' I figured as Americans we could learn a thing or two about how the rest of the world views what we call justice." He ushered her through the turnstile, and they followed the signs to the special exhibit.

Curious and expectant, she wondered what his wanting to see this with her meant to him.

They entered a giant space crowded with people. Apparently, this was only the second day the exhibit had been open. Ahead the walls were painted glossy slate gray. Beyond the archway into the adjacent galleries the walls were black, matte black and opaque. There were eight galleries, each featuring the works of an artist from one part of the world outside Europe and America. Africa had three rooms, one each for art from the North, Central, and Southern regions of the continent. Asia had three also, one for the Pacific Islands including Japan, Indonesia, and the Philippines; one for China and Southeast Asia; and one for south Asia (India, Pakistan, Bangladesh). The remaining two rooms were for artists from indigenous Australia and Central Asians. Cora wondered why there was no gallery for the Middle East. If they included the Arabian Peninsula, might Raza's work be displayed here?

The art was mostly abstract, giant canvases splashed with paint and often adorned with found items—feathers, twigs, fragments of photographs, fish bones. She hoped Daniel knew more about abstract art than she did. In each gallery he picked up a copy of the guide to that room, the English version, and together they read it as they moved slowly around the spaces.

A few of the pieces included recognizable human figures, often almost skeletally thin. One figure lay splayed on sand that the artist had sprinkled onto the wet paint. Now and again a child looked out from the canvas, perhaps only an eye or a gaping mouth. Often people were depicted with exaggerated features. Some of the works were garish with shouting neon colors that demanded attention. Others were dark and subdued, blending into the dark walls behind them. This was something she had never before experienced, although Mama had taken them to the Chicago Art Institute regularly when Cora and her brother Caleb were young.

The artwork seemed to fascinate them both. They didn't speak, just read the pamphlet descriptions and studied the works, each silently processing what they saw.

A painting off by itself drew Cora's attention. It, too, was dark but the spotlight directed onto it brought out a tiny glowing object made of porcelain embedded in the canvas. Looking more closely, she recognized the evil eye she had seen in Hanafi's husband's painting! She wondered what it meant and why both this artist and Raza included it.

They left when the Louvre was about to close, and Daniel guided her toward a wine bar several streets away. The early evening air had cooled, and he offered her his jacket.

The wine bar was crowded and noisy. He asked for a table as far as possible from a group of younger people whose decibel level of exuberance would make conversation impossible. Once they were seated and had ordered mulled wine and a plate of cheese, pate, and crusty bread, Cora asked him what he thought of the exhibit. Which works especially intrigued him and why had he wanted to see it with her?

He looked away, thinking about what he wanted to say. His face in the dim light of the wine bar appeared open and, she thought, vulnerable. Watching him pondering, she felt happy, grateful to be with him. She remembered how attracted to him she had been… and how Aunt Joan and Aidan had cautioned her to be careful. He was, after all, a Cook. *Okay. No harm in enjoying tonight and talking about the art exhibit.* She listened carefully to his answers to her questions.

"I loved having to work at what we were seeing, breaking each piece apart to examine the textures, the found objects included, the colors, trying to understand its statement. And then trying to relate it to the title of the exhibit, Justice Burning. I especially resonated with the piece with the skeletal person on the sand and the sea behind him full of what looked like fishbones…"

The voices of men arguing interrupted Daniel. Across the room the waiter, followed by the manager, approached the men's table and exchanged words with them. Faces flushed, the men stood, shouted at the waiter, and stomped out of the restaurant.

"That was interesting. What was I saying? Oh, yes, the skeleton on the beach and the fish bones." Daniel spread pate on a cracker before continuing. "One of my colleagues, Amir, insisted I meet with him last Saturday. He talked about the impact of the warming of the world and fossil fuel production on his country, Cameroon. That painting evoked the story he was telling me—rivers too hot to support fish, deserts expanding, and people starving from lack of their major food source and from lack of water. The conversation disturbed me and the painting did also. So bleak. Everything you count on for life disappearing and nothing left but bones. It's haunting, that image."

He refilled her wine glass and took a sip of his own. "What about you?"

"You didn't answer my third question. Why did you want to see it with me?"

"Because we haven't seen each other for a very long time, and I had no idea what you would be feeling about seeing me again. I hoped that something fresh and unusual would make conversation easier... And also, I wanted to share the experience with you because another colleague recommended this exhibit and said it was amazing."

Cora nodded, flushed from a wave of feeling that his words brought. She took a deep breath, pulled her mass of curls back into a hairband, and refocused, deciding what she wanted to say.

"I found the whole exhibit fascinating. I wish I could understand it. I don't... Did you notice the piece set off by itself with a spotlight on it, lots of darks with tiny splashes of color?"

Daniel scrolled through the images he'd captured on his phone before passing it to her.

"This one or the next?"

"This one. Did you notice this?" She expanded the image until the porcelain evil eye was visible and passed it back to him. "My friend Hanafi showed me a painting her husband Raza made—

Resistance! 135

they're from Saudi Arabia and she's also studying at the Sorbonne. Raza's piece is huge, also dark, and includes an almost invisible evil eye like this in the lower corner. Curiously, I could only see it when Hanafi darkened the room. I found that fascinating."

"An evil eye?"

"It's like a bead that looks like an eyeball with a blue iris. Lots of people wear them in jewelry, pendants, earrings, bracelets. They're sold all over the world and people wear them to ward off evil. It is still popular, especially in Turkey, even though Islam teaches that it is *haram*, forbidden, because only Allah can protect one from evil…Well, the one in Hanafi's husband's painting like the one in this painting had a *brown* iris. It must mean something."

That sparked a memory for Daniel. When Amir had paid for their coffee the other day, Daniel had noticed a small brown "eye" amidst the coins he'd pulled from his pants pocket. That memory provided an opportunity for Daniel to segue to telling Cora more of what Amir had said when they'd met. The conversation with Amir had clearly upset him, and he recounted it nearly verbatim.

"Have you heard anything similar from your other recruits?"

"Not really, but Amir and I have a special relationship. He was my first recruit and is really smart. We bonded as runners and became friends as well as working together."

"How do you feel about his not wanting to be part of the Youth Movement because he sees it as a screen to hide a new colonialism that makes his people suffer?"

"Ah, that is the question I have been trying to answer—more honestly, trying to avoid. I don't want to participate in something that is a deliberate façade, manipulating people's lives to take their resources and skills just to make the manipulators richer and more powerful. I got into this work because I want to help bring people together, to build a better world, as ridiculously naïve as that sounds."

Cora realized she'd been holding her breath while he spoke. His answer to her question was so important. It was what she needed to know about him. But she needed to know more before she could be fully honest with him. She wasn't ready. Not yet. She dissembled.

"Maybe we can look into how true Amir's allegations are?"

"We?"

"Well, I have a new job…I'm going to be working with the National Youth Movement. We'll be colleagues."

His face showed shock. "I thought you wanted to get back into studying for your PhD in AI after you take a month off."

"I did, but it is beginning to bore me. When I told my advisor I was thinking of leaving Paris and going home, she suggested I take several months off before deciding whether to drop out of the program. I saw an ad for an organizer with NYM and applied." She was lying. She hoped it didn't show. Why was it so easy to lie? Mama always said she was a bad liar, but Daniel didn't seem to notice. He smiled like a kid on Christmas morning.

A WORKING FOR THE NYM

The National Youth Movement planned gatherings in each of its eight regions to introduce a new programmatic initiative of the National Front Party to regional leaders. The meetings would take place from November through spring 2029. Daniel arranged for Cora to attend the first one in Dakar, Senegal, West Africa. They would both go, and she would be his assistant. As independent as Cora was, that was not an easy role for her.

Daniel had persuaded his boss that Cora should work in his division as a recruiter. He was pleased that Cora seemed happy with her assignment. It meant they saw each other almost daily at work, although neither of them had any free time. They were both too busy in the six weeks that followed their visit to the Louvre for more than work-related coffee dates. Preparing for eight international meetings that would occur within five months required a lot of long hours.

In mid-November they left Paris for the first regional meeting. Their flight to Dakar took place on one of the rare days when the sky was a bright cobalt blue unobscured by thick smog or lowered clouds. The Atlantic Ocean shimmered shades of green in the sunlight. As they exited the airport, the sweet scent of white frangipani blossoms and a riotous display of magenta bougainvillea and coral and pink hibiscus met them. Dakar appeared to Cora like a tropical Eden.

Their taxi snaked through streets crowded with shoppers heading for the old Marche Sandaga marketplace. Cora observed the women in long, loose-fitting caftans and boubous, some in pastel colors, others in jewel tones. They appeared to float along the streets. Many wore flamboyant head ties that matched their robes. Some carried huge trays of merchandise and produce on their heads as they maneuvered around pedestrians and vehicles to reach the market. Color and confidence everywhere. She had never seen so many elegantly postured women, carrying themselves like they exercised total control.

Eventually their taxi reached the hotel where the conference was to take place. One wall of the ultra-modern hotel's conference room was all glass and faced the beach and the sea. The view—white-capped waves, blue sea, and even bluer sky—was breathtaking. And the surge and retreat of the Atlantic Ocean fascinated Cora, who hailed from the American heartland where there was no ocean.

Daniel and Cora set up the technology hookups and conferred with the wait staff who would serve the evening meal. When everything was ready, they still had thirty minutes before the participants would arrive. Daniel suggested they walk out to the beach.

"What do you make of Dakar?" he asked her.

Cora welcomed his question. "It's my first time in Africa and that is thrilling on many levels. My mind was in overdrive as we drove through the city—the crowds of Africans conversing, moving about, shopping, walking purposefully. They carry themselves differently than Black people I see back home in the States, or even in Paris. More flamboyance and confidence, I think."

Did she want to mention to Daniel that Mama said some Black Americans protected themselves around White people from longstanding habit, hiding their feelings behind an impenetrable expression of distance? Was that really true? Or only for people old enough to have lived during Jim Crow? Anyway, how open should she be with Daniel? He had shown empathy for what Amir had told him, but she needed to see more.

He interrupted her mental processing. "I feel a bit uncomfortable asking you this, but it feels important, so I'll risk it." His eyes turned from the horizon, where the sun burned a bright red line, and looked straight at her. "How do you think of yourself? I mean, do you feel Black or White or both or what?"

"I feel like me, like both and, to tell you the truth, I'm glad I'm not just White." The words came out uncensored. Might as well test the guy right now.

He gave her a quizzical look.

"Does that surprise you?"

He took time before he replied. "I guess it does, a little. Not that I would want you to look any other way. It's just that I assumed with all the crap Black people have taken in the U.S., they wouldn't want to be Black. And you are so exotic looking you probably get asked if you are Arab or Hispanic or whatever. I mean, you can *choose* how you identify, right?"

His response stunned and angered her. Was he really so full of himself that he thought people who looked different from him would not want to look like themselves? Damn it! The arrogance! Cora had never wanted to be other than who she was, a mixed-race, Black and white person. She'd always been proud of the Black side of her heritage, prouder of that than the white side. Not that her father and grandparents were not good people who she loved deeply, but Black people had survived and overcome incredible mistreatment at the hands of whites since the first slave ship arrived in Virginia in 1619. Their survival and accomplishment in spite of everything…how could she not be prouder of that part of her heritage? *If Daniel makes this assumption about me, what does he assume about the people from across the world that he works with, people of all colors and cultures? Is he just another privileged White guy who has no idea that he is privileged?* She felt immensely irritated with him and disappointed, even as she knew she was overreacting. *Is there any common ground between us?* She dismissed the voice in her head that whispered that some of what Daniel said was true—which would make her "privileged" also, able to choose her identity unlike Aidan and her brother whose skins were darker.

"They're ready to open the doors," a voice called from the doorway to the conference room. Despite the warm equatorial sun on their faces, a cold front had settled on them. They hastened back to open the meeting, avoiding looking at each other.

The keynote speaker was the director of policy for the National Front Party. His greetings were effusive before he got into his message. "I am here to train you in the Party's new objective: forging a paramilitary presence to contain those who resist the new capitalist ideology you are introducing in your homelands. I will give you tools to resist the socialists, communists, intellectuals, and humanists who cling to outdated ideas that must be uncovered and replaced." He paused for dramatic effect, pushed his glasses higher on his nose, and continued. "Our analysts confirm that China is putting major resources into building up armed groups across your region to counter our efforts. It is therefore not enough that we recruit young people to our cadre of advocates. We must train them to protect their people from elements that would oppress them."

Listening, Cora wondered, *Am I the only one confused?*

"The Party will supply you with arms and ammunition and inform you when our intelligence locates threats that must be exposed and eliminated. Let me caution you: China is also recruiting and arming your countrymen. Discerning who is with us and who is against us will require using the most carefully collected intelligence. You can count on us to provide you with that."

It sounds like he anticipates open fighting between armed groups!

"We recognize that this is an added responsibility to what your contract with us states you will do, so we will pay a bonus to each regional leader who agrees to provide this military training. The bonus will depend on the size of the units you recruit and train. You can be confident it will be a considerable amount of money."

On the huge screen suddenly appeared an array of sidearms with ammunition clips and sniper magnification applications for each gun. The speaker launched into a description of each weapon and its particular strengths.

Cora felt nauseated. This was not what she had expected. No discussion of the man's presentation followed, no time for responses or questions. He finished with an altar call to sign up to add this military training to their agreement with the Party. "Those who sign up today will receive an extra bonus."

Cora moved through the rest of Day One handling her responsibilities like an automaton. Internally she cringed at this escalation in the Party's rhetoric. She remembered a conversation with a German student she had during her first month at the Sorbonne. He had been quite agitated as they talked over coffee, going on and on about the parallels between France's National Front Party and Germany's National Socialist Party. He pointed out that both gradually escalated their rhetoric, making enemies of "others" who were different in any way. Both banned dissent and armed cadre to rough up or even kill dissenters.

At the time she had thought he was overstating the parallels. Certainly, the National Front was not a modern version of Hitler's Nazis? But Jacques Thibault and Professor Benet appeared to agree with the German student. They were risking everything to oppose the National Front and calling themselves a New

French Resistance. Arming young people across the southern hemisphere to monitor and eliminate dissent...? What would you call a government that does that, other than fascist? When she returned to her room, she was in a royal funk.

Late that evening, Daniel knocked on her door. She opened the door and stood in the doorway.

"We've been too busy till now to talk, and it feels to me that we need to talk. I could see it on your face even across the room."

Damn. Why am I so transparent! Reluctantly she opened the door and gestured him in.

"You seemed upset by my question to you about how you think of yourself. And you looked unhappy at the speaker's message. Am I right?"

"Actually, I don't want to talk to you right now. I think you should leave." Her voice was knife-sharp and her eyes steely. Her body blocked him from coming farther into the room.

"But, Cora..."

"Just go. Now."

"So when can we talk?"

"I don't know." She pushed the door closed behind him and the lock snapped into the doorjamb with a sound of finality. She felt betrayed by him. Daniel with his engaging humor and his boyish charm. Daniel who she had come to hope might be mismatched working with the National Front. Was his charm a charade, a façade to appear empathetic and caring while he roped in people of color around the globe for the purpose of servicing White people in power, all the while denying that racism infected him?

Her cousin Aidan's family, originally Jamaican, liked to joke about this disease that afflicted so many White Americans. (Like Gran Cora, they always capitalized "White.") She'd listened to their jokes and tried to understand how they could find the stupid remarks White people made funny. To her they were rude and insulting. She'd intended to talk with Aidan about that but there had never been enough time. She remembered with clarity being at his parents' home for Thanksgiving once when she was, maybe sixteen. Jacob, Aiden's father, made a crack about Aidan needing to be sure to brush his teeth properly before seeing his probation officer because the officer would be looking for bush meat—"or human flesh"—he assumed people like them ate. The family had erupted in laughter: "Good one, Jacob !" "Dead wid laugh!" "You get dat right, mon." She remembered her younger brother Caleb had glanced at her serious face and whispered, "Lighten up, Cora!"

Lightening up was not in her skill set. Which made Daniel definitely a bad match for her, she thought now.

Sleep was elusive, peopled with White and Black people laughing while she stood among them puzzled, feeling out of place and exposed. She awoke, knowing that she must speak to the participants individually to assess what they thought of the speaker's message. She would avoid Daniel for the remainder of the conference.

THE GIRL FROM NIGER

By the final day of the conference, the questions spinning in her head were all Cora could focus on. She'd done what Daniel had asked her to do, seeking one-on-one conversations with the participants to provide support and troubleshoot any issues they might be having. She'd also added a question as she spoke with them: What did they think about the keynote speaker's new directive from the Party to begin preparing their members to resist militarily should they face opposition? She worked the question in seamlessly, innocuously, she thought, but the responses were the same—faces turned away or suddenly blank, body language conveying discomfort, and an abrupt end to the conversation. *How can I "read the room" on this if they won't talk about it? It's*

important to my assignment from Professor Benet to assess this. Why won't they talk with me about it?

She had successfully avoided more than professional interaction with Daniel these three days. *Had Daniel cautioned them not to speak about this with me?*

She offered to stay behind and clean up after the final session. Daniel accepted her offer. The meeting room emptied quickly, and she busied herself packing up equipment, paying their final bill, and checking for any items left behind. As she was about to leave, a participant still wearing her Niger nametag approached her. The woman was very dark. She moved her tall body with a certain authority, although she looked to be young, perhaps not even twenty. When she smiled, Cora recognized her. They had spoken before but, like the others, the girl's face had gone blank when Cora asked what she thought of the new directive.

The girl from Niger stood close to Cora, eyes assessing her before she spoke. "I didn't answer your question. I can now. I do not agree with the new directive." She scanned Cora's face before continuing. "In our country the military and police are quick to use force. They have nearly wiped out my people, forcing them out into the Sahara desert where life is not sustainable and shooting them if they resist removal. To train my cadre militarily would invite a death sentence for us all."

She looked out the glass wall to the Atlantic Ocean that was surging darkly under a heavy cloud cover. "I don't think the Party knows much about us. I'm not sure they care to know."

"Thank you for talking with me," Cora responded. "I don't have to leave for the airport for another hour. If you have time, perhaps we could walk on the beach and talk more about this?"

"I can't. I must leave for the airport now. Please read about Niger, about the level of violence we have experienced, and help them understand that this tactic will only bring more killing. Please?" When Cora nodded, she kissed her on both cheeks and hurried away.

The conversation was one piece of anecdotal evidence. Not much but *something*.

When she checked out, the clerk rushed after her. "Someone left this for you." He handed her a sealed envelope that she didn't open until she was in the taxi to the airport. "Keep asking that question," was hand-printed across an otherwise empty sheet of paper.

She returned to Paris early that evening and took herself out to dinner at the Tunisian hole-in the-wall restaurant around the corner from her apartment. While she waited for her food, she Googled Niger and found a story from two days ago about France providing Niger, Chad, and Senegal shipping containers of drones. Cora read that one shipping container could hold a million small drones, each carrying explosives, each with visual recognition capacity, and the ability to navigate without human supervision. It was time to report to Professor Benet.

HANAFI'S MESSAGE

Cora's phone would not stop vibrating. She was at work preparing her report on the fifth of their eight training conferences. She really did not want to be interrupted, but when the vibrating continued *ad nauseum*, she checked her phone. Hanafi's message was in all caps. "PLS COME! NOW." It was unlike Hanafi to ask anything of her. Cora closed her document and told Daniel she had to leave, not replying to his "Is everything all right?"

Police vehicles two-deep crowded the space in front of Hanafi and Raza's apartment. Two gendarmes wearing full combat gear and carrying high-capacity weapons stood in the doorway scanning the street and scrutinizing passersby. Cora texted Hanafi, who did not reply.

The door to the building opened to reveal Hanafi, Raza, and their children Khadija and Hassam with one armed gendarme in front of them and another behind. They were carrying satchels, the plaid, plasticized kind that market women use to transport their wares. From the tops of the satchels assorted family possessions could be seen: a blanket, towels, a prayer rug, two laptops, food, and shoes. Khadija, clutching her favorite doll, was crying. Hassam kept looking up at his father, his face as stoic and unreadable as Raza's.

Cora ran toward them. The gendarme pointed his weapon at her. *"N'approchez pas. Ce sont de terroristes!"*

Instinctively Cora raised her hands, her mind flashing back to Dad and Mama instructing them on what to do if stopped by the police.

Hanafi's eyes locked on Cora's. She seemed to be trying to communicate something. But what?

Hanafi, Raza, and the children were ushered into a white police van. The door closed and locked behind them, and the van sped away, the red light on its roof flashing and its siren keening.

The door into the apartment building remained open. The gendarmes had forgotten to close it.

Once the gendarmes left, Cora rushed into the building and up the stairs to the apartment. That door was also open. The place had been searched and ransacked. The family's possessions littered the floor along with books and papers. A plate half-full of mejadra sat on the table, still warm, with a basket of flatbread and four cups of tea, half full. They must have been seized as they were eating.

Cora searched the drawers for anything she could salvage for Hanafi in case the police returned to ransack it again. She could hold onto things for them. In the master bedroom she found Raza's canvas, its painted side facing the wall.

She must save the painting! She hauled it out of the apartment and hailed a taxi. It would not be safe taking it on the crowded Metro.

Back in her apartment, she found a space for it in her closet. Then she contacted Professor Benet.

"My friend and her family have been taken by armed gendarmes who said my friends were terrorists. What's happening?"

"A teenaged boy was killed in Breton. The NFP is claiming it was an act of anti-White violence by Iranian terrorists."

"But my friend is not Iranian."

"Is she Shi'a?"

"Yes, from Saudi. It is not safe for them in Saudi Arabia. That's why she came here to study."

"To the NFP extremists all Shi'a, Iranian or Saudi, are the same. Perhaps you should tell Daniel and his boss. See what they say? It would give us insight to whether there is dissent within the Party on this policy and who we might approach."

"But Hanafi and her family... What can be done?"

"I suspect they've been taken to a deportation camp. But ask the NYM leaders that question? Their answers could be important. By the way, use only the code next time you call. We suspect they are about to access our secure lines." Professor Benet clicked off.

Cora switched off her fears by summoning her problem-solving default. *OK. Back to the office. The Party would know Hanafi and I are friends. They may be watching me also.*

By the time she returned to work, it was late afternoon. Daniel was solicitous as he asked what had happened.

"I think I need to talk with your boss as well as with you about this. Is that possible?" She avoided eye contact.

"Let me check." He returned in minutes and escorted her to the office of Mme. Du Veaux who Cora had met only once, when she was first hired. She was a small, compact woman, probably ten years older than Cora and Daniel, and her dark eyes looked intelligent. She'd listened to Cora's account of Hanafi and Raza being taken away by armed gendarmes, remaining quiet for some minutes before responding.

"How well did you know her?"

Why is she using past tense? "We've been friends since we started at the Sorbonne over a year ago."

"Was there anything in her or his behavior that made you suspicious?"

"No."

"But she is Shi'a, not Sunni?"

"Yes."

"This morning, the government began apprehending all Shi'a to deport them from France. You know they are affiliated with Iran and with terrorist movements in Lebanon and Israel?"

Cora consciously restrained herself. "But she is Saudi Arabian. Surely not all Shi'a are terrorists?"

"Probably not. But a Shi'a murdered a French teenager today and there is intelligence that they are plotting to set off explosives here in Paris. In 2015, we learned we cannot be too careful. Your friend and her family will simply be deported, unless they are involved in any of this. Once deported, they will be under the jurisdiction of the Crown Prince and we won't have to worry about them."

"Are Shi'a safe in Saudi Arabia? She said they were persecuted there."

"I don't know. It is not my business and should not be yours. Thank you for letting me know." With that, Cora was dismissed.

Later, when she and Daniel were alone in his office, he asked. "Did I meet your friend at the NYM event last year?"

"Yes. Although you were never introduced."

"This must be very hard on you. But she was probably expecting it. The news has been full of the government's crackdown on Shi'a. You have any way to be in contact with her in Riyad?"

How did he know Hanafi was from Riyad? Or was he assuming?

"No. Don't you feel any empathy for her?" Cora's voice was icy.

"Of course, I do! When I was in middle school back in Kansas, my best friend was taken out of school by police and I never saw him again. My dad said the family were illegal aliens and had been deported. They had purchased a house, and Manuel was doing really well in school. I guess they lost everything by being deported. But you must realize that for at least a decade, European governments have been deporting immigrants, even to countries in Africa where they have no connections, no contacts. So I'm not that surprised.

Cora mumbled a yes and left his office. She needed to be alone to think.

That night she awakened to a loud explosion. The sky outside her window was orange and pink and the sound of sirens grew louder as emergency vehicles converged on her part of Porte Saint-Denis. She watched from the window as people scurried in and out of the hospital across the road. They were pushing a steady stream of stretchers carrying people wrapped in shiny silver blankets. The sound was deafening as ambulances screamed up to the emergency entrance and then screamed away, presumably to collect more injured.

THE DAY AFTER

Paris wore a different face in the morning. Gendarmes appeared to be everywhere. At each Metro entrance one stood with automatic weapons in hand. Barricaded streets slowed traffic to a crawl, and a number of shops with Arabic names were shuttered. On her way to her Metro stop she startled when she passed a Black man on the street who resembled Aidan. Could it be him? But he glanced at her, face impassive, and walked on. Anyway, what would her cousin be doing in Paris?

In her office everyone was talking about "the bombing." Apparently, a drone had dropped two small bombs on the same block a few streets from Hanafi and Raza's apartment. Cora was familiar with the area—there was a halal butcher, two bakeries, a clothing shop specializing in cloth for caftans and boubous, and a Qu'ran school. Press reports blamed the attack on Muslim terrorists. Why would Muslims destroy facilities their people relied on? The news reported that masses of people were gathering on the outskirts of Porte Saint-Denis carrying signs and chanting, "Muslim Terrorists Go Home" and "France for the French." For an instant Cora wondered if she was safe here, but she dismissed that thought.

When she returned to her apartment, she pulled Raza's painting from her closet and examined it closely. Now she noticed writing on the back in Arabic. Laboriously she deciphered the words using her Arabic/English dictionary app. "In the darkest dark, good people watch." What did that mean? Perhaps an explanation of the brown-iris evil eye hidden in the painting? Could it mean anything else?

REGIONAL TRAININGS

Daniel and Cora had worked frantically organizing the seven additional training events scheduled for January, February, and March. She deliberately offered to accompany him to each, hoping to learn if resistance to the Party's new policy of armed response to dissent was winning support and who might be unhappy about it. She kept a list of the individuals she spoke with in each region who expressed reluctance to participate and passed this information through their secret channels to M. Thibault and Professor Benet. What they did with it she didn't know.

Unlike the first meeting in Dakar, she found that in her one-on-one conversations more people expressed concern about the new policy. To a person, however, they said the extra payments were definitely attractive, given the circumstances of their families.

Cora wondered if Daniel had any idea what she was doing in these private conversations with participants. He did not question her about them. In fact, he went out of his way to commend her for her work. He followed her lead in their personal interactions, pursuing no more than a work relationship with her. By February, his respectful distance was driving her wild. She wished he would cross the barrier from work colleague to more.

The final training event was in Vietnam in late March. They met with recruits from Southeast Asia in Ho Chi Minh City. This time many recruits spoke out in opposition to the National Front leader's directive that they should form cadre of militia in their countries to resist the Chinese and those who dissented from the Party's program. One young man stood at the conclusion of the presentation. His face was flushed and his eyes intense.

"Our countries have many citizens of Chinese descent. We have worked hard to cleanse our nations of the racism that pitted ethnic Chinese against ethnic Cambodian or ethnic Vietnamese. What you propose would undo the important achievements our parents and grandparents have made. I cannot accept this directive."

A polite round of applause met his words. The room felt electric with tension. The speaker, obviously surprised, responded, barely controlling his anger at the young man's challenge. "Certainly you know that the best parts of your country came from your decades under French rule." His voice was shrill and his words clearly shocked his audience. "My grandfather and great-grandfather were administrators here in Saigon—yes, I will use that name! They gave their lives teaching your people—French government, French language, French cuisine, French literature. Even after you defeated the Americans, your communists copied the economic ways *we* taught you. You became good capitalists, even if you still called yourselves communists. Your threat is from China, not France. I would expect you to know that."

The room was silent except for the soft scraping sound of chair legs against the hardwood floor. Almost a quarter of the audience stood and walked out. A woman's voice rose angrily above the muffled sound of their movement: "This man is so ignorant that he speaks of the wonders of French colonialism even here in the city named for our national leader who fought the French for decades!"

For Cora, it was a thrilling moment. A sign that the young leaders of these nations would not be duped by the National Front's posturing, pretending that it intended the best for the countries that had generations ago been part of France's colonial empire.

Daniel was speaking with the Party spokesman, trying to calm him down. She decided to follow the group that had walked out and learn more about them. The next thing on the conference agenda was lunch, so she thought she wouldn't be missed.

Late that night, she contacted Professor Benet on their private channel and reported what she had learned, conveying the names of the leading dissidents and how they could be reached. When she finally settled herself under the mosquito netting and let her body relax on the crisp white sheets, she fell asleep immediately and, for the first time in a long while, her dreams made her smile.

THE PLANE TRIP

Daniel and Cora sat together on the long ride back to Paris. They had not talked since the walk-out. She thought he looked especially tired and, indeed, he was soon asleep, his head gradually slipping to the side until it rested on her shoulder. She liked the weight of his head, the soft feel of his hair against her cheek, the slow rhythm of his breathing. Something inside her melted momentarily.

When the wait staff brought their lunch trays, she lowered his tray and gently nudged him awake.

"I guess we should talk about what happened, no?" His voice was soft and tentative.

"Let's enjoy our lunch first," Cora suggested, postponing the conversation on which so much rode.

"Okay." Daniel spread his croissant with pate. "I know this would appall a French person, but I like it this way." He picked up a piece of pasta and scrunched his lip to hold it in place like a droopy white mustache, clowning for her, speaking English with a heavy French accent. "And you, mademoiselle, are you offended by my behavior?" The pasta-mustache fell from his lip onto his lap, and Cora laughed, loving this side of him, a side she'd not seen much of for the months of their frantic work on the training events.

For the next half-hour while they ate, they outdid themselves making fun of the speaker's incredibly thoughtless response to the young man's challenge. "We welcome you back to the French empire, where you are merely little yellow people made by God to obey our every command," Daniel declared, another noodle mustache bouncing on his lip.

"Don't worry. We will permit you to keep your chopsticks and your rickshaws!" Cora continued.

"*Mais, oui*. We have your best interests at heart."

"If you shoot your neighbors, you will save us the necessity." Cora watched him as she said this, but he was still laughing.

After the flight attendant removed their trays, Daniel turned to her, his face now serious. "What *do* you think about what happened?"

Cora had hoped he would go first. She made a sudden decision to take the risk. "I thought he was unbelievably rude to the young man. How stupid to discount the history of Southeast Asia and not even pretend good intent!"

"I agree. I was glad there was a walk-out. I considered joining them myself, but I knew my job was to pacify the situation—and him. And to try to salvage the training."

"Which was impossible at that point," Cora said. She was feeling giddy with relief at his response.

"I guess you're right. So, what do we do now? It's so obvious the Party's intentions with this new directive. Everything I have heard from the recruits who I have really gotten to know tells me this directive—hell, the whole approach now to non-French recruits—is demeaning and just wrong. Should we turn in our resignations? Find something else to do to make money? Go home?"

"Do you think we have a responsibility to our recruits to support their refusal to follow the Party's script?" Cora scrutinized him. The question was so important to any future they might have.

"I joined the National Youth Movement believing it would really benefit those I was recruiting. I'll admit I was astonished by what happened at this event, astonished by the racism of the speaker. At the same time, I don't know if I can do more good quitting or remaining and trying to be a voice for a more progressive policy. What do you think?"

"I think we need to amplify their voice. If not, this will snowball and the local conflicts already devastating these nations with climate change will escalate rapidly. Many will die and we will be responsible for those lives lost." Having said that, she was unclear how they could turn the tide pulling France to fascism, other than through her secret collaboration with M. Thibault and Professor Benet. But she couldn't share that with Daniel. Not now. Maybe never.

After the jet landed at Orly, Daniel asked if they could have a meal together. This time she did not hesitate. She still had boundaries, but they had shrunk considerably, thanks to that conversation and, she had to admit, thanks to the outrageous speaker from the NF Party.

The evening ended at her flat where they shared wine, listened to good jazz, talked, and savored their new intimacy until quite late.

The following day, however, Cora spent with Aunt Joan and Andre. Aunt Joan showed her a file folder of stories she had been collecting about the Cook family and Cook Industries and their support for ultra conservative causes. She cautioned Cora in no uncertain terms to stay away from Daniel Cook.

Resistance! 165

Mama called a few days later with the same message, and a day later Professor Benet urged her to be very careful about how much she shared with the NYM people she worked with.

THE TRAINING CAMP

"Mme. Du Veaux suggested you go with me next Saturday to the NYM training camp. Are you free?" Seven months later, in early December, Daniel asked Cora as they found themselves both at the coffee machine. They had seen each other daily at work but Cora had been distant since Mama and Aunt Joan's intervention the previous spring.

"I know you are avoiding me and want to know why." He did not like or understand her extended avoidance of him.

"I think it's best to keep our business and personal lives separate," she replied, sitting at one of the lunchroom tables and studying her phone.

"That's a lame, inadequate explanation!" He felt angry now, jerked around, despite his respecting her desire to take their relationship slowly. He started to leave the room, stopping in the doorway. "So will you go with me on Saturday? It's a work assignment." His sarcasm caused the woman now at the coffee machine to look at him quizzically.

"Yes." Cora did not look up from her phone, and Daniel left in a huff. The excursion to the training camp would take all day. It would, he expected, be awkward.

~ ~ ~

On Saturday Daniel met Cora at the Metro stop. Together they boarded the train to the countryside. He was troubled, both by the news and by Cora's withdrawal. Did she care about him or not? The train was crowded, and, not knowing how other riders felt about the latest news, he whispered, "Russia has moved into Finland."

"I know. Mama called late last night to urge me to return to the States. She sounded scared."

"Have you thought that maybe we *should* return to the U.S.?" Daniel asked her.

"I'm not going to let fear control my decisions," she replied. That was it. End of conversation. Feeling chided and dismissed, he retreated into silence for the rest of the ride. It was an uncomfortable forty-five minutes.

The training camp was a repurposed military facility from World War II that looked ancient. Several hundred young French men and women wearing camouflage sweats and carrying automatic rifles and handguns maneuvered across a wide field and through the adjacent forest, responding to orders they received in their earbuds. After twenty minutes they reconnoitered, sitting on the frozen ground in a circle around their commander as he evaluated their performance. "We will now practice a raid," they heard the man say. "Our target is about half a kilometer in that direction."

"That's a little more than a quarter mile," Daniel told Cora. It was a snarky remark and he knew it. Of course she would know this. He wanted to irritate her. Any kind of response from her would be better than her silence.

"Stop on the rise where you first see the buildings for further instructions. It's an urban neighborhood. You can't mistake it. Now, move!" the commander directed.

"An urban neighborhood? What the fuck?" Daniel was stunned.

"How will they practice warfare in an urban environment out here?" Cora asked but Daniel appeared as perplexed as she was.

"Let's follow them and find out." He started off at a run and she fell in behind him, wishing she'd worn her warmer, waterproof down jacket. It had begun to drizzle, one of those freak freezing drizzles that you hardly see but feel to the bone.

The rise of land where the trainees were gathered looked down on a cluster of buildings probably two-dozen streets wide. Lichen colored the buildings yellowish-green with spots of ochre. Occasionally, scrawny tree branches protruded through the jagged edges of broken windows, trees that had taken up residence in the abandoned structures. No one was in sight, other than a couple of stray dogs roaming about sniffing for anything edible.

"This must be the village the Party purchased for cheap after a virus wiped out the residents last year and made people afraid to live there. Almost looks like a movie set. I guess there's not a lot of urban space to practice urban warfare!" Daniel half-sneered.

The commander's voice could be heard in the frigid air, authoritative and demanding. "Assume everyone you find in this area is a terrorist and bring them out to the square. No holds barred. Now, *GO!*" and two hundred young French men and women volunteers stormed the streets and poured into the buildings. Ten minutes later a whistle sounded, and they regrouped, each trainee pulling one or more human sized dummies. The trainees with their non-human look-alikes crowded the square.

"All right. Good work. What do we do next?" The commander glanced from person to person until one man raised his hand.

"Put them against the wall?"

"*Exactamente!*" And they arranged the dummies against a long wall. "You don't have live ammo today, but there will be a time when you do. Aim your weapons and take them out. Remember: There is no room in France for terrorists."

The sound of blanks tore the air as the trainees "fired" their weapons into the dummies. In his mind Daniel saw the dummies quiver and jerk before falling silent. Looking more closely, he could see that many of the dummies had keffiyehs tied around their necks, the scarves worn by Muslims across the Middle East. He remembered the black and white keffiyeh Amir usually wore. He turned to Cora who he could see was trembling. He had no words and, apparently, she had none either. He took off his jacket and draped it over her shoulders, tying the hood under her chin. She did not respond, her eyes glazed and distant. He took her hand, and together they hurried away from the nightmare they had witnessed.

ALONE

The second Monday in February, the morning online media showed photos of Jacques Thibault's office strewn with shards of glass and mountains of debris. Mercifully, they did not show his body, which had been blown to bits by a letter bomb.

Cora received a coded message from Professor Benet instructing her to come to an obscure location in the 11th Arrondissement at three that afternoon. She smiled when she read the last two words, "dress warmly."

The woods where they walked were already shrouded in near-dusk. Professor Benet walked briskly as she talked, steam rising from her mouth and her voice broken after every phrase by having to take a breath. *Is she asthmatic or just terrified, like me?* Cora wondered.

"He expected something like this... He thought they had discovered he was no longer a... 'true believer' in their cause."

"Does he have a family?" Cora was remembering her second conversation with him at the elegant restaurant when he had recruited her and said he would have to take a chance and trust her.

"Yes, he has a wife and three children... who will now inherit the business... Thankfully, they each see the world and this country as he did... I think they will do what they can... to resist as he did... But his death is a huge loss... Very sad."

"Professor, I know you think it best for me not to know much about the resistance, but are there others, or are we alone in our small effort to stop France's slide into dictatorship and the world's descent into war?"

"We are not alone. We model ourselves on the resistance of our grandparents... They operated in cadres that had little knowledge ...of other cadres' identity so that if one was apprehended... and tortured, the network could remain intact."

"The media blames his death on Muslim terrorists."

"Of course. Like they blamed them for the drone attack on that street near where you stay."

"You think they set it up to stoke the anger against Muslims?"

"Yes. And those who criticize their policies."

"Are there any people in powerful positions who will speak out?"

"Everyone is afraid. I think... we must pray for a miracle... perhaps from outside France... where the danger is also great with AI compromised...and France incapacitated."

"What should I be doing?"

"Watching carefully, as you have done... Reporting. The military training you saw... is most alarming. I believe a story... will break soon about that. At least we have... some ways to expose them, even if few... of their followers believe anything that criticizes the NF."

~ ~ ~

That night Cora could not sleep. There must be a way out of this nightmare. She remembered the woman from Niger who was so against the requirement that NYM regional leaders train paramilitary groups. She remembered the note someone left for Cora: "Keep asking questions."

Daniel had mentioned Amir, Daniel's African runner friend who quit the NYM. He said that Amir had carried an evil eye with a brown iris. Might he be someone she could trust to help her think through what to do other than to observe them? The questions multiplied: *How can I locate Amir? Is he still in Paris? Dare I ask Daniel?*

That morning at the office, blurry-eyed and exhausted, she overheard a voice message from Daniel's boss. "Now, after these explosions do you understand why we must get rid of them all, my naïve American?"

At lunch, she approached Daniel and started a mindless conversation about the weather and mentioned Aunt Joan's upcoming jazz concert, testing whether he might like to go with her. He did. Three nights later, at the jazz club, she would casually inquire about Amir. It was one thing she could do, a first step.

~ ~ ~

Friday night they met at the Aux Trois Mailletz. They talked about work for a time, then about their families, and she learned more about his family's privately owned oil companies. He mentioned his father's pressure on him to take over the business. But before she could ask him how he felt about that, it was time for Aunt Joan to begin singing her first set.

Her songs were stunning, haunting. At the end of the set she sang "I'm Glad There Is You," and Daniel reached across the table to squeeze her hand, bringing back a strong memory of the night they'd spent in her apartment. *Get a grip, girl. That is not your purpose tonight,* she told herself.

Resistance! 173

Between sets, she introduced him to Aunt Joan, who charmed him as she did everyone. But Cora could tell Aunt Joan was looking Daniel over with a skeptical eye. It was the same look Aunt Joan gave her when Cora returned from Tallinn and Aidan had not heard that Cora was delayed "in Turkey" and would not be available to meet him when he arrived in Paris.

After the second set, Cora asked Daniel about his friend who had quit the NYM. "Are there others who have left? Do you keep in touch with them?"

Daniel sighed. "Yes, others have left, sometimes without explanation. More in the past month. I don't think any of ours have been deported. They just chose to leave the Youth Movement. I especially regret losing Amir. I think he's still in Paris, working as a waiter at Chez le Libanais. That's in your neighborhood, right?"

Cora nodded and changed the subject. She had learned what she wanted to know.

Walking through the chilly night air to the Metro, Cora startled, thinking she heard the stars tinkling like tiny bells. Daniel put an arm around her. "Cold?"

"More nostalgic. My dad used to say some nights you could hear the stars talking to each other, like the sound of small bells. I thought I could hear them just now."

"Your dad sounds like an interesting person."

"He was."

"I'd like to know more about him if you're comfortable telling me."

Was this part of his seduction act or was he really interested? Should I trust him with my most private memories? Trust your intuition, Gran always said.

"My father was a gifted composer as well as a conductor. His compositions included all sorts of sounds, including tech-generated ones. He would say, 'like Beethoven who was the first to use the foot pedal.' He was also a very gentle, kind man. As a child, I thought he and Mama were perfect together."

"You had second thoughts?"

"No, but when he was murdered and Mama almost didn't survive losing him, I thought I would not want to pay such a heavy price for a perfect love relationship. Too much pain when you lose it."

Daniel stopped and turned her toward him. "Thank you for telling me this. It explains a lot. Like why you avoid me when I always want you in my life." He kissed her there on the street while the stars chimed above her and her heart beat furiously, more terrified than by any terrorists.

When they reached the Metro, he held her face in his hands. "I'm not going anywhere. I'll be here if and when you are ready to risk it." Then he boarded his train and she, struggling to control her heart, boarded hers.

A BROWN-EYED IRIS

On Saturday, she made her way to Chez le Libanais, entered, and took a seat in the back.

She asked the waiter if Amir was working. When his eyes looked questions at her, she added that she wanted to talk with him about brown-iris evil eyes. The alarm in his eyes startled her. Had she made a mistake?

The waiter did not respond, other than to ask what she wanted to eat. She thought he was pretending he had not heard her. While he fetched her drink, she thought about what to do next and was still puzzling when a tall, dark-skinned man approached from the kitchen and slid into the chair opposite hers.

"You are looking for me?"

"Amir?"

He nodded, his face very serious. "What is it you desire, Mademoiselle?"

"I have a friend whose family was arrested and taken to a deportation camp months ago. I've tried to find out what has happened to them but can learn nothing except that they will likely be deported. Her husband is an artist. One of his paintings has an evil eye in the lower right corner, but not the usual evil eye, a brown-iris evil eye. I am hoping I can help them. But I need to understand what this means."

"This is not something to discuss in public, Mademoiselle." He spoke softly and his eyes looked away from her as though seeking how to respond to her.

"I am distressed by what is happening here." She deliberately said "here," not identifying if she referred to the restaurant, Paris, or Porte Saint-Denis. "I wish to find others who are unhappy with whom I can collaborate."

"Are you a spy for the National Party?" His face froze and he studied her intently.

"No!" She glanced around the room and, seeing no one within earshot, suddenly decided to risk it. She could see Jacques Thibault clearly in her mind at their lunch meeting and hear his voice as he decided to trust her. "I must take the chance that I can trust you. Can I?"

His demeanor changed. He passed her a card saying loudly enough for others to hear, "I think you will like this bakery. Ask for their Balah el Sham. It is the best in Paris! But they close in two hours. Best of luck with your party, Mademoiselle." He stood and strode back to the kitchen.

She studied the card. She knew the area where the bakery was located. She could walk there in forty-five minutes. She would have to trust that he would alert someone there who could help her. She finished her latte, paid, and left.

~ ~ ~

A young boy leaned against the window of Shabazz Bakery. He spoke to her as she came near. "Balah el Sham?"

"Oui," she responded and followed him through a door beside the bakery and up narrow stairs to the third floor. The boy rapped twice on a door and a woman opened it and motioned her to enter. The woman bowed and gestured to a cushion on the floor where Cora sat. The woman sat on another cushion across a woven red rug from Cora. A low table with a hammered copper top held sweets. Another woman came through the doorway carrying coffee in copper cups and a bowl of sugar cubes that she offered to Cora. Both women were dark brown like Amir. No one had yet spoken. They sipped coffee in silence and Cora wondered if they could hear the banging of her heart.

She heard the doorknob of the outside door turn and saw with her peripheral vision a large, familiar-looking, dark man enter, remove his shoes, and exit the room. After she heard water running, he returned, wiping his hands on a cloth. It was Amir.

"Daniel told me about you."

How was that possible?

"You are the scholar of AI, at the Sorbonne?"

"I was. I am taking some time off."

"And you work for Daniel now?"

"How do you know this?" She watched him closely. His face was veiled but strong, like his body. He sat cross-legged facing her and poured her a refill of the aromatic coffee.

"For now, that is not important. You asked about the brown-iris evil eye. What do you know about it?"

"I have a Saudi friend, an artist, who painted it into one of his paintings so that you only see it in the dark. I saw another painting in the exhibit at the Louvre with a brown-iris evil eye. I am alarmed by what is happening here in this country. I want to stop the fascist takeover. Daniel said you quit the NYM because you felt it was contributing to the destruction of your mother country. I am desperately looking for others who feel as I do. With my friends arrested and perhaps already deported, you were the only person I could think of who might know others who seek to resist." *Am I telling him too much? I must be careful.* She felt a momentary surge of fear and considered leaving, fleeing back to the relative safety of her flat.

But he was smiling broadly, his teeth dazzling in his dark face, like a light suddenly turned on.

"The brown iris is our sign. It is how we recognize each other. We use first names only. And yes, there are others who feel as you do, many others. A dozen at least in Daniel's program."

This stunned her. "What do you do?"

"The events of this past weekend require us to speed up our answer to that question. The escalation in the rhetoric the NF Party is using against Muslims. Anti-Muslim violence. Escalating arrests of so-called terrorists. The explosion at Lagardère that killed M. Thibault… It is time for us to act."

Cora waited for Amir to say more. *Is he weighing how much to trust me? He would be taking a gigantic risk if he did.* Eventually, he continued, ticking off on his fingers the parts of their strategy. "We must coordinate with people back home. Their pressure and ours must be synchronized. We want to see AI workers outside Europe and the U.S. go on strike simultaneously in the four countries where we are organizing and we have been assured that they will.

"We've asked for help from other democracies, including yours. We've asked the Americans for *covert* help, of course. They don't want to be seen as challenging the elected government of sovereign France. We have made contact with them but don't know what they will do.

"Because France left NATO, we need not worry that NATO will use its military force to support the NF.

"The sites we target for sabotage must be selected carefully and we must strike after workers have left for the day. We do not want civilians to die."

He had raised four fingers of his left hand as he spoke. Now he touched his thumb to make his fifth point.

"The missing piece is persuading corporations that NF fascism is bad for international business. Forty years ago, when the people of South Africa defeated the fascists who led the white-minority apartheid government there, they combined all these elements. Of course, they had the charismatic leadership of Nelson Mandela!" Amir smiled at Cora, shrugging his shoulders as if to say, but what can we do about our lack of a Mandela? "We are using their struggle as our model. By the mid-1980s corporations were hurt by the South African apartheid government's policy of reserving all management jobs for White South Africans—there were not enough Whites to fill those jobs! Today the workforce in France is heavily immigrant, and when the NF deports immigrants—which is part of its anti-immigrant platform—we believe that action will generate concern about the shortage of laborers caused by deportation of immigrants. Hopefully, there will be an international outcry and businesses will speak out. We are preparing for the deportations to begin," he closed his fist, "to generate support for our resistance."

He chuckled. "Of course, our plan has many holes and among us there are a limited number of fingers to plug them." Cora was amazed that he could see any humor in this deadly serious plan he was laying out

Amir's analysis impressed her. The resistance had clearly thought through their strategy. Their courage both scared and moved her. After a few moments of silence, she spoke.

"I may be able to help with corporations. I can, I think, learn who M. Thibault was recruiting from his corporate colleagues. At least I can try." She was thinking that Professor Benet might know this from her close work with M. Thibault.

"We will meet at 13:00 Monday night at another bakery. We alternate where we meet, depending on which bakery makes the tastiest pastries." His grin told her he was teasing her. He dug in his pocket and pulled out a brown-iris evil eye no bigger than

Resistance! 181

half a marble. "Here. If you are unsure who to trust, casually let them see this and watch their response."

"Are you worried the NF may use a catastrophic military response to eliminate you?"

"Of course. That is possible, even probable. You saw the young French men and women being trained for urban warfare."

How did he know about that? Was he still in contact with Daniel? Did he trust Daniel?

"I must leave now. You, also. Wait five minutes after I am gone before you leave. We will meet Monday night?" He passed her a business card for Du Pain et des Ides. "No matter the odds, we have a heritage to give us courage. Remember that." He winked conspiratorially. "I'm sorry you didn't get to taste Balah el Sham! See you the day after tomorrow."

He was a brave man, and he was kind. She felt awash in emotion. She was no longer alone. She blinked back her tears, and when her vision cleared, he was gone. She heard his feet slapping the stairs as he hurried down them and away.

Taking the Metro to her stop, she thought about Professor Benet's grandmother, who was part of the French Resistance. She thought of Amir's inspiration from the freedom struggle of South Africans. And she remembered the Coras, her ancestors by adoption. Then she thought, *It isn't blood that compels us to resist. It is a passion for freedom. That is our common heritage.*

THE DEPORTATION CAMP

Conditions in the camp appalled Hanafi. She was, after all, accustomed to living in comfort as a citizen of Saudi Arabia from a highly educated family, even though as a Shi'a she faced discrimination. This camp was a cluster of canvas tents grouped along dirt streets with a toilet and laundry tent for every thirty family tents. Residents grouped themselves by country of origin: There were "Little Algeria," "Little Gulf States," "Little Cameroon." Tent neighborhoods stretched for as far as she could see.

Another resident told her France had established thirty of these administrative detention centers, mostly on the outskirts of airports. In some, no longer utilized barracks held families. Unfortunately, the camp Hanafi and Raza's family were assigned to was one of the five established in the past month before there had been time to construct barracks. Women and children were confined in one area and men and older boys in another. That made Hanafi nervous. She assumed the government was treating the men as suspects, terrorists. What would they do to Raza?

By her fourth day in the camp Hanafi had taken charge of her brain and forced it to adapt to their circumstances. She visited other families, holding Khadija and Hassam's hands to keep her children beside her. She asked about the experiences of her new neighbors, determined to learn all she could and identify anything she might do to resist this abuse of her basic human rights. She could barely contain her outrage at the way they'd been treated.

A woman in the tent beside theirs was eight months pregnant. Overwhelmed by this abrupt change in her circumstances, she could not stop weeping, her sister told Hanafi. An older woman two tents down said her husband was a chemistry professor in Nice, where they had lived for two decades. Nevertheless, gendarmes had suddenly arrived and evacuated them to this camp. How could that be?

PART 3

A ESCALATION

When she opened the door to her apartment, Cora saw a folded paper on the floor. Seeing it carried her back to London and the note left under her door that took her to Highgate Cemetery. This note was almost as brief as the one that led her to the statue of Karl Marx.

"The cavalry is coming."

There was no signature, and she didn't recognize the handwriting. *No one writes notes anymore. Who would know the code for the outside door? Surely this wasn't from Aunt Joan*, the only person Cora could think of who knew her door code.

She sent a coded message to Professor Benet asking for a meeting the next day, Monday, at noon. The reply was cryptic: Bois de Boulogne, Luis Vuitton Museum.

The next morning, Cora was still trying to identify who could have left the mysterious note.

At the office she scrutinized Daniel from across the room. *What does he know? What side is he on?* She fingered the evil eye in her pocket, considering whether or not to let him see it. She decided not.

While she walked with Professor Benet in the expansive woods of Boulogne, she recounted her meeting with Amir. She asked if there were any business owners prepared to speak up.

"Yes, I do know who is sympathetic. Jacques left me instructions to contact them if something happened to him. He believed they would take action if the NF Party acted in a way that was obviously not in their interest. If the leaks the media is reporting are true, this week the NF will announce a policy of reserving professional jobs for French people only."

Worry lines wrinkled Professor Benet's face. "This is not my France. She swiped a hand across her eyes and Cora thought how painful Jacque's death must be for her. In a moment she was resolute again. "I will set a meeting with those on Jacques' list for Wednesday."

They didn't talk long. Cora was on an early lunch break and had to get back. On the Metro Cora thought that reserving professional jobs for French people might generate corporate outrage from corporations employing many foreign-born professionals. It might be the missing piece Amir had mentioned.

When she returned to her office, everything was in turmoil. "There is no Wi-Fi," a colleague called to her before she'd removed her coat. "No communications. Period."

Through the glass partition she saw Daniel's boss pacing. The woman's hands gesticulated jerkily, and Cora thought she looked furious. She spoke rapidly to someone, apparently on her Bluetooth earbud.

Daniel's face lit up momentarily when he saw Cora. "Fifteen minutes ago the internet went down all across France. Nowhere else in Europe. Just France. The President was about to make an emergency speech announcing some new decrees when everything went off. Thank God for our stand-by generators. They're keeping the office warm and supplying some power."

Had the Party been about to announce job reservation?

With no Wi-Fi, the office closed early. Cora returned to her place and warmed leftover ratatouille for her dinner. While she sat at the small kitchen table dipping crusty bread into olive oil with zaatar, she studied the note again. She hadn't before noticed the tiny silhouette of a fir tree drawn below the words. "The cavalry is coming."

The internet was on and off, never on for more than five minutes.

She tried to nap. The meeting at 11 p.m. would make for a short night. Her mind moved like a robotic vacuum circling her brain to pick up scraps, collecting them, and trying to make connections.

At 10:15 she left for the bakery.

Twelve men and women sat on the floor of the scantily furnished third-floor room over the bakery. Some looked African, others Middle Eastern, three were European, French, she assumed. Amir began the meeting invoking Allah, God, and the spirits of the ancestors to guide and bless them.

"We believe the failure of the internet is attributable to intelligence agencies in the European Union. Three more nations have agreed to join the international strike, which will begin as soon as the announcement of the National Front's job reservation policy. We seem surprisingly prepared for the international strike. Ayo, what can you add?"

A slender Black woman wearing her hair in long braids coiled on top of her head glanced around the room making eye contact with each person before she spoke. "History teaches that movements for freedom are most often undermined from within. People who are plants, moles, informers. What is at stake in the next few days is whether future generations will experience the benefits of freedom: freedom of choice about their lives and their partners and where they live, and freedom from oppression and harassment, imprisonment and even death if they disagree with their government. It is essential that there be no Judases in our movement. Look deeply within yourself and understand that lives are at stake, our lives and the lives of those who come after us. You must be true. You must not betray this movement. No matter what. *A luta continua!*" She raised her arm, hand closed into a fist and outstretched. "The struggle continues… no matter the consequences. May we see ourselves as one with of that great stream of freedom lovers whose work for justice and peace included people of all nationalities, religions, races, and, yes, sexual identifications."

She lowered herself gracefully to the floor. The faces of the others around the circle reflected the sober but joyous expression on Ayo's face.

Cora swallowed hard several times, knowing the history of revolutions, including the famous one that began here in Paris in 1789. Often they produced rivers of blood, shed by idealistic young people who believed they could make a difference. Well, she was part of them now, whatever the outcome.

Amir explained how they would know when resistance began. He described the plan for communicating and for provisioning neighborhoods cut off by the military. He acknowledged that they would have to be creative individually in recruiting people to join. "I know you can do this. You have an abundance of good ideas," he told them. At one a.m., the meeting ended.

Singly or in pairs participants left the room in silence and made their way through the city to the locations they were responsible for. As Cora walked back to her apartment through the quiet of the early morning darkness, she fingered the brown-iris evil eye in her jeans pocket. She decided that she must locate the German student, as well as other students she had met at the Sorbonne. The students must be notified that it was time to rise up and protest. She wished she wasn't such an introvert.

The following morning, she awakened early, called her office to say she was ill, and made her way to the Sorbonne. She saw few familiar faces among the busy students scurrying to class. She spoke to those she recognized, asking them to come to the student union, top floor, back right corner, as soon as their class ended. "It's about the change in policy to charge tuition to attend universities in France." She had read about this new policy and knew students would be upset about it.

Two hours later, a dozen students showed up. She spoke about the change in policy and asked for their opinions. Their response was passionate.

"Not charging tuition is a long-standing tradition in this country. How dare the government end it?"

"I will have to drop out and work next term. And every year will be the same—having to work half the year to be able to afford to attend university the other half. I know I won't be able to stay with it. It will take too many years. I'll eventually decide my parents were right to urge me to learn a skilled trade."

A young woman Cora had had coffee with said she was already working to support her widowed mother and could not afford tuition no matter how hard she worked.

"How can they do this to us? I have one year to finish. If I am forced to leave university now, it will all be for nothing."

Cora assessed the mood of the group and, after everyone had spoken, asked the question she had planned to ask: "What would it take to stop the National Front from executing this new policy? Talk about this. Let your ideas flow and don't evaluate them for now."

Responses came slowly. But they came.

"They would have to be removed from office, but the next election is far off."

"There is another way to remove them—the National Assembly could pass a vote of no confidence in their leadership."

"We could raise holy hell and attract world attention to embarrass the NF. It might convince them to pull back the policy."

"We could invite the Prime Minister to campus and hold him hostage!" Everyone laughed at this suggestion.

"We could organize a city-wide march on the National Assembly."

"Yes! My family owns a company that builds small aircraft. Maybe we could borrow a dozen planes to fly around the city dropping leaflets to inform people of the march."

"How about luring the Prime Minister to the steps of the Assembly and forcing him into one of those planes. Fly him into the wild blue yonder!" More laughs.

"Seriously, could we recruit professors to join us in a national strike?"

Cora asked them to pick the ideas that they thought could work and, sitting in groups of four, to develop those suggestions into a plan. What would they need to carry it out? Make a list. How could they procure what they needed? Who would do what?

The room buzzed with their conversations for the next forty minutes. Then each group reported to the full group. All of the groups had come up with the same strategies: massive campus demonstrations and collection of signatures on petitions calling for a vote of no confidence that they would deliver to the Assembly at a national rally held on the steps of the National Assembly. Protesters to be recruited through leaflets dropped from small planes they would secure. Leaflets printed by…? This they had to figure out.

When should the planes drop the leaflets and when should they hold the rally at the Assembly? Yet to be determined. Probably immediately after some additional outrageous action by the National Front.

Cora was pleased by their strategies and their enthusiasm to carry them out. Before they broke up, they identified a team of coordinators and a chain of communication. They set the day and time for their next meeting. When she left them, she went to Amir's restaurant, to the service entrance at the back, knocked and asked for him. She reviewed the results of the campus meeting, which seemed to please him. "I am to notify the lead coordinator when they should hold the rally. Can you safely let me know the moment we launch our resistance?"

"Of course. If possible. We don't know how far they will go to silence us," he replied.

~ ~ ~

She was one street from Rue de Bartholome, walking to her apartment, when she felt the vibrations beneath her feet. Turning onto her street she was accosted by huge, black shapes that she could not identify. The vibrations were audible. The shapes moved toward her throwing circles of very bright light in front of them.

What was happening? This is no video game. These must be tanks! Dark silhouettes that must be soldiers in black combat gear, their weapons ready to fire, walked on either side of the tanks. The headlight of the first tank illuminated her. Terrified, she crouched close to the ground to escape its interrogating glare. She remained prone and unmoving, counting to herself the twenty tanks that rolled past her with their flanks of soldiers. *They are caging the bear that is Porte Saint-Denis!* She looked up. Above her, lights came on in apartment windows as residents awakened to the invasion.

She tried but could not reach Daniel. No cell service. So she crouched there, waiting for the moment when she could slip into the shadows of the buildings unobserved and move from building to building as she made her way to her apartment.

JACQUES THIBAULT'S LIST

Professor Benet arose at dawn and began contacting those on Jacques Thibault's list, blind copying so they would not have the identity of others on the list. "Today there will be an emergency virtual meeting of *Appels Historiques* [Jacques had named his list History Calls]. At noon on the secure server. Address enclosed. All cameras off." Jacques had assured Professor Benet that they would recognize the email codename he had provided her and know this was a legitimate call to action. To protect their anonymity, she asked for no replies, only attendance. Coded initials would replace screen names. Only she would know who responded.

The internet was again spotty. She invoked the spirit of her *grand-mere* to assist her, throwing in a prayer to God that Jacques' list would receive the message. Who cared if she had a history of skeptical and haphazard belief. They needed all the help they could get.

News of the military occupation of Porte Saint-Denis came across the government-controlled news channels. It was brief: "To protect the people of Paris from terrorists, the military has occupied Porte Saint-Denis." Billboards went up in record time featuring armed gendarmes and the words: "ANYONE ON THE STREETS OF PORTE SAINT-DENIS OR LEAVING THE AREA WILL FACE ARREST."

Professor Benet drank too much coffee, paced the floor of her apartment, and tried to think clearly. These people she was assembling would know more than she did about what was happening on the ground across the city and beyond Paris, even beyond France. They did business globally. She would begin by asking for their reports, then review what was at stake and the need to act jointly within forty-eight hours. Whoever was causing the internet breakdown would likely be apprehended soon, although she hoped it would take much longer to apprehend them. The chaos of intermittent internet was generating public animosity toward the National Front, which was good.

When 12:00 arrived, fourteen business leaders showed up on a screen of black boxes identified only with letters. They reported their workers were striking in eight countries. The strikes affected maintenance of routine tasks necessary for the functioning of the internet. The bots used to identify users were controlled by workers in Mali, Cameroon, Vietnam, Cambodia, Burkina Faso, Niger, Chad, and Algeria who had all walked off their jobs and closed their offices. This news was covered within these countries and elsewhere around the world. But not in France. The National Front suppressed it. The strike by workers was having a major impact. Hackers were having a field day. Monetary transactions were paralyzed because users' identities could not be confirmed.

Jacque's widow spoke next, and to everyone's surprise, she turned on her camera, showing her face. "I now own Lagardère. I propose we go on air tomorrow evening with a special bulletin,

'Breaking News,' to announce that France's largest corporations have lost faith in the National Front and in its policies. We can explain what is wrong with job reservation and deportation from our perspective—losing skilled laborers that the nation and our corporations depend on. We can say that militarizing areas of our country endangers the democracy our forefathers and mothers fought for in the Revolution and through two devastating world wars."

M5V responded. "I can say that the people of Paris are at risk of starvation if these policies continue. I own the largest retail grocery chain in the country." Those on the call heard an audible in-take of breath as participants realized who he was and how significant his participation was to their prospect of success. M5V continued. "50% of our workforce lives in Porte Saint-Denis and are unable to get to work. Consequently, the NF occupation and curfew will soon have a devastating impact on access to food in our city. Add to that the general strikes in eight countries that supply France with food stuffs, and you have a nationwide catastrophe in the making."

For a moment no one spoke as they absorbed the importance of what M5V had told them.

Then R19 jumped in. "Madame Thibault, I do not think you should appear alone before the public. I believe we should all be with you, those who are willing. Success depends on convincing Party leaders that a large number of their supporters are withdrawing their support, particularly supporters with money and constituencies who listen to them. What do others of you think?"

One by one the black boxes revealed faces as the participants turned on their cameras. Their faces were familiar to each other. Silently Professor Benet blessed Jacques for his savvy, prescient planning and for selecting these people to invite to join him in resistance.

One screen remained black. D8B spoke now and his words were chilling. "And if we fail? If they close down Lagardère? If we are all arrested?"

Resistance! 197

The silence was deafening until Madame Thibault spoke. "My husband lost his life resisting fascism in our country. He believed and I believe that this struggle is worth risking everything for. Jacques was in the inner circle of the National Front. Some of you are also. And you have seen what they are doing. You know it must be reversed. Freedom is contagious once some people find the courage to speak up. Others will join us—or take our places if we are silenced. There are others right now who have already taken action—the striking workers in Africa and Asia, who have sabotaged the internet and stopped export of food stuffs and other goods to France."

The fourteenth screen remained dark, but the voice attached to it said huskily, "Merci, Madame Thibault. I will join you also."

OCCUPATION

Living in Porte Saint-Denis felt like living in a war zone. Electricity, cell service, and Wi-Fi were all hit-or-miss, on-and-off, meaning Cora still was unable to reach Daniel. The scene outside the apartment resembled a dystopic landscape, with military men, looking like aliens in their excessive gear and high-tech weaponry, patrolling the streets. Tanks loomed on every street corner, their turrets revolving as they watched for suspicious activity.

By Wednesday, the second day of military occupation, a loudspeaker announced that residents were permitted to be outside for one hour, between noon and 13:00 hours. The rest of the time the arrondissement was under a round-the-clock curfew.

Cora, like all the residents, could not go to work. She decided to ask Aunt Joan if she could move her essentials to their apartment.

Joan and Andre both responded, "Of course, you should come. Better to be together with family for whatever is ahead."

At noon she hurried down the street and around the corner, stopping only to purchase bread from a bakery that had hastily opened. The owners lived above their shop and recognized that people would be needing food. When she reached Joan's, she felt great relief. It was so much easier to keep her fear in check when she wasn't alone.

As she approached Aunt Joan's building, she heard the strong scatting notes of her aunt's voice serenading the neighborhood. People came to their windows and leaned out, craning their necks to see who was performing these familiar songs of love and longing. There stood Aunt Joan on her balcony, dressed splendidly, as though she was singing at one of Paris' finest jazz clubs. The fear and terror on people's faces lessened with the notes she sang that caressed the air and calmed anxiety, if only for this moment.

Cora stood with a large group from the neighborhood, looking up, entranced by the voice and the presence of this American/French woman who was known to many of them as one of the city's celebrity performers. Aunt Joan sang for nearly an hour. Even the soldiers lowered their weapons and moved to where they could see and hear her.

At two minutes before 13:00 hours, Cora entered the building and mounted the stairs to Aunt Joan and Andre's apartment, a long loaf of bread sticking out of her canvas tote like an extra elbow. On the street, people scurried to reach their homes before the siren that sounded to announce the resumption of the curfew. The hour respite was too brief, yet there seemed to be something different about the people. Was it only Cora, or did they too feel more hopeful that they would survive this crisis after hearing Aunt Joan's singing?

"You are amazing! How did you realize how much people here needed your music?" Cora enthused, hugging her aunt. Andre beamed with pride at the near miracle his wife had brought to this fraught time just by doing what she knew how to do well, despite the chaos and uncertainty surrounding them.

They gathered around Andre's ancient shortwave radio to see if they could learn anything about the world outside the tenth arrondissement. The radio sputtered and wheezed. Radio Marrakesh came on briefly with a report on the striking AI workers in that Moroccan city.

"AI workers have gone on strike, apparently in dozens of countries," the reporter sounded surprised, and Andre could hardly contain his elation as he turned to Joan and Cora, his face glowing. Dialing to seek other stations on his shortwave, Radio China came through, but none of them understood Chinese.

"I think the National Front is blocking the signals from surrounding countries. Last night I got Radio Brussels, but nothing today." Andre continued turning the dial and fussing with the antenna, determined to find some station that had not been jammed.

"They raided the apartment on the corner this morning and carried off a dozen young men and three women. They were rough with them." Aunt Joan's face was noticeably tense. "The cries of the women awakened me, and I watched them through the window. That's why I had to sing."

"The loudspeakers have broadcast that thousands have been arrested in Porte Saint-Denis. Maybe it's true, or maybe they are putting out propaganda to reassure their base. Truth-telling has never mattered much to them." Andre had taken a break to bring them each a glass of wine before he resumed diddling with the shortwave.

At 15:00 (3 p.m.) Andre turned up the volume on the shortwave. "This is the BBC with breaking news. In Paris today a group of businessmen chaired by the widow of Jacque Thibault, owner of the largest conservative media organization in France, held a press conference to denounce policies of the National Front government, a government Madame Thibault and her husband had supported. They said the NF is destroying freedom in France by ruling through martial law and rounding up asylum seekers and immigrants at the rate of a thousand a day. In an unprecedented move, the business executives pledged non-cooperation with their government for as long as these policies are in place. This comes when electricity, cell service, and Wi-Fi have been virtually nonexistent for four days. Meanwhile, workers in French-speaking Africa and Asia have refused to service the giant Artificial Intelligence companies that employ them to maintain the identity of users of screening devices. The BBC has learned that general strikes have begun in at least five countries that formerly were part of France's colonial empire. The French Minister of Finance denies there is a crisis, but our reporters have learned of runs on banks and other financial institutions, dramatic increases in identity hacking, and panic among financial elites. Areas of Paris with sizeable immigrant populations are under a twenty-three-hour curfew with tanks and soldiers patrolling the streets and incarcerating young men who the National Front claim are terrorists. Stay tuned. You will hear it first on BBC."

Andre, Joan, and Cora danced around the room, whooping and cheering. "The outside world *knows!*" Cora found herself weeping. Jacques had come through from the grave. Even blowing him to bits could not stop his commitment to ending fascism in France.

But the snippet of news Andre was able to find two hours later showed it was too soon to celebrate. The National Front's official media channel put out a bulletin that evening saying that Hungary's president was dispatching troops to Paris to reinforce French troops. The NF had announced that anyone challenging the government's authority would be committing treason. No exceptions.

The three of them ate a light meal while the buzz and crackle of interference on the shortwave provided white noise.

Over coffee, Andre reflected aloud. "France has a revolutionary history—many revolutions, frequent resistance, usually unsuccessful and always bloody. My parents sometimes talked about the partisans who fought secretly against the occupying army of Hitler, how the Germans hauled them out to the central squares of towns and neighborhoods, executed them, and left their bodies to rot with signs around their necks labeling them communists and traitors. We can't be sure this will end well. We should have a plan."

Joan moved to the balcony and stood looking out. It was nearly dark. Wearing a bright blue caftan, her hair braided with small bells, she looked exotic and royal, like an African queen. She appeared to be talking to herself. "People need hope to continue resisting. My singing seemed to please our neighbors. Maybe we can get them to join in. And maybe we can keep it going."

Cora jumped in with an idea. "What if every day during the hour before dark and the hour of first light in the morning, you sing. And Andre and I can beat on pots and pans and wave the French flag. A twice-a-day protest. What do you think?"

Joan liked the idea. "If we do this, maybe it should be at six in the morning and again at eight in the evening? There's a large cardboard box next to the trash bin. Can you two use it to make a sign we can hang on the balcony stating the time to join in singing with me? It will need to be in giant letters so people can read it. It's not much but it is one thing we can do from here during our house-arrest."

Joan didn't wait for them to answer. She checked the time and, as it was already eight, strode onto the balcony and began to sing. She sang love songs and then union organizing songs.

> Freedom doesn't come like a bird on a wing
> Freedom doesn't come like the April rains,
> Freedom, freedom is a hard-won thing,
> You've got to work for it, fight for it …
> Day and night for it,
> And every generation has to do it again.

She sang for nearly an hour while Andre and Cora found the box, located markers and rope, and constructed a rough sign that they could hang out before she finished. They drew a

French flag on the left side of the cardboard box with colored markers. Andre printed in French, making the letters bold and black, "At 6 a.m. and 20:00/8 p.m. SING FOR FREEDOM." They lowered the box-sign with the flag and lettering from the balcony with the rope they attached to its two sides. While they secured it, Joan sang on, going through her repertoire of favorite French songs and including an occasional American civil rights protest song. The sign hung at the second story level where the words could easily be read thanks to the streetlight that illuminated it. People began to cheer. They sang along with Joan and clapped after each song.

Once they had secured the cardboard sign by looping the rope that held it through the balcony ironwork, Cora and Andre grabbed pots and spoons to improvise a rhythm section.

People in adjacent apartments and across the street joined in. Joan closed with, "Ain't Gonna Let Nobody Turn Me 'Round," a song from the U.S. Civil Rights Movement that she had learned from her brother Reggie.

When Joan finished, she called out, *"Demain Matin!"* ["Tomorrow morning!"] People cheered her and shouted "Tomorrow!" and "Freedom NOW!"

As Joan stepped back into the room, Andre wrapped his arms around her and held her close. "I have no words in French or English for how brilliant you are," he declared. Watching them, Cora felt a rush of longing. *I want that. Even if someday I must lose it.* The thought startled her, and she pushed it aside for the moment.

As they sat together in the living area evaluating their impromptu protest, Cora suggested they might think of a stronger message.

"I think ending with 'La Marseillaise' would do that." Andre had stood and was pacing as he thought through the likely impact of singing the rousing French national anthem. "It was first sung as the people declared their independence of the monarchy in 1792, and it's been the theme song of every revolutionary movement since then."

"But isn't it a really violent song? If we write a message that sounds too radical, won't the gendarmes close us down before we start," Joan asked.

"Violent, yes, but the country was invaded by troops from Prussia and Austria. Things were desperate. This song motivated young men to come forward and join the resistance to oppression. And even though Napoleon later banned it, 'La Marseillaise' was resurrected again and again because it inspired and celebrated resistance to tyranny. We French love our national anthem. *No* Frenchman would object to it being sung. We might even hear the soldiers joining in!" Andre's passionate explanation persuaded Cora and Joan. They began memorizing the words, Andre prompting them when they forgot a line.

> Allons enfants de la Patrie
>
> Le jour de gloire est arrivé!
> Contre nous de la tyrannie
> L'étendard sanglant est levé
> L'étendard sanglant est levé
> Entendez-vous dans les campagnes
> Mugir ces féroces soldats?
> Ils viennent jusque dans vos bras
> Égorger nos fils, nos compagnes!
>   Aux armes, citoyens
> Formez vos bataillons
> Marchons, marchons!
> Qu'un sang impur
> Abreuve nos sillons!

"Tomorrow," Joan asserted, "we will end with the 'La Marseillaise.'" The response to their impromptu singing protest had been so enthusiastic, and the plan to generate hope through daily performances of this act of resistance, left them giddy.

At six the next morning there Joan stood, flamboyantly dressed in red, blue, and white, the colors of the French flag. From windows across the street people waved French flags or scarves in the national colors. Joan positioned herself on the balcony, took a deep breath, and began singing. Soft songs at first, love songs, progressing to labor union and civil rights protest songs. She had prepared a program to sing for them. Andre and Cora banged on pots and pans behind her when the song was exuberant, which caused neighbors to fetch their pots and pans and join in. Again, Joan sang for nearly an hour while children and adults banged and sang, dogs barked, and military whistles tried without success to stop them. She closed with "La Marseillaise." Cora saw Andre wiping his eyes as she sang the chorus: *"Aux armes, citoyens."* As Andre had predicted, some of the soldiers joined in. She could feel the emotion in the music and suspected others listening or singing along were, like her, teary.

When they moved back inside, Joan escorted her niece to a seat at the table and sat beside her. "Before we eat breakfast, I want you to know why I sang those American freedom songs. My big brother Reggie was a leader in the Civil Rights Movement—you know that he was your mother's birth father. I felt we should draw on his commitment, his passion to feed ours." Her hands held Cora's and her eyes bored into her niece's eyes. "The struggle for freedom is never over. It just shifts shape, morphs into a new location, a new set of evils to contend against." After a long moment she let go of Cora's hands. "Now, what shall we have for breakfast?"

In the early afternoon Andre was able to locate the BBC. Even well-tuned and played as loudly as possible, they had to listen closely to hear over the static. "Today, in this season Christians are observing as Lent, there is more breaking news from France. The fourteen business executives who held a press conference yesterday to condemn the state of emergency declared by France's National Front government have been arrested. The Party spokesperson would not reveal where they were being held or what would be done to them. France has only once in its history been under a declared state of emergency. That was nearly seventy years ago when General Charles De Gaulle ordered a state of emergency during the Algerian war, expecting an Algerian attack on France…

"In other news, Hungarian troops arrived in Paris to support the National Front government. The National Assembly, France's parliament, is on its Easter Week recess. It will resume meeting on Tuesday after the Easter Monday holiday. Will the Assembly question the way the government has operated? Or will they fall into line behind the National Front Party? Stay tuned. Hear it first on BBC."

During the night the pzt-pzt-pzt-pzt-pzt rapid firing of automatic weapons kept them awake much of the night.

A PRISON

Friday morning, Professor Benet arrived at the prison to see Mme. Thibault. She said she was Madame's housekeeper and needed directions for what to do about the house while Madame was in prison. The slip-on shoes she wore were dirty and down-at-the-heel. Her hair appeared to have been beaten with a whisk. Combined with her scruffy clothing and sagging stockings, she looked like a woman hanging on by her fingertips to being working class.

The guard felt sorry for the woman. She reminded him of his aunt, the one that was the butt of family jokes. There could be no harm in letting her see Mme. Thibault, he concluded.

Professor Benet walked stiffly and kept her head down, shoulders curled in, as he escorted her through the halls and into the cell. Only after the guard left did she make eye contact with Mme. Thibault, who startled when she recognized her husband's professor friend. "I'm here, Madame, to learn what you want done with the house while you are 'gone,'" Professor Benet said obsequiously. Mme. Thibault adopted behavior that fit the charade.

Their conversation was coded, instructions about the house having a double meaning. When Madame listed groceries her housekeeper should purchase, the professor memorized them so she could compare them with the codex Jacques had left for her to use in case he didn't survive the Resistance.

Visits with high value prisoners like Mme. Thibault were limited to fifteen minutes, so soon the weary "housekeeper" limped back down the halls and out of the prison, keeping up her disguise until she reached the Tuileries gardens, where she had hidden a bag with her regular clothes and shoes in the bushes beside the public toilet. Thank goodness it was still there. Seeing herself in the stainless-steel mirror, she grimaced with distaste and changed out of her disguise quickly. She was accustomed to looking age appropriately svelte. She stored the disreputable clothes behind a toilet and returned to her apartment.

DANIEL'S PARENTS

A week had passed since Daniel had seen Cora. He'd texted and called, even emailed, to no avail. Of course, cell towers were disabled many places in Paris and Wi-Fi functioning only off-and-on, he reminded himself. And, she lived in Porte Saint-Denis, which was under twenty-three-hour curfew every day.

He continued going to the office and trying to contact his regional youth leaders, which was a challenge because many of them also lived in Porte Saint-Denis and were unable to leave their apartments or communicate virtually.

Daniel's boss called him in for a private meeting. He was surprised to see her let loose her fury with the coarsest words he'd ever heard her use. She railed at him for Cora's absence from work and for the resignations from the National Youth Movement of his recruits. Resignations had accelerated rapidly since the declaration of martial law and the roundup of immigrants for deportation. Could he be completely honest with her? Tell her that the National Youth Movement had been hemorrhaging young recruits ever since the new policy of arming cadres was announced? He decided to tell her, no matter how upset she was. She fiercely corrected him.

"We are *not* losing recruits. Only your recruits are resigning. The National Front is *gaining* support, and we are *gaining* new NYM members. I don't know where you get this information, but it is false. The French people are emerging from their homes to vocally support us. Even in Porte Saint-Denis they are singing our national anthem from their apartments. But you are an American. I shouldn't expect you to know anything about French people."

He felt his color rising. How long could he keep absorbing her hostility, her nasty remarks, before he stood up to her or quit? He forced himself to cool down. He held a job within the Party, which should provide a good vantage point for observing what was happening. He and Cora had agreed that they would remain in Paris, but he needed to know where Cora was, whether she was safe. He was worried.

Daily staff meetings reinforced the spin that the National Front put on the acts of resistance taking place inside and outside of Paris. Anything negative said about the situation brought a barrage of corrective "information" from the boss and her lieutenants and a caution that the most dangerous terrorists were the ones within—"Never forget what happens to them! Jacques Thibault, his wife, and fellow travelers are either dead or in prison, as they should be." Jacques Thibault had morphed from a national hero to a terrorist in the Party's rhetoric after Madame Thibault went live with her criticism of the Party's policies.

By remaining at work in the offices of the National Youth Movement, Daniel expected that he could learn what was happening with the Party leadership, policy shifts and actions, before they were public. Instead, the office was full of propaganda and warnings to toe the Party line. Nevertheless, he chose not to quit.

One night his parents were able to get through to him in one of those rare windows of cell and Wi-Fi service. Apparently, they'd been trying every day for a week to reach him.

"What the Hell is going on there, Daniel? It sounds like a whole lot of pigs rolling in shit." His father's colorful way of talking amused Daniel, although that had not always been true. When Daniel was a child, Dad's language embarrassed him and made him feel afraid. *Dad bullies by bombast*, he thought.

"Danny, can't you come home on the next plane? We hear that nothing is functioning in Paris and that military police have occupied the city." Mom's language was predictably more restrained.

"Things are really crazy here, Mom. No one knows what's going on. In fact, *you* should tell *me* what *you*'re hearing! The government rules by decree now and considers any degree of dissent treason. Whole areas of Paris are blockaded and patrolled by troops with tanks, both French troops and Hungarians." Before Daniel could continue, his father interrupted.

"Well, we read that the chief executives of fourteen corporations spoke out and were immediately imprisoned. You know I support conservative causes, always have, always will. Your great grandfather started the petroleum company that carried our family from poverty to wealth, and I'm proud to be a capitalist. No apologies from me! But the National Front seems to have lost its way. It's no libertarian party anymore. Shit! Where do they get the idea that deporting the people they need in their workforce helps build a stronger France?"

"Calm down, Charlie," his mother interjected to no avail. Daniel could almost see them, Dad refaced and blustering, Mom trying to keep the focus on Daniel.

"I had questions when they pulled France out of NATO and took over the AI program at the Sorbonne. Private is always

Resistance!

more productive than public. Remember that, Daniel. And military alliances are what fuels economies. Hell, wars bring us millions more in profits! Nations at war rely on the products we make from petroleum! Drones, fire retardant uniforms, boots, weapons—all made from plastics. The National Front appears to have its head up its ass, if you ask me. Its policies go against its interests. They're downright stupid."

Daniel poured himself a beer and leaned back in his easy chair, enjoying Dad's rant. *You gotta love a guy so passionate*, he thought. Suddenly, he stood, his posture upright, like he was ready to begin a race. *Could my dad, owner of the world's largest privately owned oil company, have ideas about what could be done to salvage the chaos France is in?* That possibility had never before occurred to him.

He decided to ask him, which shut Dad up for a couple of minutes. Then, when Daniel was about to speak, Dad started in again.

"They may be fascists, but they are still capitalists. And capitalists don't like instability. Keeping things stable is their bread and butter. They don't want chaos, open protest, boycotts, strikes, or bad press calling them out for their human rights violations. And they're getting all of that instability in spades right now."

"You think they might decide to let up?"

"Maybe. A lot depends on what happens when the National Assembly meets the Tuesday after Easter. If there are other business leaders, other than the ones they've jailed, who want them to restore democracy and moderate their policies, *they* could force a change. If not, Parliament will likely reinforce the National Front. In that case, I expect you'll see more arrests, maybe even executions, and punishment of those outside of France who've dared to resist by work slow-downs and boycotts. Which is why we think you should come home. Now."

"Yes, Son," Mom added.

Suddenly, the connection was lost. Daniel pondered their conversation. Instability. But if the NF countered instability with a militarized crackdown on those causing it, wouldn't that give the Party more power?

By overnight mail a thick packet of material arrived at Daniel's apartment from his father. Dad explained that he couldn't be confident Daniel would receive digital communications in this time of turmoil.

Daniel had never received a physical letter from his father. He settled himself at his kitchen table and unfolded the ten pages his father had printed off and mailed to him. "EYES ONLY" was the header on each page. The communication was bulleted. The heading read:

Our Family Concerns.

1) We oppose government regulation here or in any of the 80 countries in which we do business.

2) Russian expansion in the Baltics means Russia has more access to energy markets. Russia is a major producer of fossil fuels. As it moves into countries with these resources, our company's access to them is limited or ended. Russia acquires more power to control prices.

3) As the world's largest family-owned oil and gas company, we remain under the radar of internationalist forces that want to regulate our production. We make public only what we want the public to know. We are a family business. That prevents us from feeling pressure from stockholders. We have no stockholders, only our family. <u>We want to keep it that way</u>.

4) However, we <u>are</u> vulnerable to the shift in public opinion toward support for lowering greenhouse gas emissions. Consequently, we are channeling some of our research to support that new direction. It is prudent to do so.

Each point was accompanied by source citations and images—maps, tables, graphics. Daniel felt like he was back in Business Economics 301. His head hurt. Did he really want to plow through all this material? *Can't Dad be personal in communicating with me in this time of crisis?*

He stood, refreshed his coffee, and grabbed a croissant on his way back to the table. Before returning to the document, he took two ibuprofens.

5) We value political stability. But if Russia begins constructing undersea pipelines from Finland or Norway (which I believe is its next target), that will so advantage them and so hurt our business, that military action to stop them may become advisable.

6) Our company has pursued a policy of recruiting people from immigrant populations and training them to work for us. This policy has paid off for the past ten years. We get skilled workers grateful for the chance to hold skilled jobs with us and loyal to our way of thinking. Ejecting immigrant populations makes no sense from a business point of view and only generates hostility toward governments engaging in such practices.

7) We were latecomers to the low-carbon market concept. Shell, BP, Totalenergies, Eni, Chevron, and Equinor saw the necessity of reducing their carbon footprint years before we did. I could not convince Grandpa and Grandma to take climate change seriously—DO NOT SHARE THIS WITH ANYONE—,so we have a lot of catching up to do.

8) There are incentives to shift to low-carbon production, grants and tax breaks that make it cost-effective.

9) You, your brother, and your sister will inherit this business. Therefore, you have good reason to pursue our objectives wherever you work in whatever ways you can.

10) Compare these positions with those of your employer. If you think you can help shift their policies, remain there. If not, come home. SOON. Things could get much worse.

There was no signature. But there was the hand-drawn image of Popeye flexing his muscles while a pipe hung precariously from his lips. It was the same image Dad had drawn for him and his brother and sister when he was young, Dad's special private way of communicating with his children. It was how he showed emotion. The Popeye drawing evoked memories of Daniel's days in Wichita on the family compound, of trips to Africa as an extended, four-generational family where Gigi (Great-grandma Mary) shot rhino and lions that were stuffed and transported to her home on their estate. That was when Dad had begun those drawings, when they were at a party to celebrate Gigi's return from another safari. "I'd put long, curly hair on Popeye if I dared," he'd whispered to them. At that moment, Daniel had wondered if his father was being subversive with his Popeye drawings. Might he not approve of the family's pride in killing beautiful animals?

Funny, Daniel had always pictured his dad as Popeye, liking to flex his muscles and appear tough. Instinctively they knew the drawings were Dad's way of showing he loved them, though he'd probably never say it.

Daniel wished he could talk longer with his parents. *Dad must have thoughts about how I might affect the policies of the National Front? Surely Cook Industries could do something? I'm out of my depth here.*

He needed to talk to someone about all this, and the first someone who came to mind was Cora.

A HERDING CATS

The weather was not helping. Each day felt hotter than the last. The military men patrolling Porte Saint-Denis grew irritable in their long-sleeved uniforms, berets, and bullet-proof vests. They were quick to react to the least provocation.

The rest of Paris had no idea that the daily singing had spread to dozens of streets in Porte Saint-Denis. Each morning neighbors, unable to get to their jobs, woke up early anyway to go to their windows and balconies and join in the serenade. It provided routine, order, even sanity.

In her apartment, Professor Benet had decoded Mme. Thibault's message and identified twenty-five names, new prospects to contact and persuade to join the resistance. Because her arrondissement was not under curfew, she decided to make personal visits to the people on Jacques' list. Definitely safer than digital communications. Disguising herself for her visit to the prison had actually made that trip an adventure, a relief from the heaviness of living under this repression. She would wear disguises now for these visits. She selected an assortment of clothing, hair styles, hats, and shoes to fit the personas she would take on to appeal to these twenty-five business leaders. "Dressing up" would provide some comic relief. She grinned at her image in the mirror each time she assembled herself as someone new. But she had very little time to reach twenty-five people. Easter was a week away and many families would travel for the long weekend to the countryside, or to the south of France to enjoy the beaches before the next wave of fires dirtied the air.

Most of the people lived near her in this affluent, gated neighborhood. Jacques Thibault had left her handwritten notecards for each of them that identified tailor-made arguments he thought they would find most persuasive. He even left instructions for how to gain access to them—the route they walked daily, where they ate lunch, and the name she was to use approaching them that would identify her as representing him. Bless the man!

Chevron's CEO was first on Jacques' list and the meeting went well. She made four contacts each day, but it required Herculean effort to track down some of them despite Jacques' detailed instructions. Those few she missed she would pass to one of the CEOs who had offered to help. He insisted that he was eager to stop the craziness unrolling in their beloved city.

Each conversation found her seesawing between hope and terror. Could she trust that when they said they would join the resistance, they were telling the truth? Would one of them betray her?

She returned to her apartment and stashed her "costumes" in the closet. She changed into slacks and a tunic and poured herself a large glass of wine. She put her feet up on her ottoman and rested her head against the back of her sofa. She surprised herself by muttering a kind of prayer that her effort would bear fruit.

Then, the doorbell rang. Through the peephole she saw four uniformed, armed gendarmes. They had come to arrest her.

DANIEL IN PORTE SAINT-DENIS

Daniel walked along the Seine as he returned from work, oblivious to the glorious displays of color in the park to his left and to the phenomenally cloudless blue sky. Almost ten days had passed with no response to his texts and calls to Cora. He knew the curfew in her neighborhood continued and that Wi-Fi was sporadic, but surely some of his texts were reaching her? The media reported nothing about the military's presence in Porte Saint-Denis. Like most Parisians, he assumed the tanks and troops there had been reduced dramatically by now. *So why don't I hear from her?*

His panic growing, he decided to act. Curfew or no curfew. He would go to her apartment. He would take her food and wine. And if he couldn't get out of Port Saint-Denis, he would stay with her, if she was willing for him to stay. He resolved to go that night after dark and to wear black to minimize the chance of being seen.

He stopped at a grocer and purchased kiwi, strawberries, mushrooms, cubed beef, baby onions, carrots, chard, and crusty bread, along with red wine. He planned to make her favorite meal for her. He added chocolates and good coffee to his cart. He had practiced preparing this meal during the past few weeks, eager to cook it well. Cooking was how he handled anxiety. At eight, he set out, a canvas duffle bag in each hand carrying the groceries.

He rode the Metro to the stop nearest her apartment, exited, and began walking stealthily to her apartment, moving around the barricades and staying close to the buildings, alert for gendarmes. There seemed to be no one on the street. The whole neighborhood resembled a ghost town. His mind jumped to their visit to the training camp and panic overtook him. *Could the government have gone so far as to engage in urban warfare here?*

He turned the corner onto Rue de Bartolome and picked up his pace. Her apartment was in sight, although there was no light in her windows.

"*Arrete!*" a stern voice shouted from the shadows. A gendarme in full military gear emerged, pointing his XM250 automatic rifle at Daniel.

In his best French Daniel told the man he was taking food to his beloved grandmother who was very ill and had no one to care for her. Extremely worried about her, his family had sent him to bring food to her despite the curfew. Please, please, he begged, search my bags but let me go to her.

The soldier did search his bags. Then, to Daniel's surprise, he let him pass, cautioning him to remain indoors until the noon break in the curfew the next day. "My colleagues may not have the same sympathy as I do."

Daniel sprinted across the road to Cora's apartment. The outside door was ajar, so he pushed it open and started up the stairs, the bags bumping his calves with each step. Suddenly, he remembered the first time he'd been in that stairwell. The memory overwhelmed him, how he felt holding her, the sandalwood scent of her hair when he'd buried his face in her curls.

He pulled himself together and continued up the stairs to her apartment. There was no answer to his knocking, no answer when he texted her, no answer when he called her name. He sank to the floor in front of her door, feeling like he'd been gut-punched. *Where could she be?* He placed the groceries next to the wall to his left and lay down on the worn rug, curling himself into the fetal position. He didn't care if anyone saw him, although surely they were all inside their flats and would not. He lay there all night, drifting in and out of sleep, in and out of despair. Through the long hours, one thought persisted, penetrating his anxiety: *I really love this woman.*

Daniel awoke to the sound of singing, faint at first, then louder. He stood stiffly and went to the hall window that overlooked the street. In the early light of dawn, he saw a strange sight: people leaning out of their open windows or standing on their balconies. They were singing love songs, some of the songs he'd heard Cora's aunt sing when they went to hear her perform at the jazz club. It felt surrealistic but it was truly happening. They sang for nearly an hour, ending with the rousing national anthem of France, "La Marseillaise." Then they all cheered and banged on pots and pans. *What was happening?*

He knocked on the door of the apartment next to Cora's. When an elderly woman answered, he asked her first about her next-door neighbor.

"Oh, *mon cher,* she has not been here for more than a week," the woman told him. "I saw her leaving during the time they give us to get supplies. She was carrying a bag, but I don't know where she went. Probably not far. They don't permit us to leave Porte Saint-Denis." The woman tucked some loose strands of her white hair into her bun. Her eyes appeared welcoming. She invited Daniel in for coffee, smiling warmly as she said, "This is Easter weekend, you know. Important to show charity."

Surprised by her invitation, Daniel accepted, moving the bags of food inside and setting them in the hall. The beef was starting to smell a bit ripe after its night on the hall floor. Maybe he was, too?

They sat at the woman's small, round table next to a window that looked down on what had been the outdoor market before the curfew, when people were allowed to sell and shop. It seemed like another lifetime, the woman said. He asked her about the singing that had awakened him.

She chuckled. "Today was Day #8. We sing at 6:00 in the morning and at 8:00 in the evening. A woman four streets from here started it. She has a magnificent voice. She sings all kinds of songs and her family bang on pots and pans and sing along. They hang a banner from their window—I heard this from my daughter who lives on that street. It invites everyone to join them. There are French songs and American songs. My daughter writes down the words to the unfamiliar ones and brings them to me when she brings my groceries during the noon hour break in the curfew." She shuffled through some notes on small squares of paper until she found the one she sought. "One I remember is 'Ain't gonna let nobody turn me round'—it's some kind of protest song. You can be certain we sing that one with *enthousiasme!*"

She stood and moved slowly to her kitchen counter to slice some bread for him. Her gait made him wonder if she was in pain, but her eyes, when she turned to him, danced. "The singing keeps us united. It gives us hope because we are not alone. I don't know if we could bear what is happening without the songs. That woman is our heroine!"

Daniel asked her about her expériences during these days of occupation. To his surprise she spoke of tanks on every corner. When his face registered shock, she motioned him to her bedroom window. "*Voila!* Do you see them?" Two tanks squatted at the intersection. Soldiers in camouflage and bulletproof vests carrying automatic rifles with sniper scopes leaned against the tanks, scanning the windows of the apartments.

"Are they arresting people?"

"*Mais oui*! Every day. Small numbers. They don't return."

They walked back to the kitchen table whre she scrutinized him, her brow puckered. "Where will you stay tonight?"

"I guess I will go back to my apartment in the tenth arrondissement."

"How will you do that without being apprehended?"

His face showed the question took him by surprise. He hadn't thought about that.

"I have the code to Mlle. Johnson-Allen's apartment. Since you are her friend, you could stay there, *n'est pas?*"

That solved one problem. He thanked her and asked if he could go there now to refrigerate the groceries.

"But of course. When you want company, tap on my door. I don't go out. My daughter brings my food." She started to lift one of the bags to help him, but he intercepted her. He thanked her profusely for her kindness.

Once installed in Cora's flat, Daniel unpacked the groceries and texted his office that he was ill and would not be in. He hoped his text went through. He tried Cora once again. No answer. He wondered if she would be offended at his using her space, but at the moment he was too tired from sleeping on the hardwood floor of the hallway to give that much thought. He stretched out on her bed and delicious memories of their night there lulled him to sleep.

AMIR MAKES CONTACT

Daniel's phone startled him awake. It was Amir! Amir asked where he was and could they meet to talk. "You know they monitor our phones." Daniel mumbled about being "at a friend's in 10." He didn't say Porte Saint-Denis, only the numeral of the arrondissement.

"Can we meet at the hospital during the break?"

"Yes." Amir clicked off before Daniel could say more.

While the curfew was lifted for one hour, Daniel hurried to the hospital where he found Amir sprawled on the grass outside the Emergency Room entrance. They greeted each other with an embrace and settled on the lawn.

Amir talked fast, all the while swiveling his head to be sure no one was within earshot. "Your friend is Cora?" Amir tossed him a knowing smile.

Resistance! 229

"Yes, but she's not at her apartment. I came to find her after I'd heard nothing from her, but I don't know where she is."

"Wherever she is, she is helping us... Now, about you." Amir's eyes bored into Daniel. "The NF knows they are in trouble. But change comes only when there are many active pressure points promoting it. Fascists don't give up easily. You told me once that your father owned a large oil company in the U.S." He waited for Daniel's affirmative nod. "If you are arrested, would your father raise hell to get you released?"

"I think so. If he knew. In the current situation he might never know."

"There are many pieces of our strategy already working: AI workers in a number of southern hemisphere countries are on strike. Some European Union countries refusing to trade with France, which is creating economic hardship here. The Singing Resistors of Porte Saint-Denis are boosting morale and encouraging resistance. The students on campuses are erecting camps to simulate the deportation camps, and people are boycotting French oil companies operating in Vietnam, Brazil, Iran, Angola, Senegal, Côte d'Ivoire, and Nigeria. This is huge! Boycotts of the largest French oil companies—TOTAL and ELF! In many places people have begun to make their own fuel by pyrolysis—melting waste plastics in large gas cylinders and distilling the vapor to produce clean fuel, a simple process that is spreading rapidly around the world. The U.N. has passed resolutions condemning France for putting immigrants in deportation camps. And we believe a number of major French companies will speak out against the NF next week."

"But weren't all the business leaders who spoke out arrested?"

"The first group were, yes, but we believe more will speak out. The National Assembly meets in ten days. And it is possible they may vote to challenge the party, even to discipline it. Of course, we don't know that. We *do* know there is pressure on the Party leaders, and they are nervous."

Daniel jumped in, anticipating where Amir was going. "You want me to be arrested so you can make my arrest an international incident that will raise the heat even more? And you want that to happen before the National Assembly meets?"

"Yes. We want that to happen *as the National Assembly convenes.* If you agree, we can get word to your parents. We have sympathizers at the American Embassy. Today is Saturday. Could you get yourself arrested on Monday?" Amir gave Daniel a knowing look. "That would give you Sunday with Cora."

"How is that possible? I don't know where to look for her."

"Think about it, my friend. A magnificent professional singer who sings love songs, jazz songs, and protest songs from her window. A singer who uses a microphone and amplifiers so she can be heard even beyond the streets of this neighborhood. Who is savvy about broadcasting her voice and owns the equipment. Who might that be?"

"Oh my God! Cora's Aunt Joan! Of course, Cora would go to her. But I don't know where she lives."

Amir passed him a sticky note with an address and watched with amusement as Daniel's face lit up. "What do you say? Will you join us? You should be aware that what happens to those they arrest is unclear. If our pressure points don't force them either to change policies or to step down, you could be in prison for a long time, or deported. If they think you are part of the Resistance, it could be worse than that."

"Monday?" Daniel confirmed. He knew this would be a life-changing decision. "I'll do it," he said.

"Now get yourself to that address before the curfew resumes, my friend. You don't want to be arrested before then. And give this to Cora." Amir passed him a sealed envelope, shook his hand, and kissed him on both cheeks before he hurried off.

A RESPITE

Daniel reached the address on Amir's sticky note five minutes before the resumption of the curfew. It was a very old building and still had buzzers next to a cluster of small, printed names in parallel rows. He buzzed the apartment labeled "Marcheau and Oliver," unable to recall Joan's surname. Oliver seemed the most American of the options listed. A woman's voice, melodic and in perfect French, answered. His own voice almost stuttered as he sought the right words. "I-I-I am Daniel Cook, a friend of Cora Johnson-Allen. I-I've been searching for her. Is she there? Please?"

"Detainment!" The buzzer sounded and he climbed the stairs, his heart pounding. Cora stood at the top of the second flight of stairs wearing jeans and a white poet shirt. She looked beautiful. Coiled tendrils had escaped her loose ponytail and danced around

the contours of her glowing face. Her eyes sparkled and her smile dazzled. Had any other face caused him to feel this way?

Careful, careful. Don't rush it, he told himself, but when he stepped off the top step onto the landing, she threw her arms around him. "Daniel! I am so glad to see you!"

He responded to her hug and bussed her on both cheeks, the French way, avoiding her lips by a supreme act of willpower. *Take your time, man. Don't spoil it by pushing.*

She stepped back and surveyed him from head to foot. "You look like you haven't slept much."

"I slept on the floor outside your apartment," he replied sheepishly.

Cora's eyes widened. "You violated the curfew to find me?"

"Yes. I've been calling and texting for ten days. You didn't respond and I got worried. I decided I had to chance it and come to you, curfew or not. So I did."

Her eyes misted. Was she imagining how frightening it must have been for him to go through the barricades and hide from the tanks and gendarmes? "How did you manage to get through? That was dangerous."

"When a gendarme stopped me, I said I was taking food to my beloved grandma who was very ill. He had pity on me and let me go."

"Beloved grandma?" She laughed and he thought his heart might burst with joy.

"I should have said just 'beloved.'" He grinned boyishly and she blushed.

Cora changed the subject: "Come see my Aunt Joan and meet Uncle Andre." She took his hand and led him to the apartment.

For the next several hours the four of them talked, first about what was happening in Paris and what they knew about how the rest of the world was responding, then about Joan and Andre's work. No one mentioned Daniel's work with the NF's National Youth Movement. Their interaction was mostly comfortable, except when Joan asked about his family. He could feel her sudden reserve when he talked about his father.

"I'm quite familiar with Cook Industries," Joan said, her face wary. Daniel wondered if she was a climate activist. Shortly after that Joan moved to the kitchen to prepare supper. Only an archway divided the kitchen from the living room. Daniel noticed Joan was listening closely to their conversation.

They ate early to allow time to gather the pots and pans and the banner and prepare for the evening songfest.

Daniel helped clear the dishes and took the opportunity to tell Joan what Cora's elderly neighbor had said about her. "She said you have become a heroine to the people of Paris! That is amazing. I have so much respect for what you are doing." At this Joan smiled. Soon after, she excused herself to prepare to sing. Cora followed her.

"Aunt Joan, would it be all right for Daniel to sleep on the sofa tonight? He slept on the floor outside my apartment last night and I don't want him to chance being caught. We can go to my place tomorrow at noon during the break in the curfew."

Aunt Joan smiled. "A man who risks arrest to make sure you are safe—and who sleeps on the floor outside your apartment—is welcome to my sofa." She paused, her eyes twinkling. "Is he welcome to my niece? That I'll have to think more about, but the sofa is fine! I think Andre is inviting him now as we speak."

When Cora returned to the living room, Daniel and Andre were deep in conversation. She liked the way Daniel listened attentively as Andre expressed his opinions.

Aunt Joan came out of the bedroom wearing her blue, white, and red caftan, and they took their places at the window. Cora passed Daniel a wooden spoon and a pot-drum to beat on and the nightly serenade began.

~~~

At noon the following day, Cora and Daniel set off with a shopping bag to pick up a few groceries and move to Cora's apartment. He stifled his desire to tell her that he had purchased food for their dinner. He wanted to surprise her. When they

Resistance! 235

reached her place and were unloading the groceries, she was startled to see that her fridge held a good cut of beef not too "mature" to cook, despite its night on the hall floor, and assorted fruits and veggies.

"May I cook tonight?" he asked. "I've been practicing preparing your favorite meal and think I have mastered it. That's what all this food is for."

"Oh, Daniel, that is so thoughtful," she replied and kissed him. While the beef bourguignon was slow-cooking, one thing led to another. Dinner time passed while the meal simmered. The evening songfest got their attention but they made no attempt to disentangle themselves. "We'll just be part of the audience tonight," Cora suggested. "Tomorrow morning we'll join in."

"Over a delicious breakfast of beef bourguignon," Daniel agreed, putting the pot in her frig and returning to her arms.

They talked on and off all night, learning things about each other that her months of wariness and their months of separation had prevented them from discussing. As dawn began to streak the sky with gold and orange and pink, Daniel told her of the plan he had made with Amir to be arrested Monday noon. Cora felt afraid for him, but also proud of his willingness to take on this assignment. "Are you certain your parents will learn of your arrest? Communication is so spotty with the Wi-Fi still haphazard."

"I'm only certain that Amir will do anything he can to make sure they hear…Now, let's get up, sleepyhead. It's time to sing!" He jumped up from her narrow bed and grabbed a pot for each of them.

While they enjoyed the tasty beef bourguignon breakfast that he reheated, Cora's elderly neighbor tapped softly on her door to bring them warm beignets. "I'm leaving an Easter gift for you from my daughter. I'll leave them just outside your door," she was saying as Cora opened the door. Smiling at the two of them, she retreated to her apartment.

"I think she likes us being together. She told me that she worried about me being alone so much of the time," Cora told him.

"I think she knows what it's like to be lonely. I like us being together, too." He fed her a beignet and licked the crumbs from her lips. "Let's go back to bed."

"Quelle bonne idee!" she replied nudging him out of his chair and onto the bed where she pressed a beignet to his open lips.

For twenty-four hours they allowed themselves to forget the fascists who had taken over France and feel only the romantic essence of April in Paris that poets, writers, and composers have celebrated from time immemorial.

PART 4

AMIR AT THE AMERICAN EMBASSY

Amir and his inner circle used their contact at the U.S. Embassy to get news out to the global community about what was happening in Paris. Different members collected information from their contacts outside of France—what was happening and how the rest of the world was reporting and responding to the National Party's crackdown.

On Monday morning Amir arrived early at the Embassy for a meeting with his contact. The man met him at the entrance and ushered him through security to his tiny office on the third floor. They had met several times before and developed a cordial relationship. They greeted each other warmly and sat down, the American behind his desk and Amir in the only other chair that would fit in the tiny office. Both had significant information to exchange.

The American was probably mid-thirties, brown-skinned, although lighter than Amir, tall, and gracious. The American initiated their conversation, reporting on a new development.

"The African Union has voted to launch a cooperative business venture to produce an alternative to fossil fuels. They will pay fishermen in coastal countries to harvest plastics from the ocean and heat them to make gas and liquid fuel in facilities they set up. They'll start with a pilot program in two locations, Nigeria and Angola, both set to begin before the end of this year. I'm really hopeful about this." The American appeared excited. "The resulting product is clean and more efficient than petroleum or natural gas." He had no idea that Amir had been working behind the scenes to expand interest in this form of fuel production in Africa.

Endorsement by the African Union was a major development. Amir wondered if his contacts on the continent had been behind the vote. That level of buy-in could be a game-changer. "Do you know how the African Union came to this decision?" he asked.

"What I have heard is that it was the success of local efforts in Africa and Asia, converting plastic bags and bottles into fuel by 'cooking' them in large metal cylinders, the kind they use to store gas. Apparently, this technique spread through social media and YouTube video demonstrations. It's truly a phenomenal story!"

Amir pretended this was new information to him. He didn't want to embarrass the American.

"So, last week Nigeria proposed that the African Union encourage its fifty-five member nations to begin large scale mining of the oceans for plastic refuse. They presented testimony from people in Africa and Asia already doing this on a small scale. With ninety percent of plastic refuse dumped in the oceans, killing sea creatures and polluting the water, the other countries thought it made sense. It's very promising," the American said. "Mining plastics from the ocean could slow climate change and, at the same time, grow local economies. It's a win-win."

Amir agreed. "It may also disarm the protestors living along the seacoasts who suffer from offshore drilling for oil." As he said this, Amir felt conflicted. *I don't want people to stop protesting, not until they succeed in ending offshore drilling.*

Amir had first-hand experience with coastal villages suffering from petroleum spills and leaks. He had witnessed in Cameroon how oil spills killed crops and impoverished local residents. He knew that coastal people worked for foreign and domestic petroleum companies because their fishing industry was devastated by oil exploration and the warming of the ocean. Melting glaciers raised sea levels and ocean temperatures. Offshore drilling and global warming together threatened their survival. But he remained silent, listening attentively to the American, learning as much from him as he could.

"Extracting plastics from the ocean is low-cost and can employ thousands of people. And they benefit from 'free'—or at least less expensive—fuel. It's brilliant!"

Amir saw an opportunity to raise his concerns. "You know I am from Cameroon. How will this affect the fishing industry that many of Cameroon's coastal people rely on?"

"Well, there are two answers to that question. Initially, Nigeria proposes using local fishing boats to troll the sea with wide, deep-sea nets—two boats separated by maybe an eighth of a mile, each boat pulling opposite sides of a huge net to catch the plastic. They will harvest fish as well as plastic in those nets. Over time, as consumers switch to using locally produced energy, energy produced from plastic refuse, the African Union projects that major oil companies will see the handwriting on the wall and accept that they must improve their environmental performance now and dramatically increase their investment in transitioning from fossil fuels to other forms of energy. If the big companies make that switch, it will relieve the fishing industry of the pollution from oil spills that has killed off fish all along the coast, including in Cameroon."

Amir appreciated this answer, but his own experience left him wary. If only this would happen. If only the oil companies would stop throwing their money around to buy off politicians and corrupt the process.

The American apologized for talking so much and for not offering Amir refreshments. He left the room to fetch glasses of fruit juice and a dish of peanuts. They savored the juice for a few moments before Amir asked another question.

"How is this decision by the African Union being received by the oil industry?"

"Our information is that the oil companies are scurrying to determine how best to respond. I think they realize this can be a game-changer. There's a lot of excitement in China, also, with its enormous coastline. Climate change threatens coastal towns and cities all around the world, and this presents an opportunity to fight and at the same time bring revenue and low-cost fuel to local communities. If China jumps on board, so will India, Southeast Asia, you name it. I think we'll see coastal nations across the globe starting similar plastic fishing ventures soon. Still, I don't discount the power of the big oil companies to fight it."

The American paused, gazing at nothing, then resumed speaking. "This is why I wanted to join the foreign service—to foster promising cooperative initiatives that could improve ordinary people's lives. In this time when it is hard to find reasons for hope, this feels to me like it could bring a lot of benefits."

"Allah provides," Amir agreed.

The American shifted in his chair and changed the subject. "So, what news do *you* bring, Amir?" He reached for his phone to make notes.

"Today Daniel Cook will be arrested in Porte Saint-Denis... He's the son of Hal Cook. Yes, that Cook. We need you to notify his family of his arrest. We want them to pressure the National Front to release him and use the power of their prominence in American business to publicize their son's unfair arrest and imprisonment. Can you do that?"

"Whoa! I need more information. "Why will Daniel Cook be arrested? If he has broken a law, that could be problematic."

"He will have broken no law. He simply went to Porte Saint-Denis in the tenth arrondissement to take food to his girlfriend. You know that for more than two weeks martial law has subjected that area to military occupation—the military lets no one in or out. When he couldn't reach her by phone—Wi-Fi and cell towers continue operating infrequently there—he was worried about her safety. He decided to take risk entering Porte Saint-Denis to find her."

The American's face changed as Amir spoke. Amir sensed the man was keeping tight control of his reactions. *Does he know something I don't about the Cooks? Or about Daniel? Or am I misreading his reaction?*

But the American official responded affirmatively. "I will see that the Cook family is informed. Do you know at what time he will be arrested? I won't ask you whether his arrest is part of the strategy of the Resistance."

Amir smiled and then checked his phone. "It should be happening right about now." He shifted in his chair. He had one more question but wasn't sure the American could answer him. He was, Amir knew, a low-level foreign service officer at the Embassy. "Do you know what is happening in the National Assembly?"

"They convene at one today. No news yet what they will do." The officer's phone was lighting up and he needed to go. He stood to indicate their meeting was over. "Thank you, Amir, for this information. We will hope for a good outcome." They shook hands and Amir left the Embassy.

ARREST

As it neared noon, Daniel pulled a tiny envelope from his pocket. He opened Cora's palm and placed it on her lifeline, closing her fingers around it. "Keep this. For me. For all of us. It's my pledge." He could not say more without becoming emotional. He must subdue his emotions and be brave now. He picked up his passport and phone and left the apartment.

Cora heard his steps retreating along the hardwood hall and pounding down the steps, out of the building and into the street. She moved to the window to watch him walking openly down Rue de Bartolome, as though this was not martial law and there were no tanks and soldiers on every corner. She heard a man shout, *Arrêtes!* And saw Daniel stop with his hands in the air as two gendarmes approached. They patted him down roughly, made him lie prone on the pavement, and handcuffed him. Pulling him up, they pushed him to a white van, shoving him into the caged rear and padlocking the door. Then the van, its siren blaring, sped away. That was it.

Cora turned from the window and sat down on the bed, which was still warm from where their bodies had lain. She began to weep and wept for a long time, still clutching the small envelope Daniel had placed in her hand. When she had no more tears, she sat up, spread her fingers, and opened it. Inside was an object no bigger than half a-marble, a brown-iris evil eye, and a note that read, "Keep this for me until I return."

Her tears now were tears of relief and gratitude. Daniel was one of them.

~ ~ ~

That evening her phone rang. It was her mother, Keisha.

"I've been trying to reach you for two weeks. Sometimes my call seems to go through but then the connection is dropped. What is happening? Caleb, Uncle Edward, Gran Ann and Granddad—we're all really worried about you."

"Mama, it is so good to hear your voice! Things here are scary. Maybe Aunt Joan has told you about the curfew and the tanks and gendarmes in the streets?"

"Joan's sister Femi got through to Joan last week, so I know a little about the situation." Mama paused. "Joan told her you were seeing the grandson of Charles Cook." Cora heard a steely edge in Mama's voice. "You *do* know who those people are, right?"

"Yes, but Daniel is different."

"*The Wall Street Journal* had a story yesterday about Cook Industries and their conglomerates that monopolize the production and distribution of emergency vehicles—90% of the ambulances, police cars, hearses are built by Cook and their leasing agreements lock municipalities and hospitals and mortuaries into leases that are unaffordable. They engage in a lot of questionable practices, Cora, and not just in oil and gas." Mama was on a roll and Cora wanted to be anywhere but here on the phone with her.

"I don't want to listen to this now, Mama. I've told you Daniel is different. He's risking his life to challenge what is happening here. I can't say more, and, frankly, right now I'm worrying too much about his safety to care about anything else. I am all right, as all right as anyone living in this occupied neighborhood can be. But France is *not* all right, and I hope you will do whatever you can to make your legislators know how bad it is and to persuade them to pressure the National Front to release all political prisoners and stop deporting immigrants."

Her hand was shaking. She had never stood up to Mama this forcefully, at least not since she'd run away from home at fifteen. "I need you to understand what is important in this moment, and it certainly isn't the Cook conglomerates. I'm going to hang up now, Mama. Please do what you can. The situation here is serious. I'll be in touch." She ended the call and lay back on her bed. She pushed aside her momentary regret at hanging up on Mama and tried to focus on Daniel, tried to recover the bliss she had felt during their brief time together. She spoke the words aloud: "Get yourself together, Cora. This is no time to indulge yourself." She would shed no more tears.

THE NATIONAL ASSEMBLY CONVENES

The 577 members of the lower house of the National Assembly took their seats. The chamber hummed with hundreds of conversations, some of them heated. This was an unusual session, and members were agitated and ornery. The President had sent troops into a section of the nation's capital city. The law required the National Assembly's approval for continued deployment of troops. This session the Assembly would review that presidential action and decide whether to approve or disapprove the deployment of troops in the nation's capital.

The delegate elected from Porte Saint-Denis was on his feet first. "Mesdames and Messieurs, the constitution of France explicitly reads in Article 1 'France...shall ensure the equality of all citizens before the law, without distinction of origin, race or religion. It shall respect all beliefs.' The dispatching of troops to Porte Saint-Denis where they have arrested as many as one thousand Parisiens and put the remainder of the arrondissement under house arrest—unable to go to work, to be outside their homes, to walk their streets, or to leave their district—this is an appalling violation of our constitution. This district is our most diverse, people of different races and religions who are supposed to be equal before French law. Many people there have been arrested without cause and detained indefinitely without charge—and those people are predominantly young people of immigrant origin, predominantly people of color, and Muslims. Is this 'equality of all citizens before the law without distinction of origin, race or religion?' *It is not!* I offer this resolution: 'The National Assembly opposes the government's deploying troops anywhere in France and calls for those deployed to be recalled and demobilized by May 1, 2030 and Hungarian troops to be sent back to their country.'" He passed a paper to the clerk who read the resolution aloud. It was seconded and debate began.

Delegates of the National Front Party were prepared to defeat this resolution. They jumped to their feet to be recognized to speak. One reminded the Assembly that the President and Prime Minister had the power to declare the National Assembly dissolved. It was a threat, and everyone knew it.

The leader of *Changerons!*, the primary opposition party, reminded the Assembly that the state of siege declared by the Council of Ministers began almost two weeks ago and that the constitution required approval by the Assembly for its continuance after twelve days. "Technically the state of siege under which the government has operated by decree ended on Easter, yet the Prime Minister and his Party continue it without the approval of the Assembly, thereby violating our constitution. They should resign and new elections be called for this outrageous behavior." The delegate returned to her seat to applause from one section of the chamber.

Other voices, cautious and fearful, spoke of the need for strongman government when the world was in such disarray and faced the prospect of international war, with the Russians taking territory, and with the hordes of refugees coming into France illegally. Strong measures are needed, they argued.

"What of the deportation of our immigrant population, rounded up like cattle regardless of their status, sent to camps to be deported? Are we a reprise of France, governed by Nazis? That's how they started with Jews. This government is behaving toward Muslims, Hindus, Buddhists, and even Christians the way Hitler's people behaved when they began their occupation," another female delegate stated. Her voice trembled with emotion. "I know this from my grandparents. We must not repeat this shameful part of our past!"

The National Front delegates had an answer for every challenge. "We are not France under the Nazis. We are nationalists who will not stand by while our country is overrun by foreigners. They pollute our culture, marry—or rape!—our women, produce mongrel children, and dilute the French blood of our population. If we allow this to continue, there will be *no* true French people."

Blaming the immigrants for their party's actions, another shook his fist as he spoke. "These people are terrorists. You saw what they did to Jacque Thibault, one of our Party members. Blew him to pieces. Is this what you wish to see across Paris, assassinations of leading citizens, bombing, assault on our beloved patria?"

Jacques Thibault's commitment to ending the excesses of the National Party was unknown to the public and the Party had determined to keep it quiet.

Another female delegate rose to announce that *Changerons!* sought support for a resolution of no confidence. Under Article 49 of the constitution, one tenth of the Assembly, 58 delegates, could bring such a resolution.

She was ruled out of order and reminded that there was a resolution under consideration. Nevertheless, the chamber buzzed with delegates talking to their colleagues about her bold proposal. Everyone wondered how many delegates had already signed on to a resolution of no confidence. How close were they to the required 58? If there *were* enough votes to bring it to a vote, would the votes be there to pass it? In 2023 a no confidence resolution had failed by nine votes.

When they recessed for the day, no one was clear how much support the National Front and its state of siege had, and neither side dared risk a vote. The debate would continue on Tuesday.

A WICHITA, KANSAS

On Tuesday morning, the phone rang just after one a.m., Central Daylight Time, in the Cooks' bedroom. Mona and Hal Cook were already asleep. "Let it ring," Hal mumbled, "It's just someone asking for money."

"At one in the morning?" Mona would not let it ring. She had slept fitfully the past two hours, worrying about her youngest child disrupting her usual dead-to-the-world sleep. Daniel had always been the family's unpredictable one and she feared he might feel compelled to get into the thick of what was happening in Paris. That greatly alarmed her.

"Hello?" Did her voice sound as hesitant and anxious as she felt?

"Mrs. Cook, this is Mr. Weston from the American Embassy in Paris. How are you today?"

"A bit nervous to get your call, Mr. Weston. What has happened?" Mona had no interest in engaging in small talk at this hour in the morning, given the level of her anxiety. Receiving a call from the U.S. Embassy in Paris triggered all her fears.

"Mrs. Cook, I am sorry to inform you that your son Daniel was arrested yesterday and taken to prison. There have been no charges yet, but he was arrested in the area of Paris under military occupation. He was outside during the hours of the curfew." He waited for the news to sink in. "We believe he is safe," he added, "but we are concerned about this action by the National Front government. We are hoping you and your husband can contact the National Front Party, Amnesty International, Human Rights Watch, and as many media outlets as you can to call attention to Daniel's imprisonment. The more public attention his case receives, the more likely he is to be released, or at least treated appropriately for a foreign national who has broken no law."

"Just a moment, Mr. Weston." Mona jerked Hal's arm repeatedly forcing him awake. "Wake up and get on the other phone," she insisted. "It's Daniel."

"Just put him on speaker," Hal grumbled, wondering why a call from their son would be so urgent that she had to awaken him from his REM sleep. Grudgingly, he sat up, leaning back against the headboard. He rubbed his face vigorously and compelled himself to pay attention.

"Could you please repeat what you just told me, sir. My husband is now on the call too."

"Certainly. Mr. Cook, I'm Mr. Weston from the American Embassy in Paris. I'm calling to let you know that your son Daniel was arrested in the Porte Saint-Denis district yesterday for being on the street during the curfew. That area is under military occupation by French and Hungarian troops. We think he is safe, and no charges have been issued so far, but he is in prison and the French government has issued a state of siege, so it is impossible to predict what they may do. They are ruling by decree. They have arrested nearly a thousand people in the past week, and we have it on good authority that they intend to arrest many more over the May Day holiday. We believe maximum media attention to Daniel's situation will help ensure that he is treated as fairly as can be expected. Mr. Cook, can you follow up with local and national media and human rights organizations and call the French embassy here in Washington? I can provide the phone numbers."

Hal Cook was unaccustomed to being told what to do. Usually, *he* was the one giving directives. It took him a minute to absorb this new information and what was being asked of him.

"I told him to come home immediately. He just wouldn't listen. Never has… What has the Embassy done about this? Have you registered a formal complaint?"

"Yes, sir. The Ambassador is meeting with the President of France in three hours. Any media coverage you can generate before then will strengthen the Ambassador's hand."

"I will get my press office on it immediately. Where are they holding him? How long has he been in prison? Don't they know he's working for the Party, damn it, recruiting for its National Youth Movement?"

The official patiently answered all their questions. When the conversation wound down, he stated again the urgent need for protest. "If you have other concerns about the National Front's behavior, this is the time to express them, Mr. Cook." He gave out the numbers and his own direct line, should they want to get back to him. He thanked them for their time and reassured them that Daniel was safe, for the moment. Then the call ended.

Hal dressed and in five minutes was on the phone to his staff. Mona, listening to him, had to smile. *I must remember to tell Daniel how his dad responded*, she thought. *Hal rarely expresses his feelings, but when his children are endangered, he becomes a Mother Bear, though he would hate my saying so.*

Within an hour press releases were issued condemning the behavior of the National Front Party of France in arresting an innocent American young man who had worked for nearly three years in Paris for the government, helping the country's youth. All U.S. news media were alerted to Mona and Hal's availability to be interviewed. Hal made a call to Amnesty International's executive director, getting the man out of bed to ask for his help. Cook Industries issued an order to their affiliates around the world to publicize that Cook Industries would stop doing business with France until further notice.

Calls began coming in by four a.m., requesting interviews on Zoom with the Cooks. Mona cautioned Hal not to shave. "Better to look like a haggard, distraught father. It makes you more sympathetic," she advised, and he followed her instructions.

Mona and Hal sat at their computers scanning everything they could find about the National Front Party's behavior that they might use in their interviews. At five a.m., they brought televisions from their other bedrooms into their room to monitor the coverage. And coverage there was. Every outlet's BREAKING NEWS headlined Daniel's arrest and the French government's outrageous violations of rights guaranteed by the French constitution. Hal had called in 47 of his staff, including some who were on vacation, to assist in this full-scale media campaign.

Late Tuesday night, when Mona and Hal fell wearily into bed, Hal commended himself for the fast response. "I couldn't do that if I had a board of directors that I had to consult before acting," he told her. "Dad was right to keep our company off the stock exchange and family owned."

STONES OR FLOWERS?

Seven members of the small circle of resistors that looked to Amir for leadership gathered in the family kitchen of a supporter who ran a bakery in Porte Saint-Denis. They met above the bakery on the third floor. Because of the curfew they had to walk across rooftops and climb down fire escapes, staying in the shadows, to get there. It was unsafe to risk taking the streets, too easy for the gendarmes to apprehend them. After precariously making her way there without being detected, Cora joined them.

The room was small, without enough seats for them all. Some sat on the floor, leaning against the legs of those seated on chairs. Amir began the meeting asking for reports from each of them about what was happening.

A woman described the "Songbird of the Revolution," the woman who led the people in songs of resistance twice a day. A man reported that the AI workers' boycott was now extended across Southeast Asia. Another man informed them which European Union countries were boycotting trade with France, and Amir shared what he'd learned about the vote of the African Union to fund the recovery of fuel from plastics.

Cora reported on the students' protest at the Sorbonne, the encampment they had constructed to simulate a deportation camp, and their plan to leaflet France with a call to a rally against the National Front on the steps of the National Assembly.

Several people had heard the BBC's coverage of the American arrested and imprisoned. They reported that the coverage was surprisingly extensive and effective. "His father's company has stopped all business with France," a man seated on the floor added.

Another man reported that he and his colleagues had assembled two dozen Molotov cocktails that could be dropped on tanks by drones. "Before the crackdown we purchased ten drones—you know, the ones lots of people use as toys. It's time to escalate our resistance," he asserted. His statement provoked a heated discussion.

Some agreed with him. Others were adamantly against using any form of violence. The women were especially vocal. "Acts of sabotage will bring the full force of the French military down on this district," one asserted. "Violence will cause people to side with the government. We will be labeled terrorists."

"We already are," the drone advocate responded.

"The military will incarcerate even more immigrants. It will be the perfect excuse to escalate the occupation. They'll incarcerate many more of us," another added. "We will lose all sympathy from the outside world and from the troops. We'll alienate many of our neighbors, too."

The woman from the Philippines added her voice. "My grandmother told me that when President Marcos was overthrown in 1986, the people carried flowers and food to the soldiers, walking in the streets in front of the tanks singing. She said she was carrying her youngest child with her other two boys holding onto her skirt and walking beside her. She said she was weeping, but despite her fear, she had to join her neighbors as they tried to win the soldiers to their side. And they won the soldiers, who laid down their weapons."

A man seated on the floor could not contain his irritation. He stood and paced while he spoke. "Name one revolution that did not use some sort of sabotage to get the oppressor's attention. Those women in the streets of Manila with their children taking food and flowers to the soldiers came after years of sabotage by the New People's Army. I have studied these revolutions. It is just like women to think flowers and food will disarm a military force." He sucked his teeth, making a scoffing sound, shook his head, and spit into a Coke can to show his disgust.

By midnight the conversation had exhausted them all and raised the temperature in the small kitchen. They had identified pros and cons of various strategies but could agree only that it was time for some sort of new action.

Amir called them to order, speaking soberly and slowly. Every eye was on him. "We are all exhausted and worried. I want to express my conclusion after listening to all of you. Hear me out and see what you think. If we use violence, even if we only target equipment, someone is bound to get hurt. And the NF will attack us with a vengeance just as the National Assembly is increasing the pressure on them to change their policies or be forced to resign. Think of the impact on the National Assembly members who are undecided how to vote? I believe that if we use violence, they will say it is proof that we are terrorists and that the state of siege should not be extended. They will commend the NF for its foresighted policy of dispatching troops and deporting immigrants... The Assembly's deliberations will probably continue into next week. I think they will take a vote before the May 1 national holiday on Wednesday. I propose we wait to see the outcome of that vote. If the vote goes our way and they are forced to resign, then we take to the streets with flowers and food. If the Assembly supports the NF, then we escalate to sabotaging tanks. That gives us more days to locate additional drones—perhaps we can check with people in our buildings who may have them? Waiting until the vote allows time to assemble more Molotov cocktails. That way, if we must use sabotage as a last result, we will be able to attack more of their tanks."

Around the room his words were met with nods of agreement. No one was smiling. The serious prospect of having no recourse to a war pitting homemade mini-explosives dropped from several dozen drones against one of the world's best equipped armies terrified them all.

WHAT WE CAN DO

After Daniel's arrest, Cora moved back to Aunt Joan's. There was no word from him, but, of course, there would not be. Neither could she reach Professor Benet or her mother, or even the unpleasant woman who was their boss at the National Youth Movement. Even if she could notify their boss, would the woman intervene and put in a good word for Daniel with leaders of the party? Probably not. Having to wait for the National Assembly vote, unable to do anything to affect the outcome, depressed her.

One evening, Andre located the Voice of America. They listened while eating supper, before it was time to sing. The broadcast featured several minutes of an interview with Mona Cook, Daniel's mother, and they lay down their knives and forks to pay full attention.

"My son is good hearted. He went to France to help young people around the world receive training for jobs that would improve their lives. He has never broken a law, never received even a speeding ticket. Yet the French government has locked him up without charge, violating its own constitution that protects the rights of individuals. I ask the people of the world to boycott all French products until the National Front removes troops and tanks from the streets of Paris and frees my son and the more than a thousand others the government has wrongly arrested. Please use the hashtag #BoycottFrance on your social media to spread the word."

"Wow!" Joan was stunned by the woman's interview. "She seems to see the bigger picture, that it's not only about her son. I'd never expected that from the Cooks."

Andre stood up and rooted in the closet, returning to the table with a white sheet. "Time to change our sign," he said. He wrote with large block letters, "**#BOYCOTTEZ LA FRANCE. TRANSMETTEZ-LE**." He secured the sheet to the balcony, first tying stones from their succulent window garden into the lower corners of the sheet to weigh it down so it would remain flat and readable. He lowered the large new sign and let it unfurl. He was pleased that his ingenuity worked. The stones kept it fully furled and readable.

"Before tomorrow's songfest I will add the rod from our shower curtain to the bottom of the sheet so it will stay taut," he said, proud of his cleverness. He grinned at Joan. "You never guessed I was so talented, did you?"

Mona Cook's words—and Andre's new sign that expressed them in letters big enough to be seen all along their street (and copied and texted to others)—gave them new hope.

Still, Cora was worried, and tired, though she didn't say so. She excused herself after the singing and went to bed early. Joan and Andre sat together on the couch speculating about the future. "As hopeful as Mrs. Cook's interview made us, we know that everything rests with the National Assembly. Will enough of them have the courage to oppose the Prime Minister, the President, and the National Front Party? I am not confident they will, my love," Andre told Joan as he stroked her hand.

She reached up and kissed him. "I know that. We have no idea what may come, how ugly it may get. Whatever comes, we know we have done what we can. Knowing that helps us face the future." Then Joan grinned at her husband teasingly. "Besides, who would ever have thought that by marrying you I would get the title Songbird of the Revolution? If we get through this, my career may be on a fast track, husband! Unintended consequences can be quite nice."

With that they, too, went to bed.

A PRISON

The Fleury-Mérogis prison in a southern suburb of Paris held all of those arrested since early April. Its three facilities held women, men, and youth. The fourteen business leaders who had been arrested after their press conference, Professor Benet, Daniel Cook, and more than a thousand others had been added to the prison's population since April 8th. Their numbers stressed the facilities' capacity. The inmates joked, "It must be time for another Bastille Day!" They were referring to the opening of the prisons to release prisoners during the French Revolution. Jokes were important to prisoners' morale, especially for those incarcerated for political reasons.

Madame Thibault and Professor Benet saw each other in the yard of the women's facility during exercise time. Mme. Thibault greeted her husband's friend warmly. Despite her husband's assassination and her own incarceration, she remained a person who always looked for the silver lining. "There are always compensations, *n'est ce pas*? One compensation I've found being here is seeing the women with babies. They are allowed to keep their children with them, which I think is an improvement we can be proud of. These mothers are generally women with too little to live on, hardworking women who struggle to survive. At least they can feed their children 'inside' and be fed themselves."

"It is interesting that only here in prison do we experience 'how the other half lives,' and how privileged we have been. It is an education we need to remember when—if—we return to our comfortable lives, my friend." Professor Benet hoped her words did not offend Jacques' wife. One never knew how far the empathy of the super-rich extended.

The televisions in the prison had been restricted to the Party's channel. Consequently, the only news they heard was propagandistic and triumphant, about how persuasive the National Front was in presenting its case for the state of siege and the deployment of troops. The newscasters reported with great conviction that the National Assembly was certain to support the Party's actions. With no other news available, speculation was the currency of communication in prison.

In the men's building Daniel found his biggest problem was having nothing to do. Out of boredom, he tried to engage some of his fellow prisoners in conversation. The young men apprehended for curfew violations in Porte Saint-Denis were mostly men with families who had left their homes to seek medical care for a child or another family member. The unfairness of their incarceration, and their uncertainty about how their families were surviving without them, left many of them depressed. Others were angry. Daniel heard one young father say, "For this we left our homelands, our aunts and uncles and cousins, our culture? For this we came here, clinging to the bottom of trains, nearly killed by lack of food and water?"

"Don't forget *why* you suffered to come here—it would be much worse to be imprisoned at home once the government knew you had tried to leave," replied another man, trying to calm his compatriot. "Fascists control many countries these days. It's hard to know where we can go and be safe, but at least here we are fed and have a bed to sleep on."

Overhearing them, Daniel wondered if similar conversations were taking place among delegates in the National Assembly. *Is everyone struggling to figure out what to believe?*

THE U.S. EMBASSY

Hal and Mona Cook flew into Paris on Wednesday, arriving late in the evening. Because they had a full schedule that began early in the morning, and because they were exhausted, they went straight to their hotel and retired for the night. Their first appointment was at the American Embassy at nine. There Mr. Weston would introduce them to Ambassador Eleanor Ellis. At eleven they would observe the debate in the National Assembly as guests of M. Allain de Guvernay, the leader of the Christian Democratic Party, whom Hal had phoned the day before to request permission to attend the session. Seats were free but hard to come by because this debate had riveted the attention of many people in France.

They arrived at the embassy early. Mr. Weston stood near the door waiting to usher them through security. The ambassador's office was lush—paneled walls with built in bookshelves and a salmon-colored velvet sofa with matching chairs. The gently curved backs and arms of the furniture, gilded and embellished with inlaid mother-of-pearl, were obviously museum-quality antiques. The room gave off a feeling of airiness and light along with traditional notions of femininity. In the corner stood a high-legged, gilded chest covered with elaborate carvings of cavorting nymphs, satyrs, and cherubs. Mona's attention was diverted for a moment. She appreciated Louis XV furnishings and recognized this chest as something one might see at Versailles.

"I'm happy to meet you, Mr. and Mrs. Cook, although I wish it were under happier circumstances." Ambassador Ellis was tall and statuesque. She wore a simple, well-fitting navy pants suit. Mona thought her eyes looked friendly. For half an hour they talked about Daniel's situation. The Ambassador's meeting with the French President the previous day had, she said, gone well, although no concessions were agreed to. "The President and Prime Minister both are 'true believers.' Just between us, they're bonafide fascists. Democracy is endangered here under their leadership. I share that off the record, of course, not for attribution."

Both Hal and Mona nodded.

"We suspect the first vote will take place next Monday. Tuesday is the last day before the May Day holiday on Wednesday. If the first vote goes against the National Front, a vote of no confidence can follow on Tuesday. In other words, we have four days until we will know anything. I understand that you will be sitting in on the session today. Have you considered making individual appointments to see delegates who are undecided?"

Hal replied, "I've had my staff research this and make appointments for us for all day tomorrow. Mona researched the current situation under the National Front's leadership, its treatment of refugees and immigrants, its leaving NATO, and how that gives Russia a free hand. She studied the French constitution on the plane so she could raise questions about how the delegates could support actions that violate France's pre-eminent legal document." He sent Mona a look that said he was proud of her. "Because of where Cook Industries does business, we've had sixteen delegates' offices respond that they will see us, so we will split up, Mona seeing half of them and me the other half."

Ambassador Ellis nodded. "Impressive! I've not known of another American to get into so many offices on such short notice."

Mona discretely elbowed her husband to warn him not to brag about the virtues of corporations that were unregulated and whose executives did not need to secure approval from their board. He understood her nonverbal message and remained silent.

Mona glanced at Mr. Weston who had taken a seat behind them. A very nice-looking young man, she thought. She'd been surprised that he was Black, not having picked that up from his voice in their phone conversations. She turned to Ambassador Ellis. "We are deeply grateful for Mr. Weston's call to alert us to Daniel's arrest and for his accessibility to us these few days." How many days had it been, she asked herself. It seemed a long time since that one a.m. call had disassembled and rearranged their lives.

Hal spoke now. "You know we have halted all our business with France." The ambassador nodded. "And raised hell with the media." Another nod. "What more can we do? They won't let us visit Daniel in prison."

"Perhaps you can think of ways to use the weekend to generate more media attention? Or find particular ways these delegates might be persuaded? I spent some time working on Capitol Hill before entering the foreign service. Remember, because they agreed to see you, they want to please you, so make sure you 'close the deal'—get them to give you their word that they'll vocally advocate and vote to end the military occupation of parts of Paris. The National Front sent troops into two more arrondissements this morning. If the delegates you see won't agree to speak and vote against the occupation, perhaps you can extract a promise that they will abstain from voting. Every abstention reduces the number of votes needed to stop the occupation. Remember, one's word means something here." She stood and took a step toward the door to signal that she needed to move on to other matters. Their time was up. They followed her lead.

As they reached the doorway, she extended her hand to each of them, saying, "If you are agreeable, I'd like Mr. Weston to accompany you on your delegate visits tomorrow and Friday, perhaps going with you, Mr. Cook? I will assign another staff member to accompany Mrs. Cook. My staff pay close attention to the National Assembly and are fluent in French. They may hear things that you may miss in the delegates' choice of words."

Mona saw her husband's hand reach for the edge of the Ambassador's desk to steady himself. She guessed that being accompanied by Mr. Weston hugely relieved Hal. One less thing to worry about.

"Of course," Hal replied. "That would be helpful. I'm afraid the one thing we haven't thought of is how to *find* the offices. With eight visits apiece to make in one day, we can't afford to lose time getting lost trying to locate the delegates."

"Okay, then. I look forward to Mr. Weston and Mr. Johnson's reports on your visits. Thank you for coming to see me. Good luck." They moved out into the hall and Ambassador Ellis closed the door behind them. They stood uncertainly in the hall while Mr. Weston introduced them to Mr. Johnson, the short, pink-skinned, balding man wearing glasses who would escort Mona on her visits to delegates.

THE NATIONAL ASSEMBLY

Later that morning they entered the impressive Palais de Bourbon, home to parliament. Mona whispered to Hal that the National Assembly originated during the French Revolution, although this building with its twelve massive columns on the portico had been finished six decades before the Revolution. She spoke with authority as she told him what she had learned. Mona had read that, although France has a Senate and a National Assembly, the Assembly is the primary legislative body. The Senate represented municipalities, whereas the Assembly represented geographic areas of the country.

Her mini lecture annoyed Hal, who was eager to get on with the business that brought them to the Palais de Bourbon. Just as he reached his limit and was about to snap at her to stop chattering—which he knew would make her cranky—their escort arrived to lead them to their seats in the gallery. *Whew!* Hal knew he could not afford to anger his wife, the only person who spoke and understood French in their little duo. Fortunately, he hadn't snapped at her. Fortunately, Mona had been immersed in what she was learning about this place and had not noticed that her spouse's short fuse was near ignition.

From the seats that Hal's contact had reserved for them, Mona looked down from the balcony and wondered aloud if the U.S. House of Representatives was modeled after the French National Assembly. "This chamber looks to me like the U.S. House of Representatives, although it has eight sections rather than two, maybe because France has more than two parties." She leaned closer. "Hal, wasn't there a Black man who completed our country's capital city by remembering the design of the Frenchman who Washington hired to design the city, when the Frenchman walked off the job and took his design with him?"

Hal shushed her. *Where does my wife find these pieces of trivia?* He often found it hard to follow Mona's lively and eccentric—to him—mind. *He* was worrying about how he would understand what was happening on the floor of the Assembly, without being able to speak French. He was *not* interested in making arcane historical observations. He chided her. "Not now. Mona, I need you to focus. You must translate for me what is happening in the debate."

Mona squeezed his hand. "I'm perfectly aware of that, my dear." He thought her voice sounded patronizing. He didn't like being so dependent on her. On anyone.

The delegates filed into the chamber filling the half-circle of seats that fanned out from the podium in eight sections. Debate soon resumed on the motion to end the military occupation of Paris. Mona said she was surprised that half the delegates were women. Hal dismissed her comment, impatient for her to translate what was being said. She could feel his impatience. It was a familiar feeling. From her purse she brought out a pen and notebook and began transcribing what they were hearing.

An older delegate stood to speak in support of the motion. "My friends, we must realize that more than one million of our *citizens* are Muslim and that four million more Muslims live among us. Conducting a military occupation in the districts with the highest number of Muslims is an action that will only increase the feeling of isolation and danger these people feel here. Be sensible. One fifth of our military troops are Muslims. They risk their lives to protect all of France. Furthermore, to extend the occupation risks alienating international businesses on whom we rely for foreign exchange. It alienates foreign governments. European Union countries are already threatening to remove their ambassadors. Many, like the U.S. have already called for their citizens to leave France. This is intolerable. The world is too interdependent for France to act in defiance of other nations."

His time was up. He walked slowly back to his seat, replaced by a speaker who supported the Prime Minister, the Party, and the policies of deportation and occupation.

Mona strained to listen closely and get the points written down. She knew it was imperative that they understand the arguments of the National Front if they were to be effective countering them when they visited undecided delegates tomorrow. Her notes were barely legible.

"Terrorists who wish to Islamify France…"

"Hordes more will arrive if we are not firm…"

"Hungary supports us now, but if we send them back to their country, can we count on them to return when next we need help?…"

"International businesses and governments need our trade as much as we need them. Wait it out and they will support us."

Back and forth the arguments flew, sometimes repeated. Hal looked sleepy. Occasionally someone interjected something new, causing Mona's pen to race across the page. By the end of the session, she was exhausted. She woke Hal up. He, of course, said he was only resting his eyes. They left the chamber and the building. She was too tired to stroll through the public rooms and admire the Louis XV furnishings.

They walked for a while in Invalides park, working out their stiffness from sitting so long. Their muscles had contracted from concentrating on the drama playing out on the chamber floor. While they walked, Mona consulted her notes. She told her husband the arguments and counterarguments she had heard. When they returned to their hotel, Mona went straight to bed, skipping the evening meal, lay down and, fully clothed, fell asleep.

Hal made his way to a restaurant near the hotel that his staff had recommended. The food was delicious and distracted him momentarily from his anxiety.

Returning to their room, he undressed and got into bed beside Mona, who was snoring softly. But it was difficult to sleep. He didn't want to take a sleeping pill, afraid it would impair his ability to think and speak clearly during the rounds of informal coffee visits with delegates that they would make the next day. Instead, he lay there ruminating until, finally, sleep came.

An hour before their alarm was set to go off, Hal dreamed he was in a delegate's office and could not find the words to express himself. Mr. Weston was in the dream also, but, although he tried, Weston could not help him. Hal panicked, terrified. Now he couldn't even remember one word of what he planned to say. He called out for Mona, but she was not there. He noticed that the delegate appeared to regard him with disgust. Hal began weeping. His lack of control, his total loss of functioning appalled and terrified him.

Still floating in a sleep coma, Mona felt the bed shaking and struggled awake. Her husband lay beside her, nearly unrecognizable. *Hal was sobbing.* He had always been in control, always the formidable CEO of Cook Industries. Never had she seen him cry, not even when his father died. She reached her arm around him, pulling herself against his back, and gently stroked his shoulder. She murmured, "It will be all right, Hal."

When his body's convulsions eased, she asked, "Do you want to talk about it?"

Slowly, haltingly, he told her about his dream, his panic.

When his words stopped, she cradled his face in her hands, her eyes compelling his to focus on the words she spoke.

"Why wouldn't you have such a dream? We are facing a situation that we cannot control. Our youngest child sits in prison. It's very scary. We can do some things—and we are doing them—but in the end, the Assembly will vote one way or the other. Regardless, we are resilient and we will get through this. Together. You will still be Hal Cook, the amazing man who can do so many things well. You will still be able to speak effectively, make good arguments, and be persuasive, like you always are. But we must recognize that in this situation, we may face limitations of our power and influence. And if we come out of this difficult time having acquired a measure of humility, that may be a good thing."

He was paying close attention. When she finished, he pulled her to him. "I have never been more grateful that you are my wife," he said, his voice husky.

Thursday and Friday were exhausting as they made their visits to delegates and, following Ambassador Ellis's instructions, pushed them to vote on Monday to deny the Party approval of the troop deployments, which would force them to withdraw the tanks and gendarmes immediately. Hal and Mona also suggested that a vote for a no confidence resolution would be best for France's allies and trading partners, including Cook Industries.

The visits with delegates went surprisingly well. They remembered to ask for something and push for a commitment, even if only to abstain on the votes. Of the sixteen delegates they were to see, one was called away to an emergency (at least, that was what the staff said); eight agreed to support both the motion to recall the troops; and three agreed to abstain. That four of the delegates they visited would make no commitment one way or the other was disappointing, of course. As Mr. Weston told Hal after their final visit, with 577 delegates, it was impossible to know if a majority would vote against a major policy of the Prime Minister, the President, and their Party. As for any subsequent vote of no confidence, "We'll cross that bridge when we come to it," most delegates said. If Monday's vote did not pass, the National Front would be secure in its leadership of France. A no confidence vote would not be possible.

They returned to their hotel discouraged. Had their efforts made any difference?

"I think we've done all we can." Mona's voice was hoarse and she said little over for the rest of the evening. Hal played on his phone obsessively, which she found irritating. *I can't stop thinking about Daniel, stuck in some prison cell for who knows how long while his father distracts himself with work!*

THE WEEKEND

On Saturday morning, Hal and Mona had informal coffee with two additional delegates, both polite but noncommittal. Afterward, Hal suggested she go to a museum for the afternoon. "It will be good for you to get your mind off this situation. And I need to attend to a work project." On his way out the door, he mumbled something about having a plan, which she dismissed as Hal being Hal, needing to be in control of what was uncontrollable. Although, the way he strode out of the room made Mona imagine Napoleon striding away once he decided to march on Russia. That had ended in disaster for the French, she recalled. Better to think about how she would spend the rest of this day.

Despair had moved in on her like a penetrating fog. She pulled herself from lethargy enough to set out for the L'Orangerie Museum and walked directly to the rooms of Monet waterlilies. She stood in the middle of each room, surrounded by wall-to-wall murals of Monet's gardens in different seasons, letting the glorious greens and blues seep into her soul. Breathtaking! And calming. Monet's paintings of waterlilies were a stunning reminder that beauty is within our view if we are open to seeing it. It whispers delight across the ages even in the darkest of times. Eternally. Just what she needed today.

She stayed in the Monet rooms until the museum closed, letting them nourish her. Then she walked along the Seine heading back to their hotel. She noticed the beauty of the spring day, grateful to be noticing anything beyond their crisis.

She heard a noise and looked up. Overhead small planes were flying with enormous banners streaming behind them. The blue, white, and red banners read—in French, of course—"TAKE BACK OUR COUNTRY!" and "FRENCH AND HUNGARIAN TROOPS OUT NOW!" and "THE NATIONAL FRONT IS NOT FRANCE!" One said, "MEET AT PALAIS DE BOURBON MONDAY NOON." Mona looked around. People stood looking up, pointing at the banners. Many were applauding.

What was this? And who was responsible for it?

Below the planes with their banners, drones crisscrossed the air dropping bundles of papers that dispersed as they fluttered to the ground. One dropped a few yards from her, and Mona hurried over and picked it up. It was a flyer, weighted with a small stone, and it read: "MEET MONDAY NOON, PALAIS DE BOURBON TO TAKE OUR COUNTRY BACK."

When she reached their hotel, the televisions in the lobby were all tuned to coverage of the "Air Revolution" falling from the sky around Paris. Curious, she watched for a time and then boarded the elevator to their floor. No one seemed to know who had sponsored these planes and drones and flyers that had attracted national attention. She found Hal in their room, on the bed, sound asleep. She didn't awaken him, choosing instead to savor the winged messages and ageless images that had reshaped her day.

~~~

Sunday was more of the same, more small planes with banners and more drones dropping flyers. Newscasts on the official NF channel criticized the paper pollution from the flyers that were scattered across the metropolitan area, but citizens on the street seemed to be enjoying this flamboyant distraction. Mona overheard one person say at breakfast, "How refreshing that these flyers and banners don't want to sell us something. They only want us to be good citizens."

Fortunately, Monday noon the sun shone and the air was balmy. When Hal and Mona arrived at the rally, they saw the area in front of the Palais de Bourbon filled with thousands of people. Mothers pushing prams, *grand-meres* and *grand-peres* leaning on walking sticks, college students, and suited businesspeople. Even members of the French football team showed up wearing their jerseys, much to the crowd's excitement. Because Les Blues played their games in the stadium in the town of St. Denis, just north of Porte Saint-Denis, the National Front Party had canceled all games in the stadium indefinitely, aggravating players and fans alike, no matter their political views (if they had any). As a consequence, they turned out *en masse* to show opposition to the deployment of troops on French soil.

Hal and Mary watched as the leader of the opposition party *Changerons!* spoke. The cheer-band for Les Bleus played "La Marseillaise," and the crowd joined in, singing lustily. Mr. Weston located them in the crowd and stuck out his hand, smiling. "Great turn out!"

"Please tell Ambassador Ellis she has made a believer out of me," Hal told Weston. "Diplomacy does work. It just requires creativity. Thank her, will you? And thanks to you."

Mona gave her husband a quizzical look.

When the speeches wound down, Mr. Weston accompanied them to the visitors' section of the balcony. The leader of *Changerons!* had come through with seats for them. The mood in the chamber was festive. Mona half expected balloons to cascade from the ceiling. Of course, that did not happen, but the tone of the debate seemed lighter.

"They must have the votes to bring the motion to a vote," Mr. Weston whispered.

They did. The Assembly voted to deny approval of the deployment of troops. They would be withdrawn and the Hungarian troops sent back to Hungary by Wednesday.

It was announced that ten percent of the delegates had signed the petition to vote on a no confidence in the government resolution. A cheer went up in the chamber at this news.

Hal and Mona remained nervous, reminded of the failure of a no confidence vote in 2023. Monday night they both slept poorly.

Tuesday morning, they were back in the National Assembly chamber. It quickly became clear that yesterday's vote to withhold approval for the deployment of troops and rule by decree had ended the state of siege. While the National Front remained the ruling party, the vote had been overwhelming, and today's vote to entertain a resolution of no confidence in the government was likewise overwhelmingly in the affirmative. The actual vote on the no confidence resolution would take place in a week, on May 8th.

Mona and Hal were confused by the procedure. What had happened? Mr. Weston whispered that this was actually great news. The numbers voting to allow a vote of no confidence to take place were so high that it would almost certainly pass. And delaying that vote for a week was no problem.

Absorbing his explanation, Hal and Mona jumped to their feet and Hal let out a whoop that brought the chamber guards to his seat to escort him out of the balcony for displaying a lack of decorum in France's most honored institution. Mona began laughing and couldn't stop. Mr. Weston took her arm and helped her up the steps and out of the balcony before the guards could remove her, too.

～～～

Paris was electric with the news that parliament refused to support deployment of troops to any area of France and that the state of siege was over. In Porte Saint-Denis, Amir and his brave band of resistors danced around the kitchen above the bakery, ecstatic. Aunt Joan heard the news on Voice of America and went to the balcony to sing, accompanied by vigorous banging, singing, and shouting from windows all along her street and the adjacent blocks.

Inside the apartment, Andre and Cora, like many in the City of Lights, poured wine for a toast weeping for joy.

On the streets below, women and children surged out of their apartment-captivity. They carried food and flowers from their window boxes to the soldiers.

No one fired on them.

A MAY DAY

In the southern suburb of Fleury-Mérogis, at ten o'clock the next morning, May First, the prison guards began knocking on the cell doors. *"Alons! Vite! Vous etes libre!"* The locks slid back and the doors opened. "Bastille Day repeats!" inmates called to each other. The festive mood at the prison truly felt like a reprise of July 14, 1789. Little attention was paid to who had been arrested by the occupying troops and who was imprisoned for other reasons.

Daniel heard someone joke cynically as the men walked out of the prison that the National Front probably released them all on purpose. It probably wanted to prove that they were all criminals. If crime increased over the next few days, the Party could prove that they were right to incarcerate them. Except, crime did not increase. Who knew why. And the guards enjoyed the May Day National Holiday, whether they had been granted leave or not.

The platform at the Paris Metro's Gare de L'Est was crowded with the newly liberated. No one seemed to mind when a train filled up and they had to wait for the next. Everywhere people celebrated. Daniel knew exactly where he was going.

His parents, however, had no idea where to find him. When there was no answer at Daniel's apartment, Hal phoned Mr. Weston.

Mr. Weston laughed to hear Hal's question. "I think I know where you can find your son. If you can wait thirty minutes, I'll pick you up and escort you there myself. The Metro will be much faster as the streets are full of people celebrating."

"You would really do that on your holiday? You've already done so much to help us." Mona was almost gushing with gratitude.

"Of course. Stay where you are. I'll see you soon." In thirty minutes, he was there in the lobby to collect them.

The Metro was crowded also, but they squeezed into the same car and stood close together so they wouldn't lose him. Once they exited and walked up the moving stairs to daylight, Mona could wait no longer. "How do you know where Daniel is?" she asked.

"I'm sure he went into Porte Saint-Denis to find his girlfriend. A friend of mine told him where to find her and they reunited before he volunteered to violate the curfew and be arrested. Your son is a brave man. I'm certain he has gone to find her now. He won't know that you're in Paris, or anything that has transpired this week. He only knows he is free."

"So you called your friend and learned where she was? How very kind of you." Mona patted his arm. Mr. Weston appeared not to notice. At least, he didn't say more.

As they turned the corner, they saw a huge white banner hanging from the third-floor balcony of an apartment and heard people singing with enthusiasm. A gorgeous dark-skinned woman stood on the balcony in blue, white, and red, singing. Her voice through the microphone that she held was rapturously beautiful.

"The Songbird of the Revolution," Mr. Weston told them as he walked them to the entrance to the apartment building below the woman's balcony. He entered a code, pulled open the door, pushed the button to illuminate the stairwell, and started up the stairs. A door on the third floor clicked open and a young woman appeared at the top of the stairs, followed closely by Daniel, who they almost didn't recognize as he had grown a beard.

"Mom and Dad???" Daniel exclaimed.

"Aidan???" the young woman screamed.

A FAMILY REUNION

Hearing the exclamations in the hallway outside her apartment, Joan came out to see what was happening. There stood her nephew Aidan Weston, and with him a man and woman she recognized from the media's coverage of what it called "The New French Resistance," Mona and Hal Cook. She embraced Aidan and shook hands with the Cooks, thanking Mona for her interview on Voice of America, and invited them into her apartment. Awkwardly, each took a seat in the living room.

Daniel appeared stunned to see his parents in Paris and especially to see them in Cora's aunt's apartment, but he soon recovered. "Dad and Mom, meet Cora Johnson-Allen. Cora, meet my parents." He waved one hand palm up at each of them with a flourish.

They sat stiffly at first, the Cooks all in a row with Cora on the other side of Daniel and her family completing the circle. For once Hal was at a loss for words. Aidan broke the silence.

"I owe you all an explanation. I have been working at the Embassy for a year." He turned to his aunt and cousin and added, "a fast-track promotion. The foreign service training program liked my work and my quick acquisition of French and Arabic. I think they thought, given the tension in France with the immigrant community, many of whom speak Arabic, a person of color might be able to get to know the leaders and cultivate reliable intelligence from the grass roots."

Turning to Mona and Hal, he continued. "When one of my contacts came to tell me that Daniel was arrested and asked me to notify you and generate publicity, I phoned you. I thought it best not to mention my connection to Daniel's..." He paused, unsure what word to use. He didn't want to assume that Cora reciprocated Daniel's feelings for her. "Friend Cora," he finished lamely. "Also, I am in France as a junior officer in intelligence assigned to the Embassy, so my family didn't know that I was here." He looked uncomfortable. "I'm sorry." It was a generic apology directed at all of them.

Cora walked over to Aidan and hugged him. "I'm so glad you're here!" She returned to the sofa, then jumped up suddenly. "It was *you!* The note. 'The cavalry are coming.' You thought I would figure it out because you are the only person other than Aunt Joan who has the code to my apartment."

Mona tossed Hal a knowing look. Apparently, Daniel didn't have the code to Cora's apartment.

Aidan smiled so broadly his fine white teeth split his face. "You got that right, Cuz," he said.

The others looked confused. Cora explained that she had returned from London and found a note under her door that read, "The cavalry are coming." She left out the fir tree that Aidan had drawn as a clue, since they had been together at Christmas. That was too complicated to go into.

Aidan deflected their attention to Daniel, asking when he'd been released and what he'd experienced in prison.

"Before we hear from Daniel," Aunt Joan interrupted, standing, "would you like a glass of wine or some coffee or tea?" She took their orders and retreated to the kitchen nook to prepare the drinks, listening closely so she wouldn't miss anything. She noticed that as Daniel regaled them with his prison experience, he held Cora's hand and Cora's eyes never left him. Joan thought about to her long-deceased brother Reggie, a civil rights leader killed by Philadelphia police in 1985. *Ah, Reggie, I wonder what you would think if you knew that your granddaughter loved the son of Hal Cook!*

From his place on the sofa, Hal jumped into the conversation with his usual authority, and Joan turned her attention back to the group gathered in her living room.

"Daniel, you need to know your mother has been a star, giving interviews, meeting with delegates to the National Assembly, listening to their sessions and translating for me." He was about to go into what he himself had done to publicize Daniel's arrest and bring the power of Cook Industries down on the National Front when he remembered Mona reminding him how dependent they had been on others to help free Daniel. He stopped himself mid-sentence and changed course.

"Mr. Weston has been remarkable. He located small planes and coordinated with students at the university to get them in the air at the same time as the students' drones, *and* he used his resources to get banners and flyers printed…" The expressions on the faces of Cora, Joan, Andre, and Daniel told him they had no idea what he was talking about. Of course, they wouldn't know. They had been incarcerated this whole time, either under virtual house arrest in the apartment or in prison. He stopped talking, looking to Aidan to help explain.

"Students at the university, organized by my cousin Cora, located drones to drop flyers all over Paris. The flyers asked people to meet in front of the National Assembly on Monday at noon to take back their country. I don't know how the students found all those drones, but there were more than fifty of them flying over Paris dropping flyers that your father paid to have rush-printed. And people showed up at the National Assembly at noon Monday. Thousands turned out."

"Even the national football team," Mona interjected.

"That's amazing, Dad. But there were other factors pushing against the National Front that were also important. My friend Amir organized a secret network of people practicing nonviolent resistance and prepared if necessary to engage in sabotage. Cora was part of their inner circle. And Aunt Joan became the Songbird of the Revolution, singing songs from the balcony, twice every day to keep people's spirits up."

Joan smiled, pleased that Daniel understood the importance of what they had been doing and pleased he called her Aunt Joan. "Don't forget the vastly talented engineer who made the signs that announced Mona's hashtag and our daily singing times," she called from the kitchen.

From the street below music drifted up to them. As a group they moved toward the balcony where they saw families strolling the street, carrying the traditional May Day flowers and singing the songs they had learned from Joan's concerts.

Resettling on the sofa and chairs, Cora spoke, her voice low and full of emotion. "Don't forget the French businesspeople who were part of the resistance. Jacques Thibault gave his life…" She had to pause a moment before continuing. "And his wife and those he recruited who spoke out nationally on television were imprisoned for their courage."

Aidan moved back to the balcony to watch the crowd surging through the street. "Also, Ambassador Ellis," he added. "Without a U.S. Ambassador personally sympathetic to bringing down the National Front, I could not have been involved."

"You make a good point, Mr. Weston," Hal said.

"Please, call me Aidan."

"Aidan it is. If you call me Hal."

Andre had been listening to the assortment of factors that had brought an end to the state of siege. "It seems there was no one reason this resistance worked. We might argue which was most important, but to me the central reason we have prevailed (so far) is that a community of people united by their commitment to keeping France a democracy came together to each do what they could do."

~ ~ ~

That night, as Cora and Daniel lay on her narrow bed, she spoke, her voice serious. "I know you realize that it is not over yet, that we still have a lot to work through."

"You and me or France and the world?"

"All of the above."

MAY 8, VICTORY DAY

In the week that followed, the National Assembly voted on a second motion, this one a vote of no confidence in the National Front Party that had been leading the government for more than three years. Like the vote to disapprove of deploying troops and end the state of siege, this vote overwhelmingly opposed the NFP. Forty more delegates voted for it than the 278-majority required.

A no confidence vote had not been successful for sixty-eight years, although no confidence votes had often been attempted.

Immediately after the vote, as required by Article 50 of the Constitution, the Prime Minister submitted to the President the resignation of the National Front Party government, including the Prime Minister and the Cabinet. The President would remain in power, but the remaining National Front Party leaders, those who had been leading the government, were out of office. Analysts pointed out that the French President's responsibilities are primarily foreign policy.

As her last act, the Prime Minister dissolved parliament. Her action required new elections for the National Assembly within twenty to forty days.

To everyone's relief, cell and Wi-Fi services came back within a few days. Cora and Daniel's employer, the National Youth Movement notified them that it had closed its offices while new leaders redesigned the organization. They no longer were employed.

~ ~ ~

With the sky again thick with smoke from more European fires, Cora and Daniel spent much of the first week in May introducing his parents to their favorite Paris haunts. All of them wore face masks because of the smog that covered the city. Hal asserted that he and Mona had visited Paris several times. His body language made it clear he was tolerating these young ingenues' "takes" on a city he knew from long experience.

One afternoon, after walking through Luxembourg Gardens, Cora led them across the street to Café Tournon. There, she told them, Black writers Richard Wright, Chester Himes, and James Baldwin had regularly met to nourish each other's writing and talk ideas. It was a genuine Paris salon. She told them Duke Ellington made his Paris debut there, and this café gave birth to the *Paris Review*.

Hal surprised them by being full of questions. His first—Why were Black Americans in Paris?—gave Cora an opening to teach them some of this history that her mother had taken every opportunity to teach Caleb and Cora.

In the Saint-Germain-des-Prés area she showed them the café where James Baldwin wrote his first novel and where he and Richard Wright had an argument that marked the end of their friendship. Mona took out her notebook to take notes. Hal had never heard of either James Baldwin or Richard Wright. He planned to ask Mona about them in the privacy of their hotel.

At the Arc de Triomphe on the Champs-d'Élysées, Cora told them about the Black American who had fled the U.S Jim Crow South on a steamer and joined the French Foreign Legion. Eugene Bullard then became the first African American pilot to fly planes in World War I. Bullard settled in Paris, owned bars and restaurants, and, when Hitler took power in the northern half of France in 1941, Bullard joined the French Resistance. In 1954, France invited him to kindle the flame at the Tomb of the Unknown Soldier, a high honor.

Another day they had lunch in a café that in the 1920s was the premier location for hearing American jazz by Black expatriate musicians, who were all the rage in Paris. Cora told them about Josephine Baker. Baker served as a spy for France before it was occupied by the Nazis. Hal vaguely remembered watching a television documentary about her that Mona had insisted they view. He hadn't realized she had spied for France before the Nazis occupied the country or that she continued spying for the French Resistance while France was under occupation. All he recalled was a photo of Baker, wearing nothing but a string of bananas. That Josephine Baker received France's highest honor, the French Legion of Honor medal, shocked him. Cora's voice pulled him back from his mental image of this handsome Black woman performing nearly nude. "She is quite respected here. France interned her remains in its Pantheon."

Another day they visited the Louvre. When they ooo'd and ahhh'd about the spacious, beautiful rooms that displayed its incredible art collection, Cora mentioned that a Black graduate of the Harvard School of Design was part of the architectural team that redesigned the Louvre in the 1980s and 1990s.

Hal stopped and stood still, causing a near-collision with the group of tourists walking behind him. He stared at Cora.

"You are an amazing young woman," he said, as though he was surprised. "What you have been telling us is brand new to me. It makes me wonder what else I don't know about my country that you could tell me."

"I could probably tell you a lot about *our* history." Her correction of his possessive adjective was not lost on any of them. "Actually, my mother is the expert on that. She's a history professor at Northwestern University."

"And, Dad, Cora's field is computer science. She's working on her Ph.D. in Artificial Intelligence. She was studying at the Sorbonne. Maybe she still is?" Daniel's face questioned her. They had not had time to talk about what would come next in their vocations.

"Not sure," Cora answered him. "Tomorrow I must try to locate Professor Benet."

They moved on through the gallery to the special exhibit that Daniel had taken Cora to see, Justice Burning. And there stood Amir. Amir and Daniel embraced warmly. Cora thought Amir's lovely smile confirmed the closeness of their friendship. Daniel had invited Amir to join them so he could meet Daniel's parents and go through the exhibit with them. He expected Amir's observations would help them all see this art from Africa and Asia with new eyes. He wasn't disappointed.

At the painting with the brown-iris evil eye, Daniel, Amir, and Cora simultaneously pulled out their evil eyes and laughed at their shared secret. It reminded Cora of Raza and Hanafi. "Oh, no! How could I have forgotten to search for Hanafi and Raza and their children? Has anyone heard what's happened to the deportation camps?"

Amir had heard they were being evacuated. People were being returned to their homes in France. "It is likely to take a month or longer. So many were held there."

They explained to Mona and Hal how the government had incarcerated many thousands with the intent to eventually deport millions of immigrants. Then they explained the significance of the brown-iris evil eye.

Hal said nothing. He seemed stunned. Later, when he and Daniel went to the men's room, he reached for Daniel's arm, looking at him gravely. "All three of you were part of the Resistance?"

"Yes!"

"I don't know what to think of that, but I doubt I would have had your courage," he muttered. Daniel had never seen his father so subdued.

After a meal, Hal and Mona returned to their hotel, and Daniel and Cora to her apartment.

Although Hal wanted to spend their last night in Paris with their son, Daniel insisted that Amir join them, and Hal gave in. Amir would join Daniel and his father for dinner on the 8th, the Victory Day national holiday commemorating the defeat of the Nazis in World War II.

"I want to talk to Dad about my future. We need to have this conversation, no matter how difficult it may be, and I need Amir there, both as moral support and because what I plan to propose to Dad involves Amir," Daniel told Cora on the Metro heading back to Porte Saint-Denis. He refused to say more. Instead, he kissed Cora and whispered, "You really wowed my dad, which few people can do, and you didn't even intend to."

"My intention was to educate him while I had the chance," she whispered back, but the squeal of the train's brakes drowned out her comment.

~ ~ ~

Back in their hotel Hal and Mona reviewed the day. Hal admitted he was quite impressed with Cora and with the fact that Amir, Daniel, and Cora had been part of the Resistance. Mona, who was removing her makeup and getting ready for bed, turned to her husband, amused by the note of envy she heard in his voice. After thirty-five years with him she thought she knew his little vanities, but this was the first time she'd heard him be

Resistance! 301

sympathetic to *any* revolutionary. She grinned through the layer of face cream she had been smoothing into her skin.

"Hal, you and I have also been part of the Resistance, even though we were latecomers. We contributed money and connections to help unseat the fascists." As Mona anticipated, her observation pleased and pacified him.

~ ~ ~

In Cora's apartment Cora and Daniel also discussed the day... and Daniel's parents. "I'm glad I was able to raise your father's awareness that Paris has had a multicultural population for several centuries and is proud of welcoming Black Americans who came here to escape segregation and race discrimination in the U.S." She was wrapping her hair in a silk scarf as she spoke.

"To tell the truth, I'm surprised my father was willing to hear what you were teaching him. He's such a single-minded person, so focused on being in charge and on making more money. I haven't seen him listen to other perspectives the way he listened to you. Maybe there's hope for him yet. Way to go, Cora!"

"We come from very different families. Your dad may have accepted what I told him today, here in Paris, but what would he be like in Kansas, in his native habitat? And you don't know my family. You know only Aunt Joan, Uncle Andre, and Aidan. Mama doesn't tolerate ignorance well and doesn't hide how she feels. I think we don't yet know if our relationship will stir up a firestorm."

He pulled her to him. "I guess we'll have to research all the unlikely couples in history whose love overcame their differences and lay it out for your mother and my father," he said playfully.

Their conversation had suddenly crossed a threshold and they both knew it. They were talking about a future together. Each knew that more than family differences lay between them. In that moment each contemplated this uncertainty. Their lovemaking felt awkward and unsatisfying, and they fell asleep without saying anything more.

Cora's phone rang them awake early May 8th. To her surprise, it was Professor Benet inviting Cora to lunch. Jacques Thibault's widow would join them. "We have so much to share about the past month," she said, after telling Cora where and when to meet them.

They met at the same restaurant where Jacques had taken Cora when he asked her to join the Resistance. They took seats at the table, Cora across from Jacques' widow.

Cora felt her eyes brimming. "Madame Thibault, forgive my emotions, but this is where I met your husband several months ago. I am so sorry for your loss. He was a most impressive man. I will never forget him."

Madame Thibault reached across the table to touch Cora's hand. "Thank you, *ma chère*. Jacques thought very highly of you. He talked about you with me. He believed you will do great things in this life."

For a moment, no one spoke.

"It was a month ago today that he left this world," Madame continued. "Could any of us have known the courage and hope that would be required of us during this time? But we found both courage and hope. Thank God, we got through it."

In the restaurant, spirits were high. People wore small circles of pleated ribbon they called cockades—blue at the center surrounded by a circle of white and then a circle of red. Diners conversed animatedly and Cora wondered if their behavior was unusual, or was this how the French usually celebrated this holiday. When she asked, both women grew serious.

"You know, Cora, we celebrate May 8th as a national holiday because this was the day Hitler and his party's control of France ended. How appropriate that we also celebrate *our* May Victory on that date!" Mme. Thibault played with the stem of her wine glass and her face grew sober. "Will this achievement last? Ah, this is the question we are asking ourselves. Will a coalition of parties be able to hold the line against the National Front Party in the upcoming elections? Will the National Front Party respect the democratic process? Or will they get a fresh breath and be more effective in the future? I think the struggle is not over."

"Perhaps it never ends." Professor Benet waived the approaching waiter away. *Was she still afraid to speak openly?*

"When our colonies fought for their independence, they fought against long odds and they knew it, but they persisted. I was in Angola in 1975 when Angola received its independence. I was a cub reporter, sent there because I spoke Portuguese to interview the first president of independent Angola, Agostinho Neto. Neto led the Popular Movement for the Liberation of Angola in its struggle for independence from Portugal *for thirteen years*. He told me that his movement's mantra was, 'A luta continua. In English, The struggle continues.' He said their children memorized this simple sentence 'so they will never forget that their struggle is never over.'" Mme. Thibault's eyes glowed remembering. "I'll never forget that."

Cora could picture her as a twenty-year-old, participating in this important historical moment. She felt moved by the power of Mme.'s memory.

"My experience with that idea was much more mundane, but I will never forget it." Professor Benet pulled from her wallet a worn piece of paper that she reverently unfolded. "When I was in the U.S. on a Fulbright Fellowship, I went one Sunday with my host family to their Protestant church. I was there reluctantly, not being particularly religious, but they sang a hymn that struck me powerfully. I copied down the words." She read from the worn paper—

> Once to ev'ry man and nation
> Comes the moment to decide,
> In the strife of truth with falsehood,
> For the good or evil side;
> Some great cause, some great decision,
> Off'ring each the bloom or blight,
> And the choice goes by forever
> 'Twixt that darkness and that light.

It captivated me. There was such truth in those words." She refolded the paper carefully and returned it to her wallet. "I think this year we lived through one of those moments."

"Yes, my friend." Mme. Thibault had the last word, which felt to Cora like a benediction. "This time France did it right. But there will always be a next time."

The waiter had arrived with their lunch. They shifted in their seats and refocused on their bowls of bouillabaisse. While they ate, they shared stories from the past month, the press conference, their arrests, the time Professor Benet visited Mme. Thibault in prison pretending to be her maid. They laughed as Professor Benet recounted her visits to the remaining business leaders dressed in various disguises. Even the arrival of the gendarmes to arrest her seemed amusing now that the National Front was no longer all-powerful. They spoke of what they had learned during their time in prison about the basic humanity of prisoners and of the poverty that drove so many women and their babies to be incarcerated. Cora told them about Aunt Joan's daily singing, and they asked to meet Aunt Joan to thank her for what she had done.

When the waiter brought them *mousse au chocolat* and cappuccino, Professor Benet changed the subject.

"Cora, the University informed me that the A.I. program is no longer controlled by the government. They want me and the others they fired to return and rebuild it. Your place is open for you to return also. Do you wish to?"

There it was, the question that had haunted her. "I need to know more. My research in Tallinn and London showed me that A.I. is very close to being able to operate without human input. You know that my interest has been in how to prevent false information from being deliberately put into A.I. and skewing what it reports. Frankly, I am wondering now if it is too late to prevent this from happening. It is a grim scenario, A.I. telling us what it thinks we should know rather than giving us even-handed data and assessments."

"You are thinking that if it is too late, you might as well focus inward, have babies, and find your meaning in family rather than in your work?"

Cora flushed, embarrassed to be so transparent. She nodded.

"You may not like my response. You are correct that we are very close to what many predict will be a point of no return. But human wisdom, even among the greatest minds, is only partial. Often in the past people predicted the end of the world or at least the end of civilization, yet some kept working to change the outcome. And we are still here." Professor Benet took a long sip from her coffee cup, allowing herself time to process what she wanted to say next. She wiped her mouth, sipped some water, then sipped more cappuccino.

"Many young people today feel hopeless. Because of climate change, Russia's aggression against its neighbors, and the growth of extremism. They feel that there is no evidence we will be able to survive. They are joining alternative communities, living in the countryside, learning the skills of their grandparents' generation in the hope they will be able to survive the apocalypse. I cannot tell you what to do, Cora. No one can. You must make your own choice. As I said, personally, I cling to the belief that positive change is possible and that it requires us to invest our lives in producing it, however we can."

Cora let out a long, audible sigh. It was so complicated. Here with these women who stimulated her intellect, she felt rejuvenated, excited by the possibility of digging back into the work she had longed to do. Then there was Daniel…

"When do you need to know my answer?"

"When you are ready."

Cora found herself smiling as she boarded the Metro. *I have such respect for Professor Benet and Mme. Thibault! To work with her now, knowing her as I do after sharing this time of crisis, would be such an honor.* She was still smiling as she mounted the stairs to her apartment, but as she opened the door, her smile faded. A question had taken hold of her thoughts: *What will returning to the Sorbonne and A.I. research cost me?*

A DANIEL'S FUTURE?

At Daniel's suggestion, he and Amir walked with his father through Invalides park. It gave each of them time to think without facing each other across a table in some restaurant or café. As a runner, he found that he thought more clearly when he was physically in motion.

His parents would fly home to Wichita tomorrow, so he could not postpone the conversation any longer.

They chatted about Hal and Mona's time in Paris, their impressions, what they had learned and noticed. Hal asked Amir about his family and about Cameroon. Daniel was pleased that Amir did not modify his answers to avoid unpleasant truths. Amir spoke about the impact of fossil fuel operations offshore and about the impact of the misuse of carbon credits on his country. To Daniel's surprise, his father listened.

When their conversation eased, Daniel used that moment to segue to what he really wanted to talk with his father about—his own future.

"Dad, I believe Cook Industries can play an important role in leading the world away from fossil fuels to renewables by supporting local and national efforts south of the equator to produce renewable fuel from cast off petroleum products, from plastics." He did not give Hal time to reply. "Amir and I have talked about how to help the world make this transition in a way that doesn't simply replace one form of exploitation with another." He knew he was on shaky ground now as his father was bound to have a knee-jerk reaction to the word "exploit." He kept going. "I have a great group of young leaders from across that part of the world who I could work with on this, the very people the National Front selected and recruited as the most promising young leaders in their nations. Working with Amir, I believe we can make an important start at forming new alliances, new businesses, and rewarding innovation within these nations to produces low carbon fuel *and* lowers global temperatures. There are already small-scale operations in place: producing clean fuel from burning and cooling waste plastics, for example. Ocean farming of plastics dumped into the sea. We can support this innovation and foster more." He paused to take a deep breath before playing his best card. "Cook Industries, if it takes such a direction, can be on the cutting edge, like Steve Jobs and Bill Gates were in developing the internet or (Cora had helped him come up with this one) John D. Rockefeller in finding and developing the oil industry."

He glanced at his dad to assess the impact of what he was saying. Hal's face remained unreadable. There was an awkward silence.

"I hope your silence means you're considering what I'm proposing." Daniel was unaccustomed to his dad ever being silent for so long. "Of course, I don't expect you to say yes right away. I know you have to talk to others about it, but I make this proposal because it is the only way I see myself working with Cook Industries, and I know my siblings have each found their careers doing other things, so, if you want Cook Industries to continue as a family business, I think I'm your last shot, Dad." He said it lightly but seriously and waited for an explosion.

"My legs are getting tired," Hal said. "Can we sit for a while?" They found a bench and sat. Amir simply observed. Daniel's tension showed in the erect way he carried his upper body. He crossed his legs, uncrossed them, fiddled with his phone, pulled out breath mints that he offered to the others, crossed his legs again. Had he ever had such a long and honest conversation with his father? He thought he could hear time ticking by on his superwatch. He wondered what Amir was noticing but didn't dare look at him. He kept his eyes on the grass at their feet, only occasionally raising them to acknowledge the people passing by on the path.

Hal cleared his throat and coughed a little. Daniel thought his father must feel uncomfortable sitting with Daniel on one side and Amir on the other, like he was surrounded. Maybe he should suggest they walk some more?

Hal cleared his throat again. Finally, he spoke.

"You make some good points, Son. Especially about being the only one among your siblings to carry on the family business."

Was his father joking? Was that all he heard?

"I'm teasing you," Hal said. "What you propose is intriguing, and I do like the idea of capitalizing..." he paused realizing they might not like is choice of words. "*developing* innovation by the best and the brightest of the Third World..." Would this choice of words offend them? It was so difficult to talk with other generations. They didn't even use the same language. Words had different meanings for them.

"Okay, my bottom line..." Damn! He was really lousy at this. "You are correct that I need to give it more thought, but I am open to your proposal and will take it seriously. Is that enough for you for now?" He turned to Daniel and Daniel was surprised

Resistance! 309

at the expression on his father's face. He looked at Daniel with a kind of vulnerability and with respect.

"It is, Dad. Thank you for taking this seriously."

"Of course, I can't *commit* to support your ideas."

"Here's where I remind you, Dad, that you always brag about being a solo player who needs no okay from a board of directors." Daniel didn't want to sound overly snarky, but, after all…! He felt a sudden need to move his muscles, but Amir had told him to be sure they got a commitment from his father, if possible. Daniel stood. Amir stood after him and stuck out his hand. Hal shook Amir's hand.

"Can we shake on it? And, Dad, when will we hear your decision? We are fleshing out our plans and may need to look for other backers."

Surprised and rather stunned, Hall shook his son's hand. *My boy knows more about the corporate world than I gave him credit for.*

"Amir, I'm very glad you are onboard with Daniel in this," Hal said, reassuming the driver's seat. He turned back to Daniel. "I can get back to you in… Is two weeks soon enough?"

The younger men smiled their assent.

After they escorted Hal to his hotel, had dinner with both Mona and Hal, and said their good-byes, Amir and Daniel returned to Porte Saint-Denis, to Amir's apartment. Both felt a buzz from Hal's response, even if it wasn't a full-on commitment. They talked that night until very late about how they might execute their proposal and identified a fallback strategy in case Hall would not fund them. Amir would be the CFO freeing CEO Daniel for the work that he loved, meeting and inspiring the dreams of young people. Ideas flew like popcorn from a renegade popcorn popper.

"Paris has changed you," Amir told him when Daniel left in the early morning for Cora's apartment. "I believe you are finding your own voice, my friend. Congratulations."

A FAMILY

Cora and Daniel had planned to spend May 9th together. Each had news to share, so they took turns listening and talking. Both were excited about the other's encouraging conversations on the previous day. Unaddressed was their future as a couple.

When their conversation subsided, they lay side by side in her bed. Cora kissed him and whispered, "I am so glad for you and so proud of what you proposed to your father. Even if he is not interested, there will be other ways for you to pursue this dream."

"Thank you." He kissed her back. "So, Cora, I have a question. How will **you** decide what to do?"

"I want to go home to see my family, talk it over with them. It's been three years, and I really yearn to see Mama, Caleb, Uncle Edward, and my grandparents. Aidan's family, too."

Daniel felt uneasy about what he needed to say to her, and it took him a few minutes to get it out. "Would you be open to me going with you? I'll understand if you don't want that, but I would really like to meet your family and have them meet me."

Cora sat up, swinging her legs on the edge of the bed and Daniel prepared himself for disappointment. "I love the way you asked that. It shows you respect my need to do things on my own."

He tried to hide his disappointment.

"Actually, I would love for you to come with me. I thought I'd ask if Aidan can get leave to come, too—all my favorite people together in one place. Dad and Gran Cora not counted, of course. You cannot imagine how much I longed for that during my dismal time in London, buried under the blizzard of the century." Her eyes lost focus as she recalled those miserable months. "I was so lonely I cried nonstop." She kissed him again. "Oh, Daniel, please *do* come with me."

He basked in her delight before fetching his phone to locate flights and Cora texted Aidan.

"Hey, we could also take time to see your old haunts in Montreal so you can return to being Elise Brevard," he joked. "You still have that passport?"

~ ~ ~

Two weeks later, they flew to Chicago. Aidan flew on a different flight but his time in Chicago would overlap theirs by five days. Cora's mother Keisha met their flight, accompanied by the elderly Black man Cora called Uncle Edward. Daniel struggled to keep everyone in her family straight. Keisha said Uncle Edward was Cora's great grandmother Cora's son and that Uncle Edward had been close friends with Aunt Joan's brother who was Keisha's birthfather. That left Daniel totally confused.

Keisha drove them to Evanston and Cora cried when she saw the home she'd grown up. Daniel observed each of them carefully.

Cora hugged her mother and they held onto each other for what seemed a long time. Noticing their closeness, Daniel felt a moment of envy. He heard Cora say, "I've changed so much during these years in France, Mama, but this is still 'home' deep inside me. I half expect Dad to bound down the steps to welcome me with a bear hug."

"I still have that experience, too, honey, even after so many years."

Daniel observed, *They're more affectionate than my parents, but they have been through a lot of loss. Or were they always close? How did they manage that?*

~ ~ ~

The flight exhausted Daniel and Cora but Cora stayed up to talk with her mother. Daniel had excused himself and gone upstairs to bed.

When Cora entered her room a while later, he stirred, eager to hear what had transpired downstairs while he'd been dozing. "Mama seemed glad to hear my feelings," Cora said as they undressed.

"Does that surprise you?"

"Kind of. That whole year after Dad was murdered—funny, I'm using that word now! For that entire year sadness submerged all of us. It nearly destroyed Mama. She was so overcome with grief that she hardly noticed Caleb and me."

"So maybe she's changed? You said you have."

She didn't answer his question. "It feels strange to see everyone looking older. Also strange not walking on eggshells around Mama."

"Good strange?"

"Yes."

"Well, it's been a number of trips around the sun for all of you. I wonder how she feels about us."

"I guess we'll find out. Mama will want to know everything

Resistance! 313

about you, but she won't push if you say you don't want to talk about something. She respects boundaries—most of the time."

In the morning, over a bountiful breakfast, Mama began a friendly but persistent interrogation of Daniel.

Cora listened to them talk for an hour before leaving them to it. She wandered the house, looking for the artifacts of their life as a family. Her brother, Caleb, joined her in Mama's bedroom.

"She still keeps Dad's keyboard under the window," Caleb pointed out.

"Remember when she finally gave away his clothes?"

"Except for that flannel shirt with the elbows out. I think she still sleeps in that."

"It must be a rag by now."

"Can I change the subject? Are you really serious about this guy? Mama said his father owns Cook Industries. I mean, Cora, they are retrograde! This family has prided itself on not being rich, but this dude reeks money and power."

"Yes, I am serious about him. He's not like that, although it took me a long time to trust him. I met his parents in Paris. It surprised me how nice they are, but then I have to remember that they were there to rescue their youngest child."

"I suspect you've been drinking the Kool-Aid, Big Sister. I mean, they've been propagating legislation for states to pass restricting books and outlawing abortion and equal rights for trans people."

"I know that. Aunt Joan and Aidan gave me a lot of articles to read about them when I first met Daniel three years ago. But his passion is to help young people across the world, especially in Africa and Asia, help them innovate solutions to global warming that reduce and eventually eclipse the dominance of billionaire-owned corporations like his father's. His best friend is a brilliant guy from Cameroon who he plans to work with on this. Give him a chance, Caleb. You'll see he isn't what you assume."

"The acorn doesn't fall far from the tree, Cora."

"Actually, in this case, the tree itself may be changing, thanks to Daniel."

"That's impossible. You'll have to find a better metaphor. Trees don't change."

"But they do communicate with each other, and they can learn to grow in unnatural places, which means they can change." She pushed him, teasing. "I learned that from Amir, Daniel's friend."

"Still the same old nerdy Cora, playing at being big sister even though we're only fifteen months apart," Caleb teased. "Never to be out-argued!"

"So what about you, Caleb. What are you doing now?"

"Go ahead, change the subject. But you haven't convinced me."

The siblings slipped into a less fraught conversation, both grateful to shift topic. Caleb recounted his work with a startup architectural firm designing *avant garde* structures that were so well insulated using natural materials that they required little to no heating or air conditioning. He grabbed a paper and pen from Mama's night table and drew her some of his models. Caleb had clearly found his niche!

Seeing her smile, Caleb stopped mid-sentence describing one of his designs. "I've been a late bloomer, but I've found the path I want to pursue. Maybe not as exotic as yours, but right for me." He grinned impishly, then pulled her into a sideways hug.

~ ~ ~

The third day of their time in Chicago, Cora's grandparents arrived from Cleveland. Gran Ann wore her eighty years well, but Grandpa Don looked somewhat frail. Uncle Edward joined them for dinner, bringing bread he had baked. The evening was quite spectacular as Cora and Daniel regaled the group with their stories of their France's Spring Resistance.

The following night Mama added extra leaves to the dining room table to accommodate Aidan and his parents, Femi and Jacob. It was a festive time. At least it was before Caleb, with his predictable bluntness, asked Aidan what he thought of Cora's

Resistance! 315

boyfriend. Caleb chose to ask this when Daniel had excused himself to use the toilet.

The room went silent. Typically, Caleb was naming what everyone was wondering about. Was this Daniel Cook the real deal or a closeted reactionary? Should they allow themselves to warm to his charm and the loving way he treated Cora?

Aidan took his time answering. He poured himself a tall glass of water and drank it. He folded his napkin and crossed and uncrossed his legs while tension took hold of the room.

"I was very wary of Cora seeing him when I saw her at Christmas 2027. Aunt Joan was, too. When Amir came to me to tell me Daniel Cook had deliberately been arrested by the fascists, I didn't know what to think. I respect Amir and his commitment to democracy over autocracy and plutocracy. So, I did what he asked and contacted Daniel's parents. They went into action immediately. To my surprise, in her media interviews his mother criticized the National Front Party and its policies. She didn't only advocate for her son's release as any parent would do. She called out the Party for rounding up and deporting immigrants, arresting innocent young people, and occupying the most diverse neighborhoods in Paris."

"That doesn't say much," Caleb interrupted. "It's Hal Cook who is evil incarnate."

Aidan appeared weary and terribly serious. "Hal worked with me to secure small planes and drones that flew over the city with banners and flyers calling for a national demonstration against the fascist National Front government. Not the kind of action a wannabe fascist takes. I didn't know what to think."

Around the table he heard sudden intakes of breath and exclamations of "No way!" and "Really!" Aidan heard his father's voice with its strong Jamaican accent: "BLOW WOW!" Even his mother Femi had slipped into patois, but her voice was softer as she exclaimed "Geezaat!"

Aidan continued. "Daniel knew he might wind up dead when he deliberately provoked arrest and imprisonment. He has plans to address climate change by assisting young people to build their own innovative alternatives to fossil fuels. He's determined to do this whether or not his father agrees to realign Cook Industries to fund him. To me, he is the real deal."

Cora had not been certain how Aidan felt about Daniel. She had sat rigidly upright, feeling fearful, wanting to protect Daniel from Caleb's words. When Aidan finished speaking, she went to him and hugged him.

Just outside the doorway to the dining room, Daniel exhaled audibly, drawing all eyes to him. He had overheard much of the conversation from down the hallway when he had started walking back from the bathroom, but he was so uncomfortable that he'd remained out of sight so he could listen unseen to what they would say. His heart pounded his ribcage, but no one had noticed him, not until this moment. Flushed from embarrassment at hearing Aidan's final sentence, he finally stopped holding his breath. He wanted to disappear.

Cora's mom went to him.

"No need to hide, young man. You've passed Caleb's test with flying colors. And you passed mine. Come on back to this family, where you belong."

Caleb was not convinced.

A CRISIS AND OPPORTUNITY

The downstairs was deserted, except for Daniel and Cora. Keisha, her parents, and Caleb had gone upstairs after saying good night. Daniel sat in the living room, holding tightly to a sofa pillow with red fringe. He pulled his fingers through the fringe, fidgeting, and the fringe falling through his fingers looked like blood.

He avoided Cora's eyes.

"Are you all right?" She lowered herself to the sofa, sitting beside him.

"Your brother really dislikes me. I've been trying to figure out what I've done to deserve that."

"It's not what you've done. It's who you are."

His head swiveled toward her. "What do you mean?"

"You come from a very rich family that made its money

mining resources of indigenous land here in the U.S. and around the world for three generations."

"Whoa! Wait just a minute. My family paid for the right to drill oil. They provide jobs for people and pay them decent wages. They give generously to charities. And they believe in America." The intensity of his voice steadily increased and his face flushed. "Besides, I am committing myself to the conversion from fossil fuels to energy sources that will stop or at least reduce global warming." He shook his head vigorously, his anger mounting. "And I can't change the fact that I am White. To dislike me for that reason is racism."

He stood and paced the room.

Cora could not respond. Here it was, the barrier that since the start of their relationship she had half-expected to rise up and shatter their connection. How could she expect him to understand? His world, his whole life experience, was so different.

Daniel continued. "I know you will say I have no idea what Black people have gone through. But I am here in your home with your family, who are each accomplished people with good jobs—Aidan a foreign service officer, his brother a lawyer, his mother a teacher, your mom a professor... They live well, Cora. I don't know about Caleb. We have not talked, and not because I haven't tried to get to know him... And Amir, my best friend, is Black."

As though that last remark sealed the deal, he sat down with a flourish and resumed fondling the fringe while his eyes bored into her.

"This is why I resisted your charms for so long." Her voice was barely audible. She did not look at him and when he tried to take her hand, she pulled away. "Are you really as clueless as your father?"

He looked stunned. Silence stretched like a taut and tenuous thread connecting them.

Finally, she spoke. "Mama told me that Dad was clueless. When they first got together, she was tired of re-educating white folks and his ignorance was so offensive that she came close to sending him away. But she didn't. And he learned, from her and on his own, reading Black history and literature and discussing it with her until he got it." Cora seemed to be talking to herself. She turned to Daniel, tears in her eyes.

"Your privilege is like a curtain that hangs between us keeping you from seeing the world that I see, that my people experience."

"But half of your people are white, like me."

"True. But for hundreds of years the U.S. has defined one drop of African blood as the determinant of racial identity. It still is. So people identify me as Black, Daniel, and I am proud of that identity. Do you understand that?"

"I understand that is how you see yourself."

"But you don't see me that way, do you? You see me as 'exotic.'"

He appeared assaulted by her words, wincing visibly, then looking away from her, his eyes on the photo of her parents on the piano across the room.

"*They* figured out how to make it work. Can't we?"

"I don't know. I *do* know that I cannot marry you until I feel clear about that." Cora reached for his hand. "I love you very much, Daniel, but love will not be enough to get us through what the world is experiencing now, the surge of fascism and repudiation of 'otherness.'"

"So I'm on probation?"

"No! That is offensive. We are on hold while you see if you can get to a place of understanding and while I see that I can trust that you do understand. Okay? You come from a very wealthy, powerful family. I come from a family that views your family's wealth and power as dangerous to them and others less powerful and wealthy. Those are big differences." Her eyes sought his and he raised his head to meet them. She was determined to be brave, but tears slid down her cheeks and dripped from her chin, making dark marks on her blouse.

"Okay. I love you, but I understand that I have work to do and am ready to do it."

"Maybe you can begin by getting to know Caleb before we leave for Paris? He's an architect designing homes that don't require air conditioning or heating, but on Saturdays he counsels low-income young men, helping them with job placement. Ask him about his work. You might learn a lot."

The conversation had exhausted Cora. She stood, her face showing her weariness. "Let's leave it here for now. I need sleep." She turned from him and climbed the stairs, holding onto her sobs until she reached the bathroom, where sound of the pounding hot shower covered her. When she entered the bedroom, Daniel was in bed, his body curled toward the window. She suspected he was not asleep, but neither of them spoke.

~ ~ ~

Five days later, Cora and Daniel prepared for their flight back to Paris. The media was full of stories about Russia's threat to use nuclear weapons if Poland did not 'return' its territory along the Baltic Sea to Russia. Russia demanded the land from its major port of Gdansk to just north of Berlin, three hundred miles north to south and one hundred miles into Poland. If Poland complied, Russia would be 483 miles from Germany's capital city and would control the sea around Denmark's capital as well.

The world was in an uproar and fear cut knife-sharp into ordinary life in every home.

As they said their good-byes at the airport, Mama asked if Cora had decided what she would do.

"Yes," Cora answered. "I have the skills and intelligence to possibly make a difference. I'm returning to the Sorbonne. Even if the odds are long, it's what I want to do."

Keisha held her daughter for a long time. Cora could tell she was trying unsuccessfully to hold back her tears. "And what about Daniel?"

"He supports my decision. We both feel our 'calling,' as Gran would say. We'll both stay in Paris, together. We'll see what comes."

Her mama hugged her again. This time there were no tears. "You know that my mother met my birth father in Mississippi fighting for Black people's right to vote. In your own ways you and Daniel are joining that stream of courageous individuals determined to right wrong. May God be with you," Keisha whispered.

"*Mama?* I never thought of you as *religious*." Cora pulled back to see Mama's face.

"Honey, I'm not 'religious.' But Daniel told me that when he was in prison, one night, he heard the stars chiming. It's something your father would have said. I'm not sure what I believe, but I do know that in times like these, even folks like me are looking for 'signs.'"

THE END

ACKNOWLEDGEMENTS

I am immensely grateful to the readers who carefully read various versions and sections of this book and gave me essential feedback. Thank you to Sally Timmel, Meg Tuggle, and my Sunflower Scribes writing group for insights on Cora's behavior and feelings. Thank you to Doug Lippoldt, whose twenty-two years living in Paris greatly helped my descriptions of Paris and my use of French and whose close reading caught several important inconsistencies. Thank you to Katie Mitchell-Koch for insight into the chemistry of climate change and plastics.

Thank you also to those who have read my novels and shared with me their appreciation of them, including William South, Brian Daldorph, and Mary Ann Verrow. Writing is a solitary profession. The writer inhabits a world with their characters and lets them lead. Hearing from readers how much they enjoyed a book connects the writer to the world beyond the words on the pages and keeps us writing.

Special thanks to Laura Tillem, my favorite editor, dear friend, and resource on all things literary and political. We have co-edited prose books together for ten years and I am most grateful for her presence in my life. Finally, thank you to my go to Beta reader Ronda Miller, a wonderful poet and writer who has supported so many writers with her editorial skills and encouragement. Ronda loved the characters in my three Crossings Series novels, *Maybe Crossings*, *Dark Crossings*, and *Resistance!* She did not want me to stop writing their stories. Like Laura Tillem, she remembered details of their lives and asked after them as though they were real people, encouraging me to keep them alive by writing another book featuring them. Indeed, this book would not exist were it not for Ronda and Laura's encouragement to write it. Ronda's sudden death in late 2024 left all who knew and loved her feeling acutely their loss of continued interaction with this generous, gifted woman.

My poet-husband, Michael Poage, whose seventeenth book was published this year, always inspires my writing. For him and for the rest of our family I am ever grateful.

Wichita, Kansas
January 20, 2025

ABOUT THE AUTHOR

Gretchen Cassel Eick is a writer of history, biography, and fiction whose life-long fascinating with people from elsewhere began when at nineteen she studied at a university in Sierra Leone, West Africa. She traveled extensively as a human rights and foreign policy lobbyist before earning a PhD in American Studies and becoming a professor of history. She wrote two prize-winning nonfiction books—*Dissent in Wichita: The Civil Rights Movement in the Midwest, 1954-72* (University of Illinois Press, 2001, 2007, 2023) and *They Met at Wounded Knee: The Eastmans' Story* (University of Nevada Press, 2020)—and six novels, *The Set Up, 1984, Finding Duncan, Maybe Crossings*, Dark Crossings*, Where is Ana Amara?* and *Resistance!** (*Resistance!* is the third in her "Crossings" Series along with the other two asterisked novels). With her husband, the poet Michael Poage, she teaches university level history, travels the world, and writes.